# Framing
# Noverta

Robin Weaver

**Framing Noverta**

ISBN: 9781943601332
ISBN-13: 194360133X

# DEDICATION

Dedicated to my late grandfather,
Fern Hall Strange

# ACKNOWLEDGMENTS

A special thanks to my fabulous critique partner, Linda Lovely. Your feedback and editing make my books so much better. Also, thanks to Tony Turner for your help; much appreciation to everyone who critiqued this book or offered comments on the cover. Publishing a book truly does take a village.

# CHAPTER 1

*Sunday, November 6*

The Georgian house loomed bright in the dark night, a big wooden ghost warning Calvin Henderson to turn back. Only Cal couldn't turn back. The call had come in and being the newly elected sheriff, he had to respond. Even when investigating meant going to your best friend's house at two a.m.

Cal pulled his brand new '38 Packard onto the grass, barely avoiding the ruts in the gravel driveway. Thanks to the gully-washer that rolled across the Tennessee hills just after dark, he'd have to spend his Sunday afternoon cleaning the mud off the shiny black paint.

Lights blazed at the Randolph residence. That couldn't be good. Turning off the engine, Cal rolled down the window and listened.

Quiet. *Too quiet.*

He listened harder. Exactly what did he expect to hear? No crickets—but it was November. No cars on the road—Noverta Randolph and his wife lived too far out in the sticks. So what was missing?

Barking. Noverta's dog should have alerted the house of his arrival.

*Damn.* Every instinct warned Cal nothing good would come from climbing out of his automobile but he eased his door open. He rotated his shoulders, wishing he could ignore that little twinge in his midsection. There could be a million reasons for all the lights. Just because Ida Simmons, the Randolph's next-door neighbor, called about "a loud noise" at an ungodly hour didn't mean anything, right?

It probably did mean something, though—something Cal would rather not know about. With Noverta out of town, Lily Randolph probably partied again. At some point, Cal would have to do the right thing—tell his best friend the little wife was pitching woo outside the marriage bed.

Cal hesitated, not keen on going inside. His gut insisted something sinister waited. His gut was rarely wrong.

He climbed out of the car, shivering as the wind howled across the Mississippi River. After grabbing his flashlight and Remington shotgun out of the automobile, he headed up the brick path toward the house. Another chilly gust sent the porch swing into frantic motion.

"Damn." Great, his gut had him talking aloud like some country bumpkin. He needed to listen, observe—not speak. In response to his self-lecture, his tight gut tightened more.

Cal stopped short.

Noverta Randolph sat on the brick steps holding his head in his hands. His friend should be fifty miles away, at the cattlemen's convention in Memphis. Why had Noverta returned home early?

Cal shined his light at the shed where Noverta parked the Randolph Ford. He saw taillights.

"Vertie?" he ventured, using the boyhood nickname Noverta never managed to outgrow. "What's that in your hand, Noverta?" Cal stopped breathing for a second as he eyed the snubnose.

Noverta's eyes seemed to stare right through him. Cal hadn't seen eyes like that since he'd left the force in D.C. a year earlier.

Tightening his grip on his double barrel, he shook Noverta's shoulder with his left hand. "What's happened here, Vertie?"

No response. His friend continued to stare straight ahead, apparently at nothing. Did Noverta even know Cal had arrived?

Something was wrong. Very wrong. The silence grew louder.

Cal laid his shotgun down on the pavers. Pulling his shirtsleeve over his hand, he removed the handgun from Noverta's grip and placed the weapon on the gray porch. The snub-nose stood out like a giant June bug, only the thing packed the deadliness of a thousand yellowjackets.

"Vertie. Talk to me. Where is Lily? Is she all right?"

"What?" Noverta blinked for the first time since Cal's arrival.

"Vertie, where's your wife?" Cal repeated, unable to keep his voice from increasing in volume. "Where's Lily?"

"Lily is…" Noverta's catatonic eyes came to life, no longer dead but not quite human either. "I didn't kill her!"

*Kill her*? Cal tasted bile as he pointed toward the gun. "Vertie, is that yours?"

The weapon certainly didn't seem like something Noverta would own. As far as Cal knew, his friend didn't own a single handgun.

Noverta looked at the snub-nose, as if it were a rattlesnake ready to strike. "No. It's Lily's."

*Damn.*

Cal had come back to his Tennessee roots to avoid murder and that kind of dung. He hadn't become a small town sheriff to deal with more corpses. Especially a corpse he knew. Sure, a bum wrist meant he couldn't play major league baseball anymore, but there were at least twenty other things he could have chosen other than Leeton County law enforcement.

Still, he had signed on. Best if he checked on Lily. Maybe Noverta was wrong. "Vertie, I have to look around. Promise you'll stay here, okay?"

Noverta didn't speak. He began to rock back and forth.

"Stay here, Vertie. You hear me?" Repeating the obvious probably wouldn't help.

Nor would it change whatever waited inside. Cal picked up his shotgun and headed inside the normally friendly, but now threatening, Georgian. Hard to believe the eerie white house was the same place where he and Vertie played hide n' seek as youngsters.

"Lily?" He prayed for a response. Nothing.

He made his way down the entrance hallway toward the back of the house, his boots thumping in rhythm with his racing heart as he tread across the oak floor. The bedroom door stood slightly ajar.

"Damn." He was talking aloud again. He took a breath, but every inch of his body rebelled against going inside. He knew what awaited him in that room. Or rather, what didn't await him. Lily wouldn't be greeting him with a smile.

He tentatively poked at the mahogany door with the butt of his shotgun. The door swung wide. Lily sat on the four-poster bed, propped against embroidered pillows.

Cal's breath whooshed out. He *was* wrong. Thank God.

Only... Why wasn't she moving?

Raising his shotgun, Cal inched closer. Then wished he hadn't. Lily's chest had no rise and fall. The brown eyes that once sparkled with so much life now wore a vacant stare. She was dead.

Cal stared at the ceiling, determined to keep the contents of his stomach intact. The thing on Noverta's bed couldn't be the Lily who had stripped down to her undergarments and dived into Pickwick Lake when they were teenagers. That Lily convinced the entire gang to follow her into the still chilly water on that spring night. That Lily made everyone feel alive.

Over the years, that Lily had turned to ice. When Cal first heard she'd cheated on Noverta, a few crystals formed around his heart as well. Being loyal to his best friend, Cal had avoided Lily. Maybe he shouldn't have been so quick to judge. If he'd communicated with her instead of looking the other way, insisted she talk to her husband and work things out, would things have turned out different?

He'd never know. Cal gagged, covering his mouth in an attempt to regain his composure. And control over his digestive system.

*Detach*. He had to detach. He'd investigated enough murders in D.C. to know the drill. He stared at the corpse, determined to think like an investigator, not the man who'd known Lily before discontent set in. Poor woman wasn't just dead, she was a murder victim.

Perfume lingered in the air, the floral scent stifling in the midst of death. Lily's long black hair hung loose around her face, but a small bullet wound in the middle of her forehead marred her porcelain beauty. The pillows weren't embroidered with fancy pink thread after all. The rose-shape stain on the linen came from the exit wound. The red circle enveloped Lily's head like a macabre halo. No need to check for a pulse. The doll had already gotten life's big kiss off.

Cal ignored his queasiness and walked around the four-poster bed with precise steps. He noted nothing unusual on the floor. Blood on the wall by the door, not a spatter, but a smear. That blood couldn't have come from Lily. She clearly hadn't gotten up again after the bullet pierced her head, so where did the blood come from? Did the killer touch her and then touch the wall? Or had he been injured? Cal would have to check the hospital to see if anyone had been admitted. He'd also needed to check Noverta's body for wounds or blood.

Below the blood smear, a clump of plaster covered the braided rug. On the wall above, he spotted a hole. Cal took a closer look. A bullet, most likely a .38 caliber. He found another bullet in the trim around the window.

Had Lily fired at her killer? Surely Lily didn't just sit there while her assassin fired three bullets. Or did the murderer take the gun away from the small woman and use it on her? That theory fizzled like an out-of-play foul ball. No sign of a struggle, other than the rumpled bed.

Cal searched the entire room. Using the barrel of his shotgun, he pushed the red velvet quilt away to look underneath the bed. Nothing.

His stomach gurgled. Needing a minute, he leaned against the wall, being careful to avoid the blood smear. The bedspread lay on the floor and the wrinkled sheet had been shoved toward Lily — pushed to one side as if someone had left the bed. The feather pillow next to the unblinking woman had been flattened and propped up against the headboard. She'd had company, but who? Probably not her husband since Noverta still wore street clothing. Had a lover shared her bed and then shot her?

That didn't make sense. Cal's mind raced, looking for any explanation other than the obvious one: a lover had lain next to Lily and Noverta made his wife pay for that indiscretion.

Cal took a closer look. No hair that he could see on the second pillow to provide the clue he needed.

Hell's bells. He'd seen his share of death in his fight against crime in the big city, but Lily was his first dead woman. Ever. He'd have to call in big city help on this one. The Memphis Police Department had expertise no county sheriff's office possessed. Only five minutes into his investigation and already Cal knew he had a big mess on his hands.

Methodically, he made his way through the rest of the house. The back door was still locked. The windows showed no signs of forced entry. Nothing to suggest anyone else had been inside. No wineglasses, no half-eaten food, no indications of a struggle, and no candles burning in anticipation of a romantic interlude. Yes sir, a real who-could've-done-it-besides-Noverta?

Cal's mind formed a question he didn't want to ask. If Noverta wasn't the killer, why didn't he call the police? Why did he grab the murder weapon and sit down on the front porch?

Wasn't looking good for Noverta. Not good at all.

Robin Weaver

# CHAPTER 2

Using Noverta's phone, Cal called the Memphis Police Department. Knowing the switchboard operator would repeat everything, he provided only the essential information—assistance requested for a 187, followed by directions to Noverta's residence.

Cal hurried back to the front porch to wait. He'd get some grief from the county mayor for calling in the city boys, but Noverta was his best friend and he'd take all the second opinions he could get. Memphis had the highest murder rate in the country, thus the MPD knew a hell of a lot more about homicide than he did, despite his two years with the D.C. force. The Memphis unit had nabbed Machine Gun Kelly in '33. Besides, being the sheriff, he didn't *technically* report to the county mayor.

"Vertie, you all right?" Cal knew he should ask for details, but Noverta's answers might be something he'd have to repeat in court.

Noverta remained mute. Thank God. The man stared into the dark fields with unblinking eyes, clearly in shock. But was his the shock of the victim or the regret of a villain?

Cal glanced toward the side of the house but couldn't see much. He really should look around— he'd done a quick check of the perimeter after he'd discovered the body, but he should check again, ensure he hadn't missed anything.

"Who'd do this to her?" his friend moaned.

Cal blinked, wondering if he'd heard correctly. The surface evidence pointed toward a crime of passion, toward the wronged husband pulling the trigger, but was that a true picture? Could Noverta actually be innocent?

Only if Noverta hadn't killed Lily, who had? "Listen, Vertie. Don't say a word. You hear me? Not a word."

Noverta didn't answer. He sat perfectly still, staring that thousand-yard stare so popular among shock victims.

"Why not?" a woman asked.

Cal jumped at the unexpected voice. His hand automatically reached for his shotgun, no matter that the voice was feminine and familiar.

"Why?" the woman repeated, barely more than a whisper yet it boomed in Cal's head. "Why shouldn't he say a word?"

*Grace.* Grace Randolph. No, Grace Randolph Gardner. Ernest Gardner's wife.

Cal had longed to hear her voice for years—ten to be exact. He'd heard Grace talking to other people since he returned—at church, at ballgames, and at Avers Groceries. A few times, she'd even addressed him with a polite "hello." Only they hadn't really talked since he'd left town ten years earlier. While he wanted a real conversation with her more than he wanted his next breath, he didn't especially want to hear her voice now. Not when her brother might be the murderer.

"Grace, what are you doing here?" he asked, glancing at the neighbor's house. Had a shadow crossed the upstairs window?

Of course. That would explain Grace's arrival at Noverta's house.

He directed his gaze at her. "Ida called you?"

Who else had the old woman called? Cal was losing control of the crime scene. Worse, Grace had walked up behind him and surprised him. He'd thought his senses were on hyper-alert, but he hadn't heard a thing.

Maybe he shouldn't beat himself up, though. As kids, Grace had always been the best hunter of their group. You couldn't tell by looking at her peaches-and-cream complexion, but her grandmother had been a full-blooded Choctaw. She could sneak up on a polar bear.

Not important. He needed to get control of the situation. And Grace needed to explain exactly why she just happened to show up at her sister-in-law's crime scene.

"What are you doing here?" he repeated.

She turned in his direction. The years closed in quickly. "Vertie's in trouble. Where else would I be?"

Cal ran a hand over his hair, feeling guilty for feeling so relieved. He hadn't believed, even for a second, she'd been involved in the murder.

"Only, why shouldn't he talk?" Grace asked. She twisted her head toward her brother for a second then turned back to Cal. "Well?" Her tone had taken an edge that rivaled the sharpness of a Cy Young curveball.

Cal swallowed. What should he say? He'd scripted every single word he planned to say to Grace if he got the chance to talk to her alone. Only in his planned scenarios, there hadn't been a dead body propped on the bed.

Would Grace be upset about Lily's murder? Or only concerned about her twin brother? At one time, Grace and Lily had been friends, but if rumors were true, Lily had alienated most of her female friends.

"Cal, where is Lily?"

He swallowed again. For all his big city training, he couldn't think of the appropriate response.

"Fine," Grace said, propping her hands on her hips. "I'll check on her myself." Grace dropped her arms to her side and marched up the steps.

"Grace, stop," Noverta's voice croaked, unexpected and creepy as hell. "Don't go inside. Lily is… Don't go inside."

"Vertie?" Grace reversed direction and sat down next to her brother. "What's happened to Lily?"

Noverta started swaying, the motion more chilling than the unseasonably cold weather. "I didn't shoot her, Grace. She was dead when I got here."

"Lily's been shot?" Grace turned her profile in Cal's direction. "Is she…?"

Cal nodded, grateful he didn't have to say anything more. He watched Grace swallow once, then swallow again.

"I'm so sorry, Vertie." She gave her brother a little hug. "Cal, do you know who…who did that to her?" Grace's tone held a challenge. Shadows concealed her face, but Cal sensed she glared.

Message received: *Leave my brother alone and find the killer.* Making it impossible to say what he was thinking—Noverta killed Lily.

"I haven't drawn any conclusions," he said instead, speaking the truth. No conclusion didn't translate to no theory.

Grace nodded. She didn't question him further, just stood and started up the stairs again.

Cal bolted forward and grabbed her arm. "Grace, you can't—"

This time he could see her face. She definitely glared.

Time seemed to freeze. After several seconds, Grace's shoulders drooped. The anger seemed to blow out of her with the gusting winds.

"I understand," she said. "I'll just sit with Vertie, if that's all right?" Grace glanced at his hand.

Cal released her bicep. He couldn't recall any specific statute, but suspected it wasn't *all right* to let her sit with Noverta. His friend clearly needed his sister's support, but Cal couldn't afford any distractions and Grace distracted him to the extreme. "Might be better if you headed on home, Grace. I don't want you here when the boys from Memphis arrive."

She shivered. Rubbing her arm, her fingers covering the very spot he'd touched. "Why not?"

Because the detectives would wonder what she was doing at the scene of a crime. Worse, didn't she own a small Smith and Wesson?

"Grace, please. Trust me on this one and go home."

"Forget it," she said, determination resonating in her tone. "I'm staying."

She floated past him, the scent of lavender lingering behind. She positioned her lithe body next to Noverta and tucked her skirt around her thighs. "Tell me what happened, Vertie."

If Noverta was guilty, he'd likely confess to his minute-older twin sister. There might be only sixty seconds difference in their ages, but Grace had been the closest thing to a mom Noverta had. Cal didn't want to hear a confession.

Cal huffed a breath. "Don't ask him that. He should remain silent."

Grace glanced his way, and then reached for her brother's arm. Cal couldn't be sure, but he thought her hand shook when she patted Noverta's arm.

"I don't know what happened," Noverta said, his voice little more than a whisper.

*Please don't say anything else.* Cal really didn't want to testify against his friend.

"Something must have happened, Vertie." Grace insisted.

Noverta sniffled, wiping at his nose with a starched sleeve. His shirt didn't have a single wrinkle. No stains either. Not the shirt of a man who'd just committed a murder, but then, it didn't take a lot of perspiration to fire a handgun.

"I came home," Noverta said, his voice little more than a whisper. "The front lights were on. You know how I get about that, Grace. Can you believe I was mad Lily was wastin' electricity? Now she's gone and I was mad about the darn lights." Noverta made a not-quite-human sound.

"Vertie, stop whimpering," Grace insisted. "Tell me the whole story. Now."

Ah, hell. Cal knew he should walk away, get out of earshot. If Noverta said the wrong thing and he had to repeat the words in court, his friend could get life imprisonment. Or worse, the hotsquat.

*No.* If Noverta said something incriminating, he'd just pretend he hadn't heard. Not professional, but Cal sure as hell wasn't about to railroad a friend.

Noverta shook his head. "Drove straight home from Memphis." The porch light glaring behind his head created creepy shadows across the dead lawn. "Didn't even think about it being so late. I called the dog, but he never came. Did you see Tanner?"

Cal hadn't seen or heard the dog. The bluetick hound was the envy of every dove hunter in the state and should have been barking up a snowstorm. Where was the dog?

What difference did it make? Lily sat propped in the bedroom with lead in her head. That had to trump a missing hound.

Grace patted her brother's arm again. "Don't worry. We'll find Tanner."

Noverta shook his head, this time with more vigor. "Dog wouldn't leave Lily, Gracie. Not with me gone. I tried to tell her she was ruining a good hunter, but she laughed at me. Spoiled that animal like one of them prissy French poodles. Always giving him bacon and—"

"Vertie," Grace interrupted. "We need to know what happened to Lily."

Noverta shuddered. "I don't know. When I got here, she was just sittin' there. Like she was waiting for me...only she had that hole in her head." He shivered. "I never saw a person shot dead before. Never. God knows I wanted the woman gone, but not like this. Who would do this to her, Gracie?"

Maybe Noverta hadn't killed Lily. Cal kicked at the edge of the walkway, trying to redirect his thoughts. His friend didn't sound like a guilty man and Noverta was no poker player. Every emotion experienced showed on his face. So if he didn't kill his wife, who did?

Cal had to find out. With Noverta alone at the scene, no one would believe his friend hadn't pulled the trigger. The story would have sounded less daft if Noverta had been hit in the head with a fastball. If the jury didn't send him to the gas chamber, they'd have him committed.

Unless Cal could do something.

"Did you kill her, Vertie?" Grace asked, and then glanced in Cal's direction again.

Noverta leaned over, covering his forehead with the pads of his palms. "How could you even ask that? You know I'd never hurt a woman, wouldn't hurt no one. Tell her, Cal."

Cal blinked. He knew Noverta wouldn't hurt anyone, but everyone in the county knew about his temper. "It's not about what we *think*, Vertie," he replied. "You were holding the gun. It looks bad."

Noverta shook his head, sending another series of wavering shadows across the driveway. "The gun was on the floor, over by the door. I just picked it up."

"Why?" Cal asked.

"I just thought the damn gun shouldn't be lyin' on the floor. I didn't know Lily'd been shot when I picked it up." Noverta made a moaning noise.

Cal wished he could offer some solace, or better yet, some hope. He couldn't. "Vertie, you must have seen that she'd been shot."

Noverta shook his head. "No. Hadn't been in the bedroom then. Gun was on the hallway floor."

Cal rubbed at the corners of his eyes with his forefingers. The killer had dropped the gun? Why not take it? "I believe you, Vertie, but we need to find something that points to someone else. Right now…"

"Then *find* something," Grace said, her soft voice filled with hard iciness. "He told you he didn't kill her."

Cal pretended to ignore her remark and addressed Noverta, "You see anyone when you got here? Any cars? See anything out of the ordinary?"

His friend shrugged. "No. I expected to find someone. I heard she…" Noverta started to sway again.

"Hell, Vertie. Don't say that to anyone else. You'll look even more guilty. Make damn sure you don't talk to any of the Memphis gumshoes when they get here. You hear me?"

Noverta swayed again.

"Vertie, tell me you understand."

Grace linked her arm around her brother's. "He hears you," she said.

"Make sure he does," Cal insisted. "Innocent people get sent to prison, too."

He waited but Grace didn't respond. She wouldn't look at him, either. He couldn't understand why she was so angry at him. Was she mad because he wasn't doing enough for her brother or did her wrath go back ten years? That didn't make sense, she was the one who'd married someone else.

Damn if he'd stand around thinking about that. "I'm going to look for the dog," he announced.

No one protested. He headed toward the side of the house and whistled, not really expecting to find Tanner. The dog would have already come running with his tail wagging if he'd been near the place. Cal wished he'd brought his own mutt with him. Lucky might not be a prize winner like Tanner, but the little rascal went crazy if another dog came within a half-mile.

No matter. Looking for Tanner had been an excuse to get away so he could think, an excuse to get away from Grace. He stared at the house, willing his mind into gear. Lights from Lily's bedroom window illuminated the yard, casting happy shadows that contrasted sharply with the ghoulish situation indoors. Cal almost turned

21

away, but he spotted something on the ground. What?

He walked closer to the window. Four feet from the foundation, he found a hat—a Leeton Mudcats baseball cap.

He'd been on the Mudcats team before he signed on with the Chattanooga Lookouts. So had most of the town's young men, Noverta among them. Only Noverta had given his hat to his father during the final-game ceremony the day the Mudcats disbanded. The picture had been in the *Leeton Herald*. At the time, Cal wondered why Noverta made the gesture, given his feelings toward Old Man Randolph.

At Noverta's insistence, Cal had accompanied his friend back to the Senator's house after the Mudcats' curtain call. They'd followed John Randolph inside. Cal remembered feeling awkward when the senator stopped by the fireplace. Wasn't cold enough for a fire. John Randolph struck a match anyway, waiting patiently until the flame caught among the pre-arranged kindling. Then, the senator tossed Noverta's baseball cap into the hearth. Cal could still envision the greenish blaze, flickering and taunting as Noverta's gesture went up in flames.

So whose Mudcat cap had he found? The hat could belong to almost anyone who'd played on that team, but since it didn't belong to Noverta, finding it outside Lily's bedroom didn't bode well. Even a district attorney as dense as Jackson

McKinney could convince a jury Lily's lover dropped the cap after Noverta chased him away, could make the case Noverta had gone crazy and punished his cheating wife.

Cal studied the ground, or what he could see of it with his flashlight beam. No discernable footprint on the wet grass to identify the cap's owner, but the crown was dry. The cap had been dropped after the rainstorm, either by Lily's lover or her killer—or maybe both roles belonged to the same man. Either way, Cal couldn't take a chance the hat would make things worse for Noverta, so he stuffed the cap in his inside coat pocket. For the first time in his life, he might have obstructed justice.

# CHAPTER 3

Grace wheezed in a long breath. With Cal out of sight, she could breathe again.

When had her life become such a mess?

She knew the answer to that. The day she wed Ernest Gardner. Grace didn't blame her husband for their sham of a marriage. She'd gone into matrimony knowing exactly what she was getting—a man without focus, ambition or the capacity to love anyone as much as he loved himself. In his own way, Ernest had tried. Only she didn't love him and he must have sensed that. His fascination with her faded mere days after the wedding night.

Cal's presence reminded Grace of her unfortunate choices, reminded her she hadn't gotten over the man who got away. How dare he return to her little town looking far better than he should? With Cal out of sight, she'd achieved a certain level of serenity.

A serenity shot to hell in one night. Damn Cal for being the sheriff. Damn Lily and her cheating butt.

No, she mustn't think that way about the dead. Grace stared into the starry sky and asked for forgiveness.

"You really should go home," Cal said.

His unexpected voice made her jump. Understandable, everything about the dreadful night made her jump. Jumping she could handle. Cal's voice shouldn't make her think about "what might have been," especially given Noverta's problems.

"I'm not going to leave…" She stopped talking to listen. What had she heard?

Cal must have heard, too. He twisted his head toward the noise. A faint wailing sound cut through the silent air, growing louder with each passing second.

"Do you hear that?" she asked, and then felt rather stupid. Of course, Cal heard. The noise had gotten so loud even Noverta had stopped swaying.

"A siren?" Cal scrunched his nose. "What the hell? It's too soon for the Memphis squad to arrive."

Headlights flashed across the cotton field adjoining her brother's yard. A car sped down the pavement, taking the turn onto the dirt road way too fast. The beams slashed through the murky darkness as the vehicle raced past Ida Simmons's house and screeched to a halt at the edge of Noverta's driveway. The abrupt stop created a monsoon of mud that splattered across the brick pathway. The driver jumped from the car and hurried up the path.

Grace squinted to get a better look. *Deputy Herbert Smith.*

Keen. Could the night get any better?

She shook her head. Sarcastic thoughts wouldn't help, although Cal seemed annoyed, too. He did that little popping thing with his thumb he'd done in high school, a clear signal he worked hard to hide his annoyance. And why did she have to remember every little detail about the man she'd tried so hard to forget?

"Damn." Cal kicked at the dirt. Maybe the popping thing wasn't working for him.

As much as Grace welcomed any distraction, Herb ranked as a wet sock on his best days. Tonight, his arrival could signal disaster. The deputy might be the only person in Leeton who didn't dote on her twin brother. Hatred, a potential murder suspect, and a hothead with a badge could never mix without creating an explosive cocktail. Worse, Herb was Ernest's friend and she didn't want anyone asking about her husband tonight.

Cal uttered a few choice words, under his breath. Words he wouldn't use unless he was really aggravated.

"You'll have to repent about that come Sunday." She probably shouldn't have said that, but the taunt was second nature. She'd used the same line often in the old days. In the good old days.

Cal actually flashed a little smile. "Guess so." His smile quickly turned into a grimace. "But hell and damnation."

The sheriff widened his stance as the deputy came within earshot. "Herbert."

"What's going on Cal?" Herb asked, propping a hand on one knee as he huffed from his exertion.

Cal didn't answer. After a couple seconds, the deputy straightened and sauntered to the edge of the porch, thumbs in his pockets.

He motioned with his head. "Is that a gun?"

Did he mean the shotgun? Grace squinted, wishing the automobile lights hadn't destroyed her night vision. Then she spotted the thing on the porch. A small handgun.

Grace felt a bit woozy. Was that Lily's gun?

Herb reached for the weapon.

"Herb, don't!" Cal yelled.

Too late. The deputy lifted the little shooter and studied it. Stupid jerk actually pointed the barrel at his own face. Grace jumped up and yanked the weapon out of his hand.

"Jesus Christ, Herb!" Cal took a step toward the shorter man, then stepped back to remove his hat and run a hand through all that thick black hair. He glared at her. "Grace, put the gun down!"

Why was he barking at her?

Herb threw his shoulders back, probably trying to make the most of his five-feet-five-inches. "We don't take the Lord's name in vain down here, Sheriff. Or did you forget?"

Uh-oh. *Down here*? That would yank Cal's rope. He had lived in the south since he was five years' old. Even so, because he'd been born "up north," he was still considered a skanky Yankee by too many of the townspeople.

"We don't destroy evidence either," Cal snapped. "You've just obliterated any fingerprints that might have been on the gun."

"Fingerprints?" Herb laughed. "Them things ain't accurate."

Dear Lord. Herbert was an imbecile. She must have made some sound because the deputy looked at her.

After a "pffft" sound, the deputy asked, "What's she doing here?"

Grace swallowed, attempting to control her spike of temper. With an effort, she ignored Herb and handed the gun to Cal, keeping the barrel down. "Here, Sheriff. I was afraid Herbie might shoot himself."

Cal made a half snort, but quickly recovered. Had he winked when he took the gun?

"Wait!" Herb's head turned right then left, then right again. "You said *evidence*. That mean we got us a crime here?"

Cal moved closer to Herb, his six-foot, two-inch frame hulking above the deputy. "I'll brief you later, Herbert. Right now I need you to drive Grace home."

She didn't intend to go anywhere, certainly not with Herb Smith. "I am staying right—"

"What do we need fingerprints for?" Herb interrupted. "Did somebody rob Vertie? Is somebody dead?"

The glee on the deputy's face made Grace want to punch him. She wouldn't have been surprised if Herb rubbed his hands together and said, "Oh, goody." The man acted like an untrained puppy, waiting for someone to toss him a bone. Only he'd want real bones. With real blood—Noverta's blood.

Herb glanced at her, then at Noverta. Her brother started to sway again. Faster.

She'd rather tangle with a tornado than deal with Herbert Smith right now. Noverta was losing it and needed her help. She sat back down and tightened her grip on her brother's shoulder, forcing him to slow his movement.

"What they doing out here?" Herb asked.

She sensed Cal didn't want to explain in front of Noverta. Heck, he probably didn't want to explain to Herb at all. Everyone knew Cal would probably have fired Herbert Smith, but the mayor insisted his nephew remain on the payroll.

The sheriff took a deep breath, and then motioned for the deputy to step away from the porch. Grace didn't hear everything, but she overheard enough. Cal had explained the situation.

Herb put his hands in his pockets. "Looks like an open-and-shut case to me." The imbecile clearly wanted to make sure she overheard. "Everybody knows sweet little Lily was fooling around. Hubby caught her doing the dirty deed and shot her. Wonder who she was screwing this time?"

Cal grabbed the deputy by the collar, yanking so hard Herb's heels came off the ground. "Don't talk like that in front of Grace. Apologize. Now."

Grace swallowed, fearing there'd be another murder if Herb didn't do as Cal ordered. Despite her fear, a little bubble of satisfaction surfaced. Cal probably would have demanded the deputy apologize to any woman in the same situation. Still, she hoped his overly physical response was because he still felt *something* for her.

"Sorry, Grace," Herb croaked.

Cal relaxed his hold, allowing Herb to get off his toes and plant his flat feet back on the ground. She nodded, refusing to give the deputy any additional acknowledgment. Unfortunately, Herb had a point. The man might be dumb as dirt, but the little crumb was right about Lily's murder. Everything seemed to point toward Noverta. If only he hadn't decided to come home early. She had to do something to save her brother.

"We aren't judge and jury, Herbert." Cal sounded stern, almost like her father.

"Right." Herb's eyes blinked rapidly. "So what do we do now, boss man? Or did Noverta already confess?" The deputy's posture slumped. "Did he admit he put a plug in his two-timing tomato? I know you and Vertie Boy here are pals, but we gotta handcuff him, right?" The deputy walked toward Noverta, his hands reaching behind his back for something. "Stand up, turn around, and put your hands behind you."

Noverta sparked to life. He lunged at Herb before Grace could grab him. The damn deputy whacked her brother over the head with his nightstick before either she or Cal could intervene.

Noverta sank to the ground.

"You jerk!" Grace wanted to deck the deputy, but Cal had already grabbed the crumb and yanked him beyond her reach. She slumped to the ground next to her brother. "Vertie... Criminy. He's out cold."

She put her hands on Noverta's neck, testing for a pulse the way her mother-in-law had taught her. The old woman might be meaner than a trunk full of rattlesnakes, but she knew a lot about bodies—both human and animal. The things she'd learned about ancient medicine might be the only good thing to come from her marriage to Ernest.

"Is he all right?" Cal asked.

She twisted her head to look at the sheriff. He had Herb in a headlock, only this time, Grace didn't think the action was overly physical. She wouldn't have cared if Cal choked the hotheaded deputy.

"Hard to tell. I think so." Her brother's pulse beat strongly beneath her fingers. She glared at Herb. Hadn't she heard the deputy was one of Lily's worshippers? "Wait a minute. Herbert," she challenged. "Why *did* you drive out here in the middle of the night? Must be at least ten miles from your house."

The deputy made a hissing sound. "None of your business."

"It's my business, though," Cal said, his soft words layered with menace. "How did you just happen upon this crime scene?"

"Darn, Boss. Didn't just happen. Adeline is on the switchboard tonight and she rang my line after Ida called you. She figured you might need some help."

Grace knew Adeline was looking for a husband, but was the switchboard operator so desperate she'd set her sights on Herbert Smith? Must be. Otherwise, why would she call the deputy?

Dumb question. Adeline probably called everybody.

Grace stared at the house next door, seeing lights in the upstairs window. So Ida had made the first call. The neighbor had always treated Noverta like a son and seemed to take Lily's indiscretion personally. In the past, Ida would have called

Grace if Noverta was out of town and another car parked outside her brother's house. Only there'd been so many calls, Grace had grown weary of them. So she'd set the old woman straight. "Lily's just lost her way, Mrs. Ida. Pray for her because I can't do anything about her visitors."

Ida hadn't called Grace again. Maybe if she'd been a little nicer, Ida would have called her tonight. Maybe Lily wouldn't be dead.

Cal relaxed his grip on the deputy. Herb yanked out of the hold and rubbed his neck, pointing at Grace with his free hand. "I ain't the only one who happened on a crime scene. How did Grace get here?"

Grace took an exaggerated breath and pointed at her mud boots. "I walked, Herb. With my *feet*. Maybe you've heard of them?"

"Enough," Cal interrupted. "Both of you. Herb, drive Grace home. Then go wake Rodney. Tell him to get over here. We need him. *Now*."

Grace fought down a surge of panic. Why did Cal think he needed a second deputy? Did he think Noverta would run? "I don't need a ride," she said. "I'm staying with—"

"You can't let her go anywhere, Boss," Herb interrupted. "Ain't she a suspect, too? She coulda killed Lily easy as pie. Lord knows she's the best shot in the county."

Holy bibles. Would she ever catch a break? And did Herb seriously think Cal wouldn't have thought to question her without his oh-so-wise suggestion?

"Herb, I've already questioned Grace. Just drive her home."

Cal had reverted to his patient voice. Grace had heard him use it time and time again when the average Joe would lose his temper. She really needed to stop remembering every single thing about him and concentrate on Vertie's problems. Otherwise, she might get herself in a real mess.

"I don't need a ride." She'd walk a thousand miles before she'd ride with that flea-covered weasel.

Cal made a weird sound—something between a growl and a groan. "Have it your way. If you don't want a ride, then walk. But you will leave my crime scene." He twisted toward the deputy. "Since Grace doesn't want a ride, take Vertie to the hospital. And no more rough stuff, you hear me? You use that stick again and you'll be facing assault charges."

"Assault charges?" The deputy sounded surprised.

"In the car. Now."

Grace hurried to position her body between Noverta and the two officers. Noverta was her baby brother, all six feet of him. "You don't need to take Vertie to the hospital. I can take care of him."

Cal took off his hat and ran a hand over his head. "He's in shock, Grace. He's going to the hospital. With Herb."

"Then I'm going with him," she replied.

"Grace..." Cal used his *patient* voice again. Directed her way, that patient voice didn't seem so admirable.

"Don't you *Grace* me, Cal Henderson. Vertie's my brother and you're not taking him anywhere without taking me, too." *So there.* She quelled the urge to stomp her foot.

Cal made an indecipherable sound. He put his hat back on and widened his stance. "You *cannot* go with him. Noverta is going to the hospital. Once he's released, he's going to the station for questioning. Alone."

"I'll call my father. You can argue with him."

Cal crossed his arms over his chest. "That's probably a good idea. Call. Then if you don't get out of the way and let me do my job, I'm going to forget I still care about you and arrest you for obstruction of justice."

Criminy. He'd called her bluff. She never intended to call her father. Things would be just fine if she never had to speak to her old man again. Well, things would be just fine if Noverta wasn't a murder suspect.

"Sis." Noverta's voice was unexpected.

She twisted her head to make sure she hadn't imagined her brother's words. "Vertie, you okay?"

He nodded, and then grabbed his head with both hands. "Don't worry about me. The lump on my head will go away. Lily's head..."

Dear Lord. She prayed Noverta wouldn't lose it again. Not in front of Herb.

"Do as Cal says and go home," Noverta said, his voice calm again. "I'll see you in the morning."

She couldn't see Cal's expression, but his body language made it clear he'd been serious about arresting her. Might as well concede game one. She had things she needed to do to keep her brother out of jail. Even if one of those things meant talking to her father after all. "Fine. I'm going."

# CHAPTER 4

Cal waited until Grace disappeared into the darkness. Then he stooped over Noverta, who sat on the stone walkway, rubbing his head. Given the events of the evening, the lump on his noggin might be a welcome distraction.

"Vertie, Herb's going to take you to the hospital."

He stared at his deputy, expecting an argument, but Herb only nodded. Cal motioned for the deputy to help him get Noverta on his feet. Together, they managed to get the man upright.

On his feet, Noverta resisted when they moved toward the car. "I can't go," he moaned. "I can't leave her."

Cal blinked, wondering if Noverta meant Grace. Then he winced. Of course he meant his wife, Lily.

No way could he have murdered Lily. So who had?

"Lily's gone," Cal said. "Staying here won't help. We have to get you to the hospital."

Noverta didn't move. "Promise me you'll take care of Lily."

Hell. "I'll do what I can, buddy. You know that."

Noverta nodded, although Cal suspected his words hadn't registered. "Find Tanner, Cal."

Herb guided the stunned man toward the car. Oddly, Noverta offered no resistance. Cal almost wished he had.

The deputy closed the door and walked back toward Cal. "I know I screwed up, Boss, but don't make me leave. Noverta don't need no doctor and I want to help with the investigation."

God help him. "Vertie's in shock," he said, drawing on what little patience he had left. "We need to get him cleared so we can question him. After you take him to County Hospital, I need you to go by and wake Rodney. Tell him to get over here." Cal desperately needed his senior deputy at this scene. Unlike Herb, Rodney Parker had six years' experience as a Memphis patrolman. He'd worked on a couple of homicides while serving with the MPD and had only returned to Leeton because Cal asked him to be deputy. More important, Rodney was Noverta's first cousin, on his mother's side. Rod would be motivated to find evidence clearing his relative.

"Why can't we just get Rodney on the horn?" Herb asked.

"Because the switchboard operator will overhear. This investigation is tough enough without half the townspeople rushing over here to see what happened." *Like you did, Herbie.* "And don't you call anyone either, Herb."

Instead of balking, as expected, Herbert nodded. "All right. I'll be back as soon as I drop him off."

Cal placed a hand on the deputy's shoulder to keep him from moving. "No. Once you talk to Rodney, go back to the hospital and wait until Noverta is released. Got it?"

Herb's shoulders slumped. "Okay." He turned and headed back toward his car. Without an argument. Maybe things were getting better.

"Wait!" Cal called. "After you wake Rodney, I need you to go to the funeral home. Get Wayne out of bed and tell him we need him to pick up the body. After eight a.m."

Getting the county's only funeral director out of bed would take some doing. Wayne slept like the dead—pun not intended—and wouldn't appreciate being awakened at four a.m. only to be told to pick up a corpse four hours later, but Cal didn't see any way around the situation. He couldn't release the body before the Memphis team investigated.

"What you gonna do?" Herb asked.

Why couldn't Herb follow instructions? Just once. "As soon as the Memphis boys get through here, I'll go talk to Ida. After that, if the hospital has released Noverta, we'll question him at the office. Either way, you stay with Noverta. That clear?"

"Sure thing, Boss."

He waited until Herb's car disappeared into the night and then pulled the string to turn off the porch light. He couldn't think with the hundred-watt bulb shining in his eyes. Noverta's parting words kept echoing in his head. "Promise me you'll take care of Lily."

Hell. Like he could do anything for a dead woman. He couldn't even let Grace comfort her brother.

Being a D.C. cop had been a good diversion after they'd told him he couldn't play baseball, but the seedier side of law enforcement had gotten to him. He'd returned to his small town and ran for sheriff, expecting peace and quiet. If Cal had known his peacefulness would end in less than a year, he might have made other plans.

He shined the flashlight on his watch, wondering how long it would take the Memphis team to arrive. Since he had a wait ahead of him, he might as well look for the dog again. His instincts said the dog's disappearance and the murder were related, but maybe someone simply stole Tanner. The dog *was* the most prized animal in the county and had to be worth a few bucks.

Cal walked toward the back, knowing Tanner usually stayed in the shed behind the main house, when he wasn't sleeping with Lily. She did pamper that dog—or rather had. Maybe she spoiled the animal to annoy her husband, or maybe she was just lonely. Either way, Lily loved the animal and Tanner guarded her fiercely.

Cal reversed directions, shining his light in a wide arc, looking for anything he'd missed before. He froze when he spotted tracks, footprints he hadn't seen earlier. Of course, the prints were new. Grace had walked to Noverta's house via the path in the woods.

He rubbed the bridge of his nose, the pain in his head getting worse. When he raised his head, he saw something. What? A light flickering in the woods?

He turned off his flashlight and waited. Nothing.

Then he heard a noise. The roar of an engine?

Definitely. In the opposite direction of Ida Simmons's house. No lights. Had someone been watching?

Hell's bells, he couldn't go after them. Because he'd sent Herb to the hospital. Could he do anything right?

He waited, scanning the horizon repeatedly. The light did not reappear.

* * * *

It was after seven a.m. when Cal walked down the hill to Ida's house, Herb on his heels.

"I told you to wait with Vertie." Lack of sleep and the direness of Noverta's situation didn't help his temper, but Cal managed to keep from snapping. Barely.

The Memphis team hadn't arrived until after four-thirty, and the deputy returned long before the city boys finished sorting through the evidence. Cal hadn't want to reprimand Herb in front of another team, so he'd held his tongue. He supposed he should be grateful Herb didn't interfere with their investigation.

"Vertie's sleepin' so I didn't see no reason to watch him snore. I locked him in a cell so he ain't goin' nowhere."

*Damn.* "Where's Rodney?" he asked.

Herb shook his head. "He didn't answer the door. I pounded on it with my stick."

Cal wanted to yell, but with a monumental effort, closed his mouth. He needed a dependable deputy and Herb wasn't the man. He suspected Herb hadn't tried very hard to find Rodney. He should drive to the senior deputy's house himself.

To be fair, Rodney probably wasn't home. Likely, he'd stayed overnight with one of his babes. Women loved the senior deputy and Rodney loved them back. By the dozen. He seemed to have a different doll every weekend.

Cal executed an abrupt about-face so he could study Herb's face. "Was his car at his house?"

The deputy removed his hat and scratched his head. "Whose car?"

"*Rodney's* car, Herb. Pay attention."

The deputy shifted his feet, a sure sign he lied. "Didn't notice."

"You didn't notice if there was a car parked in front of his house? Are you joking?"

Herb pursed his mouth and shook his head. Damn deputy probably hadn't even gone to Rodney's house. Ida opened the door before Cal could say more.

He nodded at the elderly woman, forcing his jaw muscles to relax. "Morning, Mrs. Ida."

"Come on in, boys."

A mouthwatering aroma overwhelmed his senses, temporary blotting the memory of the worst night of his life—rather early morning of his life. Scents of coffee and chocolate combined with bacon to form sensory perfection, creating a balm that made it almost impossible to believe a murder had occurred less than three-hundred yards away. Almost.

"You must be hungry," Ida said.

Cal wasn't. Even Ida's legendary biscuits and chocolate couldn't tempt him. "Coffee would be nice." He flashed what he hoped passed for a smile.

"Do I smell biscuits?" Herb asked, his tongue sliding over his lips.

"Just coffee." Cal frowned at the deputy.

As usual, Herb was too obtuse to notice. Man kept staring toward the back of Ida's house. Why had he allowed him to tag along?

"Come on back to the kitchen," Ida replied, acting as if they'd come to Sunday tea. They followed and she placed two steaming cups on the table, a look of concern on her face. She might be a nosy old lady, but she was nice.

"Sit." She plopped into a chair across from them, wincing when her hips made contact with the oak seat. The woman must be at least eighty. Her joints would hurt after being awake all night. "It's bad, isn't it?" she asked.

"What makes you say that?" Cal wondered exactly what Ida knew.

"I'm an old woman, Cal Henderson, not a fool."

He rubbed his temples while Herb helped himself to one of Ida's biscuits.

"What happened?" she asked.

"Why don't you tell us what you saw," Cal replied, not wanting to put any ideas in her head.

"I didn't really *see* anything," she replied. "I *heard* several cars last night. But then Lily always has a lot of visitors."

"Several?" Cal stopped blowing on his coffee and stared at her face. "Was that earlier? Before midnight?" Had she really been awake that late or was she merely basking in the attention?

"Well, yes and no. I try not to be nosy, but since Syd died, every little noise seems to catch my attention."

Not nosy? Cal worked hard to keep his expression blank. Ida might be the busiest of the busybodies. She'd also managed to work Syd

Simmons into the conversation in less than two minutes. Her husband passed away while Cal played for the Washington Senators during the 1934 season. Cal hadn't returned for the funeral and he swore Ida took every opportunity to mention Syd, her way of waving the guilt wand. Cal doubted Joe Cronin would have appreciated it if he'd announced, "Gee, coach. I know we're playing the Yankees but the guy's wife made us cookies."

Most of Cal's memories of Old Man Simmons were filled with "Get off my property." Ida had been different. Having no children of her own, she'd bribed them with goodies, especially Noverta. Like most grownups, Ida doted on Noverta. Cal had earned his share of lemon bars simply because he was the best friend. Syd didn't share his wife's sentiment. The man resented the chocolate chip goodies Ida baked for them.

"Exactly how many cars did you hear?" he asked, determined to control the questions.

Ida blinked at his abruptness. "Before yours?"

Cal nodded.

"Well... At least four, maybe five, but I don't know exactly what time I heard them."

"Why not?" Cal asked.

Ida shook her head. "I have trouble sleeping because of my bursitis, but I do doze off. Still, I'm quite positive I heard two of the cars just before I heard the first shots. Those were gun shots I heard, right?"

Cal didn't blink, he wanted to hear her story before he confirmed anything. She turned to Herb, probably hoping for confirmation. The blasted deputy nodded, his mouth too full of biscuit to speak. Ida was one smart coot.

"You were telling me about the cars," Cal prompted.

"Oh, right. Anyway, after the first shots, I heard another automobile."

The woman confirmed what Cal already knew from the multiple tire tracks. Finally some good news. The Randolph house was on a dead-end so the cars had to belong to people visiting Lily. Even if one of those cars belonged to Lily's lover, that still left one vehicle unaccounted for. That car likely belonged to the killer.

Cal's senses alerted. "*First* shots? You said you heard *a* shot when you called earlier. You heard more shots?"

She nodded.

"How many? When did you hear them?"

"I heard three shots in all. At least I'm pretty sure I heard three. There were two booms the first time," Ida said, squinting over her wire-rimmed glasses. "Only heard one shot the last time."

That didn't add up. Cal figured Ida must be confused. "The shots weren't all fired at the same time?"

She shook her head. "No. I'm not positive about the time, because the first two were around one in the morning."

"Why didn't you call me then?" Cal asked.

The old lady shook her head. "I went to the porch and heard laughing so I figured I must be mistaken. When I heard the next shot, I figured I'd best call you."

"You heard laughing? Who was laughing?"

"I'm sorry," Ida said, shaking her head again. "I don't know. Think it was a man."

Cal's head reeled. Did that mean someone had been clowning around? Or had the killer laughed after the shooting? "What time was the second shot?"

Ida shook her head. "I didn't look at the clock, but I called as soon as I heard it. Well, as soon as I could get out of bed and get to the phone."

That would have been around two a.m. Only why would anyone shoot and then shoot again an hour later?

"Any idea who killed her?" Ida asked.

"I never said there was a murder, Ida." Cal watched the woman's face, immediately on alert. He looked for a tic or any minute expression that might indicate she knew something more. Herb stopped eating to stare at her.

Ida's lips pursed. "Don't you go getting all suspicious, Calvin Henderson. Of course, there was a murder. Otherwise that Memphis police car wouldn't have driven over here." She paused for a second and her expression saddened. "Was it Lily?"

Cal figured everyone would know soon enough, so he nodded. Ida dropped her head—a moment of respect? Regret? Herb resumed his eating.

Ida raised her head. "Herbie?"

The deputy choked on the last bite of biscuit. Cal used the embroidered napkin to hide his smile. Everyone knew he hated to be called Herbie.

"Would you like another biscuit?" Ida asked. Without waiting for a response, she put two biscuits on the deputy's plate and ladled on the chocolate.

Cal didn't know if Ida had intentionally plied Herb with food to keep him from interrupting, or if the deputy's full mouth was purely coincidental. Either way, Cal was grateful.

"Did you see or hear Noverta's car?" he asked. "Or recognize any others?"

"Hon, I didn't see any of the automobiles. I couldn't sleep, but I was still in the bed trying to get my forty winks."

Questions about the automobiles were leading nowhere, so Cal changed tactics. "You said Lily had a lot of visitors. All of them male?"

Ida hesitated. Probably struggling with the age-old Southern dilemma: How do you be both polite and honest? "You mean before last night?"

He nodded.

"The ones I saw were always men." Honesty had apparently won. "Poor Vertie. I couldn't love that boy more if he were my own son."

Cal nodded. Might as well end the interview. If Ida knew anything that could help Noverta, she would have mentioned it already. Noverta had been her favorite as far back as Cal could remember. The woman didn't think anyone noticed, but she'd always slipped Noverta an extra cookie or given him the biggest piece of strawberry pie. Even Syd didn't get a piece as big as Noverta's. Ida's husband complained, but Cal had never minded. Ida gave Noverta refuge when life with John Randolph proved too much for a ten-year-old. That was more important than pie.

Cal stood, grabbing his hat. "Thanks, Ida. I may have more questions later. If you think of anything else, let me know." His deputy, still chomping on a biscuit, made no move to get up. "Let's go, Herb."

Herb stuffed the rest of the biscuit in his mouth and then wiped his hands on the napkin Ida held out for him. "Right," he mumbled.

"You know I'll do anything I can to help Noverta," Ida said.

Cal gave her a brief nod. "I know. By the way, thanks for calling Grace. Saved me some time."

She frowned. "I didn't call Grace."

Cal froze. Then he forced a smile, but Ida frowned.

Too bad he couldn't deputize Ida. The woman noticed something was odd about his question whereas Herb just kept eating. Didn't the joker realize the importance of Ida's answer? Good thing

51

he didn't. If Herb thought he had a reason to go after Grace, he'd swing for the fences.

Hell, he should be going after Grace himself. He had *assumed* Ida had called her when Grace showed up at Noverta's house — a greenhorn mistake. No more assumptions, he'd demand the truth.

Things just kept getting worse.

# CHAPTER 5

*Monday, November 7*

Cal parked his Packard in the slot marked *Sheriff* and turned off the ignition. He made no move to get out, needing a minute, maybe two. His eyes ached and he needed to close them, but when he did, everything still looked red. He pulled out his pocket watch, the only memento he had from his father. Eight o'clock. Hard to believe it had only been thirty hours since he'd gotten the phone call from Ida.

The Memphis team collected evidence, but refused to take jurisdiction. Which meant Cal and his team, meager as they were, had to solve the crime. He'd scheduled a seven-thirty meeting with his deputies but he dawdled. The last thing he wanted to hear were more questions when he had no answers. And he was exhausted—not from too little sleep, although that hadn't helped. He was just plain tired, bottom of the ninth losing 10-1 weary.

No matter what he'd attempted, something always gummed the works. A fellow didn't like to bellyache, but all he'd ever wanted was to play baseball. And Grace. Seeing her again, even under these circumstances, stirred old feelings—feelings best left alone.

Cal had almost had his dream within his grasp—both baseball and Grace. Then he'd lost Grace. They'd talked about a wedding after she graduated. Instead, she'd married that sissy, Ernest Gardner, only a month after he left town. Why? She'd insisted he go to Houston, said she understood playing for the Buffaloes gave him a better shot at the majors than signing on with the Memphis Choctaws. So what went wrong?

Worse, he worried she might be somehow involved in Lily's death. He shook his head. There *had* to be another explanation.

When he'd come home for a visit all those years ago, he'd tried to talk to Grace, but she wouldn't see him. He hadn't pushed. Why bother? Time clearly hadn't healed whatever ailed her. Worse, she'd become Mrs. Gardner, and was thus out of bounds. Still, he should have demanded an answer. Or maybe he shouldn't have gone to Houston in the first place.

Without Grace, he'd put his all into his baseball dream, only the major leagues lost some of the luster. Even that little bit of happiness vanished when he broke his wrist, thanks to a wild pitch and the runner on third breaking for the plate. The catcher fired the ball to the plate, making the tag a close call. "*You're out!*" the ump had called. Only Cal was out too, the collision with the runner's cleats breaking his wrist and ripping tendons in his arm.

He'd gotten a slew of sympathy cards, most under the guise of get-well wishes. Of course, most of those same wishes came with requests for autographs from Heinie Manush or John Stone. Funny, Manush had never asked Cal to sign autographs for his friends. Guess there was humor in almost anything. He could sure use some now.

After learning he couldn't play baseball anymore, he'd refused to cry foul and return to his hometown with his tail between his legs. He'd signed on with the DC Metropolitan Police instead. What he hadn't counted on was corpse after corpse. Two years as a big city cop had been enough, more than enough. Noverta came to DC for a visit and hinted Cal should come home and run for sheriff. At the time, that sounded like a good idea, except he didn't know if he could stomach seeing Grace with someone else. In hindsight, he supposed he wanted to see her more than he minded her being married, so he'd returned to Leeton, thinking he could capitalize on his big city experience but he wouldn't have to deal with murder and mayhem.

He'd been wrong. So wrong. He'd come home, hoping to finally belong. Instead, he remained an outsider and now he had a dead body on his hands.

Closing his car door, he caught sight of a Ford parked next to his Packard. "Hell." One more thing he didn't need. Cal ground his teeth, a habit he thought he'd kicked.

Herb stepped out of the office before he could walk inside. "Boss, you got a visitor. Jackson McKinney."

He already knew that, but didn't let on. "Thanks, Herb."

Why didn't Herb look tired? Cal certainly didn't want the perky deputy hanging around while he talked with the DA. Cal didn't need half the town knowing what he'd discussed with Jackson. "Do me a favor, Herb. Head over to the Town Diner and get us some of those cherry things." He handed the deputy a dollar and walked inside before the man could protest.

Cal dreaded what awaited him beyond the paneled hallway, past the main office to his smaller space in the back of the building. The district attorney would be pacing behind his oak door. Who'd called the DA? Ida Simmons? Herb? Most likely Herbert. Although the deputy should have mentioned that. Hell, Cal should have notified the DA himself. Still, he resented that someone else had beat him to the bag. Would he ever regain control of the investigation?

The way things were going, he should probably expect the editor of the *Leeton Herald* to stop by too. He'd wanted to make a quick check on Noverta, but clearly, that wouldn't happen anytime soon.

Jackson stepped aside to let him enter the office. Rodney shrugged behind the DA's back.

"I need to speak to you." Jackson had worn the same expression when he tried out for the Mudcats. The man had struck out and still had a chip on his shoulder.

"So speak." Cal said, too tired for polite conversation.

"Alone."

"I'll be going then," Rodney said, rolling his eyes behind the district attorney's head.

The deputy had barely closed the door when Jackson blurted out, "I'm charging Noverta with first degree murder."

*What*? "Good God, Jack. I've only just started the investigation."

"Noverta is my friend too, but Judge Sparks wants to start the trial next week."

Cal took off his hat and tossed it toward his desk. Judge Olsen Sparks had kept his Circuit Court seat for four elections. Known as much for his impatience as his fairness, naturally he'd want to *hurry things along.* Given enough pressure from outside the judicial system, the judge had even been known to sacrifice some of his fairness. Sparks didn't have much liking for Senator John Randolph, either, which didn't bode well for his son Noverta. Politics and justice sometimes just didn't mix.

Cal's tired stomach developed an ache. "Next week?" he asked, shaking his head. "You can't be serious?"

"Why not? If you arrested him, he must be guilty."

"I didn't arrest him!" Cal unclenched his fist, determined he wouldn't raise his voice again.

"Huh?" Jackson didn't sound like a Yale graduate. "Then why's he locked up in the jail?"

*Hell*. Cal knew he'd made a mistake. He hadn't gotten back to the office until noon on Sunday. Noverta refused to talk, wouldn't even say he wasn't going to talk, which was pretty much what Cal had advised his friend to do. He wanted to let Noverta go, but he had to play this one by the rules. He'd be pretty damn incompetent if he released a man who'd been holding the gun and had offered no explanation.

Grace had shown up, refusing to look him in the eye. "Dad got him a lawyer. The man will be here tomorrow. Don't question Vertie until the lawyer shows up." She'd left without another word, surprising the hell out of Cal. Even for the senator, hiring a lawyer on a Sunday was a big, big deal

So Cal left Noverta behind bars. "I'm only holding him for questioning, Jack."

"You haven't questioned him yet?" Jackson's mouth dropped open.

Cal shook his head. "I can't. Not until his lawyer shows up."

Jackson scoffed. "Lawyer? Why would an innocent man need a lawyer?"

"He doesn't," Cal replied, not at all sure that was true. "The senator hired the attorney."

The DA made a snorting sound. "Well, hurry up and question him then. I'll hold off with my charges until then. As long as it's today."

Cal blinked, trying to think. "You can't charge him. Unless there's some new evidence, I'm letting him go."

Jackson propped a hand on his hip, looking more sissy than tough. "Unless you have proof someone else pulled the trigger, my office will order his re-arrest. Noverta's my friend, too, but everyone knows Lily was… Noverta must have shot her. He was the only one there."

"How do you know that?" Cal demanded. "No details of the investigation have been released."

"That's not important."

"I have to disagree," Cal said, working hard to keep a civil tone. "I imagine Adeline was on the switchboard when Ida called me. She told someone. Or a lot of somebodies. Then rumor and speculation spread like wildfire. Isn't that what happened, Jack?"

Jackson looked at his feet. "Just doing my job, Cal."

"Your job?" Cal couldn't believe he'd heard correctly. "Hell, Jack, with all that booshwash, why wait for an investigation? Hell, all that talk must mean Noverta's guilty. Let's skip all that boring stuff in the constitution and get the rope to hang our *friend* right now." His polite tone had gone down swinging, only he didn't really care.

"Now hold on, Cal."

He had no intention of *holding on*. "You decided to go to trial without even talking to me and you want *me* to hold on? Go to hell, Jackson."

The DA's lower lip quivered. "Hey, look. I never expected a murder either. Who knows? Vertie may even confess."

"He's *not* guilty, Jack."

"You don't know that."

"I do," Cal insisted.

Jackson looked away, but when he looked at Cal again, his shoulders stiffened. "Cal, I don't like this either, but we have to be professional. Even if the killer is a friend. A good friend. God knows we haven't had a murder trial in this county since, well, I don't know when, but we have to do this right." Jackson clearly ranked career ahead of his friends.

"Are you implying I'm not being professional, Jack?" He hoped the district attorney didn't miss the threat.

"No, of course not. I think that … Look, I'm sorry, but your friendship might be clouding your judgment. Just a little.. Like I said, Vertie's my friend too, but first you arrest him and then you tell me he didn't do it. What am I supposed to think about that? Do you think it's any easier for me to try him than it was for you to arrest him?"

"Yes." Cal *knew* it was a lot easier for Jackson. "And I *didn't arrest him.*"

The three of them had been inseparable in high school, but he sensed Jackson had since grown more than a little bitter. In a small town where baseball meant more than brains, Jackson hadn't made the team. Even graduating from Yale didn't rate respect, not in a town where sports reigned as king.

Why Jackson had ever come back to Podunk-ville remained a mystery. The man could have signed on with any law firm in the country.

Cal experienced a stirring of suspicion about Jackson's haste. Trying a murder case would finally make him a big shot if he got a guilty verdict.

What really surprised Cal, though, was that he wasn't angry with Jackson. "Look, Jack. I may have to arrest Vertie. I know that. He has motive. He was sitting at the murder scene, alone, holding a gun. If I didn't arrest him, I'd be incompetent. However, the ballistics and fingerprint results haven't even come back yet. It's too early to make an arrest."

"Ballistics?"

Cal blinked. Jackson acted like he'd never heard the word—maybe he hadn't. The DA had gotten lazy since his college days.

"Yes, ballistics," he replied. "We need to know what gun fired the bullet lodged in Lily's head."

"Shit, Cal. He shot her in the head?"

Cal moved around his desk, as fast as he could without running. "For God's sake, Jackson, Vertie didn't shoot her." He paused for effect. "And how could you possibly think about going to trial when you didn't even know how Lily died? Christ! It's insane to charge him with murder before the investigation has even started."

"Don't bark at me," the DA snapped. "You make a big deal because I jumped to conclusions, but you can't *assume* Vertie's innocent just because he's your friend. Who else would've shot her, Cal? Who else had motive? Who else had opportunity? Lily's not going to let some stranger walk into her bedroom and then sit still while somebody puts a bullet in her head. You better get on board, Sheriff."

Cal had vowed to make no more assumptions, but he wasn't *assuming* anything. He *knew* Noverta hadn't killed anyone. Only he wouldn't be able to convince Jackson. The DA had made up his mind, had said *your* friend, not *our* friend.

He tried anyway. "Half the wives in this county have motive, Jack. That's why we investigate. There are too many gaps. Vertie's dog is missing, Ida heard a car arrive—probably Noverta's car— after she heard the shots. More important, Vertie just didn't act like he put a bullet into someone's head."

"Says who? How the hell do you know what someone acts like after he murders his wife? You ever shot anyone, Cal?"

"Don't be an ass, Jack. I'll wager I've seen a few more murdered corpses than you."

Jackson wheezed in a breath. "Doesn't mean you know how a killer thinks. Damn dog probably just ran off and Ida's an old woman. She probably hears a lot of shit that isn't there."

"And the cow jumped over the moon. You want to do your job, Jack? Then let me do mine first." Cal retreated mentally to his own dugout— in his mind, the home team dugout. More harsh words would only threaten a lifelong friendship and even though the DA was wrong, Cal didn't want Jackson as an enemy. He took a breath and tried again. "Look, I'm not asking for much. Just give me a couple weeks before you start handing out indictments."

The DA sighed. "I can't. Mayor Grimes..." he stopped speaking and started rubbing the balding spot on his head. Cal had seen the same gesture often enough, even before Jackson started losing his hair. The man was nervous.

And Cal should have known Jackson was getting pressure. "It's the feud, isn't it?"

Jackson nodded. "Yeah. Martin Grimes hates John Randolph. Judge Sparks isn't a fan either. I'm in no-man's land, Cal. I'll do what I can, but no promises."

Cal almost felt sorry for Jackson. Almost. He couldn't afford sympathy. "You can't let them pressure you. Not with a man's life at stake."

The DA shrugged. "The mayor's my boss, Cal. He speaks, I obey."

*Hell's bells*. "At least stall for a day or two. Buy me some time, Jack."

"I'll do what I can, Cal, but if your fancy ballistics report shows that the bullet came from the gun Noverta was holding, I can't get you a minute. I think both of us know that gun killed Lily, don't we?" Jackson made eye contact, but looked away quickly.

"Tell me something," Cal said. "Did Herb talk to you? Or go directly to the mayor?"

Jackson glanced at the floor, and then at the window. "You do me a favor, Cal. Try to wrap up the investigation soon. If something comes out after the trial starts, I'll look foolish."

"Yeah, Jack. That's my number one concern." The sarcasm lingered like the scent of smelly baseball cleats. Jackson McKinney was a lily-livered swine, Yale degree and all. The pig rushed to the door, so fast you'd think someone had sounded the fire alarm.

After the DA left, the walls of Cal's office seemed to close in. He counted to ten and then walked outside. Leaning against the brick building, he chewed on a toothpick. The trial would be quick. Sparks and the mayor would see to that. Both men were bitter, out for blood. If the mayor let

Jackson delay the proceedings, Senator Randolph would have time to mobilize and call in political favors. Thus Noverta's only hope depended on Cal finding out who really killed Lily. And doing it fast. Jackson McKinney could no longer be considered a friend.

"Cal?" Rodney interrupted Cal's thoughts.

Just as well. Thinking was getting him nowhere. "Yeah?"

"You coming back in?"

"Ah, shit." He'd completely forgotten about their meeting.

Rodney held open the door, but put a hand on Cal's shoulder as he tried to enter the building "Why didn't you call me? After Ida called? For God's sake, Cal. Vertie's not only my cousin, he's my best friend."

Cal blinked. "I sent Herb to your house. Where were you anyway? Herb swears he banged on your door."

Rodney jerked his hand away. "Not so. I was home all night. Nobody even knocked on my door."

Cal scratched his eyebrow. "Maybe you just didn't hear him."

Rodney shook his head. "Not possible. You know what a light sleeper I am. Besides, I had…a guest. Didn't do a lot of sleeping if you know what I mean. I don't give a shit what Herb says, nobody banged on my door."

Cal scratched his brow again. "One question, Rod. Where was your car?"

"Huh?"

"Your car. Where was it parked last night?"

Rodney frowned. "In front of my house. Where it always is. Why?"

*Damn.* Cal had always suspected Herb wasn't the twit he pretended to be. Still, what kind of game did he play? The deputy probably didn't want to share the glory of being at a murder scene, but could there be another reason for his lack of action? If Herb hadn't gone to wake Rodney, what had he been doing?

"Cal?" Rodney frowned.

Cal gave his head a little shake. "Let's go inside." He had a few other ideas, but he wouldn't slander the deputy. He couldn't share his theory with Rodney, not yet. "Do me a favor, Rod. Don't tell Herb about this conversation."

"Bull." The big deputy leaned against the door and wrapped his arms across his chest. "That screwball made me look bad. Why should I keep quiet?"

Cal huffed a breath. Rodney was correct. "For now, consider it a favor."

Rodney winced. "Damn, Cal... All right. But next time, I might just flatten the little crumb."

"Thanks." He slapped Rodney on the back, grateful he had one person willing to cooperate. "Let's get this meeting over with. You and I can talk later. After I find something for Herbie to do."

Rodney nodded, but didn't move away from the plastered wall. "There's one more thing. Don't mean to tell you how to do your job and all, but don't we need to notify Lily's folks?"

*Damn.* He'd completely forgotten a basic procedure. Especially bad since Lily's old man was Brant Carleton. Lily came from money, lots of money. Her father was the cotton king and had visited the White House—as FDR's guest. Didn't matter that Carleton had disowned his daughter before she married Noverta, the man still had to be notified.

"You know where the Carletons live now?" Cal asked Rodney.

"Yeah, down in Tupelo. Over two hours from here. Want me to go deliver the news?"

Cal considered calling the local police station, but the Mississippi boys weren't always the most cooperative fellows. "Yes... No. Let me have Herbie do that. That'll buy us four hours, right?"

"Yes, but you sure you want *him* doing the notification?"

He wasn't sure about anything, but he'd send Herb anyway. Rodney followed him back inside. Herbert Smith sat in the main office, feet on his desk and strawberry jam covering his upper lip.

"Herb, in my office."

"That where we're meeting?" Herb asked, his mouth full of brownish dough.

"Meeting's canceled," Cal snapped.

"Good." The deputy stretched his arms over his head. After he stood, he stretched again before he shuffled to the office door. "But if the meetings canceled, what you need?"

Cal sat down behind his regulation gray desk and stared out his window. Herb wasn't the only one who could instigate the waiting game.

Neither spoke. The deputy cracked first. "You aren't going to yell at me again for grabbing the gun, are ya?" Herb dropped his arms to his side, knocking papers off Cal's desk. "Ah, sorry, Boss."

"You seem tired, Herb. You need to go home?" That would buy Cal twenty-four Herb-free hours instead of only four. Having the deputy gone wouldn't fix anything, but his absence would ease the dull throbbing in Cal's head. "You've worked a lot of hours in the past two days."

The deputy blinked. "No. I'm fine."

Cal studied him. Man would probably never sleep if it meant he might miss something. "You've lived here all your life, right?" The friendly went out of his voice as he remembered Herb's "not from down here" comment.

The deputy didn't seem to notice Cal's tone. "Yeah. I mean no. Lived in this state all my life, but my folks moved all over."

"Do you know Lily Randolph's parents?"

"Nah. They ain't from around here." Almost the same thing Herb said at the crime scene. Maybe the man hadn't meant to insult him.

Cal started to say "Tupelo," but changed his mind. "Get over to the courthouse and find out where they live." The task would keep Herb busy for a while. And out of Cal's hair.

"Why don't you just ask Noverta?"

Excellent point. Not the type of logic he'd come to expect from Herb. Still, he wasn't about to tell the bozo deputy, who might be smarter than he appeared, that Noverta had never met his in-laws. No one in their circle had met the parents and Lily never talked about her folks except to say they'd kicked her out when she was seventeen.

"Boss," Herb interrupted. "I asked why we don't get Noverta to tell us where Lily's folks live."

"Can't do that," Cal replied. "Vertie's lawyer told him not to say anything, especially to us." Not exactly a lie. Noverta had actually refused to talk, but Cal hoped his friend would talk to him privately—if he knew anything—once he got a chance to talk *off the books*. "Now get over to the courthouse before I suspend you without pay. You're still on thin ice for assaulting Noverta last night." He didn't intend to let a subordinate keep yanking him around either.

"Hold on. I didn't mean—"

"Herb, go."

"That went well." Rodney said as soon as Herb slammed the door. "I have to ask again. You sure you want Herbert notifying the Carletons?"

"Maybe not," Cal admitted. He could easily imagine Herb describing Lily's body to her mother.

"Keep an eye out for him. Once he gets the address, go with him to Tupelo."

Rod grinned and reached for his hat. "So the meeting really is canceled, huh?"

Cal nodded, wondering what else would go wrong. Not much had gone right since he'd taken Ida's call. Christ but he should never have run for sheriff. "Yeah. I don't have any news to share. I'll go and talk to the senator. We can talk more when you get back from Mississippi."

Rodney followed Herb out of the office, Cal picked up the phone and asked the operator to connect him with John Randolph. While he waited, he opened his bottom desk drawer and took out the baseball cap. When he'd gotten back to his office on Sunday, he'd stashed the undocumented evidence, not sure what to do with the hat. He studied it, still unable to make sense of the thing. Did it belong to the killer or Lily's lover? In other words, was it a clue or a motive?

He needed to ask Noverta if he'd seen the cap, only Noverta really wasn't talking. According to the jailor, he wasn't eating either, scarcely taking a sip of water now and then.

Cal tugged at his collar. Noverta acted like a man already condemned, no longer functional in the world of the living. At the scene, Noverta had clearly been in shock about Lily's death, but Cal suspected he knew something. Otherwise, why refuse to talk off the record? Surely Noverta knew Cal had his back.

Unless Noverta's silence might pertain to Grace. "Damn."

What role could she have possibly played? Cal didn't want to even pursue that line of thinking.

Grace's husband was another story, though. Noverta might cover for Ernest, right? Hadn't he heard Noverta and his brother-in-law were pals? Matter of fact, Noverta might be Ernest's only friend.

Cal shook his head, wishing he could get his brain firing in a single direction. Until he got more investigation under his belt, all of the Randolphs—and anyone associated with them—would remain suspect.

The phone clicked. "Senator Randolph speakin'."

Cal shoved the Mudcats hat into his desk drawer. "This is Calvin Henderson, sir. We need to talk."

"I know, son. Not over the phone. Let me take care of some things and we can meet." The senator's words were cryptic.

"Sir… Before you hang up…"

The senator cleared his throat. "Yeah?"

"Does Noverta really have a lawyer?" Cal asked.

Silence.

"Sir?"

"I've made some arrangements." The senator disconnected before Cal could request details.

Given the secretive behavior, Cal added another Randolph to his suspect list. Hell, John might even go straight to the top. The senator was a hard man, always expecting perfection from life and perfection from his offspring. He might be the sole reason both Noverta and Grace were so persnickety. Even so, John could mistreat his offspring but if anyone else threatened one of the Randolph clan, the senator would be the first to pick up a baseball bat and start swinging. Or hire a hit man for the strike.

Cal needed to get out of the office. He grabbed his hat and headed for his car. On the way out of the building, he spotted the *Leeton Herald* on Herb's desk. The headline read:

## Local Resident Charged With Murder

Hell's bells. The local paper normally came out on Thursdays. Which meant Melvin Thompson had printed up a special edition.

Cal hadn't charged anyone with anything. Had the DA already stepped in?

Was a guilty verdict far behind?

# CHAPTER 6

*Tuesday, November 8*

Cal pounded a fist against his feather pillow, desperate for sleep. When he'd finally drifted off, he'd dreamed of Noverta strapped to the electric chair. Cal covered his face with a handkerchief so he wouldn't have to watch, only the cloth was wet.

He'd awakened to find Lucky licking his face. Cal scratched the small dog behind the ear, knowing the mutt was only trying to comfort him. The wagging tail was a welcome relief, but the sleep-induced image of Noverta in the hotsquat wouldn't go away.

No way could he get back to sleep. Might as well get up. Grace would already be awake so he could drop by and question her without Herb hovering. Would Ernest also be awake?

Probably not. The man enjoyed his booze and frequented the gin mills in their dry county. Cal didn't really think Ernest had the gonads to kill anyone, even in the heat of passion. Ernest was too lazy to work himself into a rage. Still, the man might have heard something, might know the identity of Lily's lover.

Being honest, Cal admitted he didn't want to even look at Grace's husband, let alone talk to the fink. Questioning Ernest might be priority one, but Cal really wanted to see Grace alone. Dumb, maybe.

No, definitely. He should put aside his personal emotions and behave like a seasoned investigator. More important, he needed to get it into his thick head, once and for all, Grace had married someone else.

When he pulled into her driveway, he was no closer to accepting the situation. The house looked even better than he remembered, though. A new dairy barn had been built on the property since he'd last visited. Grace had done well.

Cal couldn't imagine Ernest helping with the milking, so just what did the man do? Other than live off the cream of Grace's labor? From what he'd heard, the man spent half the day with a bottle in his hand. He'd never really liked Ernest, even before the marriage. The man had been a decent catcher, but once they left the ballfield, Cal had little use for Ernest "Mama's Boy" Gardner.

Grace startled him when she opened the front door. He hadn't even knocked.

"Cal." She ran a hand over the shoulder of her prim white top, and then motioned him inside, her face a mask. She looked a little pale and her blouse was untucked on the left side, not like the Grace he remembered. Even as a kid she'd been fastidious to a fault.

He focused on the rug just inside the room, trying to squash the memory of running his hand over the soft skin beneath that fabric. He needed to see Grace *only* about official business.

"It's early, Cal. I'm guessing this visit is about Vertie?" Her face remained stoic, revealing nothing.

She sounded so proper. Maybe she still didn't want to see him. If only he knew what he'd done, understood why she hadn't waited for him all those years ago.

He reached for her hand, amazed again at the combination of softness and calluses. She smelled good, no perfume, just clean. Some things hadn't changed.

Cal didn't release her hand. Not smart, but he'd missed her. Even after he'd heard about her marriage, he couldn't manage to stop missing her. Some things might not have changed, but the things that mattered were all fouled up.

She pulled her hand away and motioned toward the open door. "Maybe you should come inside."

He stepped inside. "Am I interrupting anything? You and Ernest having breakfast?" Damn, why had he asked that? He should be demanding to know why she just happened on the crime scene instead of making sure they were alone.

She shook her head as she closed the door. "Ernest isn't here."

"Where is he?" Ernest was already out at seven a.m.? No, more likely, he hadn't come home yet.

Grace blinked. "He didn't say. Would you like some coffee?"

As sheriff, he could demand Ernest's location, but maybe she didn't actually know where her husband was. So why embarrass her? Wasn't like Ernest could disappear in Leeton.

"Coffee sounds great. Are you doing okay?" he asked.

She made a rather un-lady like snort. "Great. If you ignore the fact my sister-in-law's dead, my brother had to sleep in the jail and the man I… The man I considered a friend put him there."

That was the Grace he remembered. "You know I had no choice," he said. "I did everything I could to stop the indictment. Right now, I'm doing everything I can to clear Vertie."

He waited. She said nothing.

"I have some questions," he said, studying her expression.

"I know." She ran her hands down the sides of her skirt. "I'm just frustrated. Thanks for not interrogating me in front of Herbie. Let's get that coffee first."

He followed her into the kitchen and sat at the old oak table which had belonged to Grace's grandmother. As kids, he and Noverta carved their initials on the underside. In those days, the house still belonged to Mammie Bumpass and remembering to take off his shoes so he didn't get dirt on the woman's oriental rugs ranked as his only problem. The good old days.

Grace put a mug in front of him and added cream. For some reason, he didn't stop her, even though he now preferred his coffee black, a habit he'd picked up in D.C.

She settled into the hardback chair, placing her hands in her lap. Her posture said schoolteacher, her full lips and creamy skin suggested something more erotic. "Go ahead with your interrogation." Her voice sounded almost hostile.

Cal winced at her tone. "Christ, Grace. Questions don't mean an interrogation."

She placed one elbow on the table and ran her fingers across her temple. "Sorry. I'm a bit on edge."

He nodded. "Why were you at Vertie's house the night Lily…died? You let me believe Ida called you, but she didn't, did she?"

Grace sucked in a breath, her cheeks puffing out as she exhaled. "You know Vertie always turns to me if there's trouble."

Damn. Cal supposed he was a heel for even questioning her presence. Only he couldn't shake the feeling she was hiding something. She wouldn't make eye contact, although he supposed he couldn't read too much into that. She hadn't looked at him directly since he'd returned to Leeton.

He'd think about that another time. "Is there anything you can tell me that might help Vertie?" he asked. "I'm out of options here and things aren't looking good."

"Criminy, Cal. You know I would have told you already." Grace's voice had a slight tremor. "Despite his temper, Vertie couldn't hurt a flea. Everyone in town should know that. Even if he did catch Lily with another man, he'd probably have said, 'Ah, Doll Face. What'd you do that for?'"

Cal nodded. That's exactly what Noverta would say. Too bad what he and Grace knew wasn't evidence.

"Ida Simmons said Lily had lots of visitors. Grace. I don't know any other way to ask this, so I'll be direct. Did you know Lily was having an affair?"

Grace snorted. "Suddenly I'm delicate? We can't talk about sex?"

Her bluntness stunned him. She'd always been direct, but a southern lady didn't say "sex" and Grace epitomized a lady. Maybe being married to

Ernest had changed her. Or maybe living with that awful Gardner woman had taken a toll. Granny could make a preacher cuss.

Damn. He'd forgotten about Granny. Cal gazed at the door leading to the dining room, wondering where the old witch hovered. He'd heard she slept until noon. He certainly hoped so. The woman had always made him feel as if he had poke salad on his teeth. He supposed Grace had to take in her mother-in-law, but he didn't like to think about the only woman he'd ever loved enduring the tirades of that tobacco-chewing cow.

"Cal," Grace said, shaking her head. "Everyone in this town knew about Lily's affairs. Even Vertie—not that I will admit to that outside this room. So, of course, I knew, but I don't have any details. With me being her *husband's sister*, Lily never confided in me."

He studied Grace's face, comparing the woman he remembered to the person sitting across the table. She'd cut her hair and the dark curls were held in place with pins, but Christ, she was beautiful—maybe even more beautiful than she'd been in school. "You sure there's nothing else you can tell me?" he asked, needing to focus on the investigation. "I'm desperate here."

"As I said before, if I knew anything that would help," she said, "I would tell you." The warmth had vanished. Her actions weren't exactly cold, but he sensed she was no longer comfortable in her own skin. His Grace had engulfed everyone with her warmth.

*His Grace*? She hadn't been his Grace for ten years. She'd been Ernest's Grace for the last decade.

He suddenly felt a little cold himself. "You don't know who Lily was seeing?"

Grace tugged at the cuff of her crisp blouse. "From what I hear, she was having affairs. Plural. There was talk of a lover from Pontotoc. More talk had her spending the weekend with another man in Marion. You know how things get repeated and embellished in this town. A person hears a lot of things but that doesn't mean any of them are true."

She hadn't told him anything. The always-direct Grace had pitched around the plate. Cal wondered why.

"What people are saying those things?" he asked. "Who told you about the Pontotoc man?"

She shrugged. "I don't remember, exactly. Even if I did, it would be someone who heard it from someone else."

"Did Vertie know about the rumors?"

"I don't know if he heard that specific one, but he knew Lily wasn't faithful. Last week he told me he thought she was pregnant and said it couldn't be his baby."

"Damn." If Lily was pregnant, Noverta had another motive. Of course the baby's father would have a motive, too.

Why didn't he know things had gotten so bad for his friend. He had no idea Vertie's marriage had completely deteriorated. He should have known, but what could he have done?

"Grace, I wouldn't mention that part about the baby."

"I'm not stupid, sheriff."

Sheriff? Ouch. Just when he'd thought they might be friends again. The awkwardness between them had gotten downright uncomfortable. Since things weren't going well anyway, he might as well force his ten-year-old issue. "Grace, I don't know what happened after I left for Houston, but why would you call me sheriff? You said you loved me once, have you forgotten my name?"

Color flooded her face. Good.

"Of course I remember your name." After a moment, she flashed an almost-smile. "It's Cal. Right?"

The weight lifted from his shoulders. Probably dumb on his part to be encouraged by a half-smile. Especially when her posture remained ramrod straight and she looked like she'd rather be chewing on a tin roof than drinking coffee with him.

He took a sip from his cup, immediately wishing he hadn't. How had he ever liked cream?

"Is something wrong with the coffee?"

Had he winced? He needed to remain straight-faced during interviews, not give away his every thought with body language. Wouldn't do to get called out by a cream-filled cup of caffeine.

"It's fine," he fibbed. A vile-tasting beverage was the least of his issues.

Their gazes met. For a second, neither spoke. For that second, ten years might never have elapsed.

She looked away. "So how *do* we help Vertie?"

Her reminder of Noverta's problems effectively closed the door on the past.

"Okay," he said, thinking aloud. "Let's assume the rumor mill has some credibility and Lily had more than one lover. One of her lovers could have motive, especially if Lover A found out about Lover B."

Grace frowned. "Even though both A and B knew Lily was married?"

"Fishing here. Maybe her lover was married, too. Heard anything about any jealous wives? I've got to have a place to start, Grace." He took another sip, and tried to hide his grimace under the guise of wiping his mouth.

She narrowed her gaze. "What's wrong with your coffee? You made that face."

She'd caught that? The woman was good. And she remembered his faces? Even better. Meant she had thought about him. That was something and something was better than the whole lot of nothing he'd been feeling.

"I... Sorry. I take it black now."

She took his cup to the sink, rinsed it, and poured a fresh cup. "You could have said something."

He flashed a little smile. "That would have been too easy."

He took the fresh cup, resisting the urge to touch her hand when he reached for it. How could they still be so connected, yet so far apart?

Best to focus on the investigation, not his personal life. He had no hope of resolving the latter. "Any idea why Noverta and Lily were having problems? I mean, they seemed happy once. Why would Lily start cheating?"

"You're joking, right?" She looked at him, waiting.

Cal didn't know how to respond. He wasn't joking.

Grace shrugged. "I guess you aren't. Vertie never talked to you? I thought you were his best friend." The tone was there again.

"Men don't talk about those things." He supposed he had a tone of his own, but her disapproval still made him defensive.

"Point taken," she responded. "I can speculate on their problems if that will help?"

It would. He nodded.

"I love my brother, but to a woman like Lily, he might seem a bit...tame."

"Tame?" He didn't understand. "If she was unhappy, why wouldn't she just leave him?"

Grace gave him a look. "Probably the same reason Ernest doesn't leave me. Again, I'm speculating, but I'd say Lily likes Vertie's money. Especially since her mommy and daddy dissolved her trust fund." Grace rose and started toward the sink.

*Reason Ernest doesn't leave me.* Was she nuts? Ernest had the best thing possible and the damn man didn't appreciate Grace? No way. The real question was why did she stay with the dweeb.

He reached for her arm. Grace jumped at his touch, but didn't pull away.

"Are you unhappy?" he asked.

She sat back down, staring at his hand. He reluctantly released her arm.

"Don't ask that." She propped her elbows on the table and then reached for the sugar bowl, twisting the red-and-white bit of pottery in a circle. "Please."

Damn. He'd hoped Grace was happy. If she loved Ernest, things would at least make sense. Only how could she put up with that man? There'd been as much gossip about Ernest as there had been about Lily. Maybe more. Ernest liked the hooch even back when they were teenagers. When Cal heard that Grace's husband had added gambling to his list of vices, he'd wanted to strangle the idiot.

Instead, Cal had avoided everything connected to Ernest Gardner. Once, he'd gotten a call from the owner of the Caged Canary—a speakeasy Cal pretended didn't exist since Leeton was one of several dry counties in south Tennessee that didn't permit businesses to serve liquor. The owner named Ernest Gardner on the complaint. Cal sent

Rodney to handle the disturbance. After his deputy responded, Cal hadn't asked about the details. Hell, he hadn't even read the report. The less he knew about Ernest Gardner, the better.

Even so, he'd never heard anything linking Ernest with Lily. If any of the rumors could be believed though, Ernest cheated a lot. Was it possible the man had cheated with Lily?

If he followed that logic, Grace would have more motive than Noverta. Could she…

*No.* He'd never believe her capable of committing murder and covering up the crime.

Grace sighed. "I really don't know why Vertie stayed with her, Cal. I'm sure Lily stayed with Vertie because divorced women rank lower than chitterlings in this town."

He opened his mouth and closed it again. Grace was correct. Was that why she stayed with Ernest? Women from families who could trace their heritage back to the Mayflower didn't get divorces.

He wanted to believe that, but he couldn't make assumptions. Grace might actually love the crumb she'd married.

"Good morning, Sheriff." Granny Gardner walked into the kitchen.

Cal spewed coffee across the table. He hadn't seen the old lady since he'd returned to Leeton. She'd been scary when he was a kid. Now, the woman was downright haggish. Her gray hair hung in clumps, somehow emphasizing her toothless jaws as she smacked openmouthed on something purple and disgusting.

Had she been hovering outside the door before announcing her presence? How much had Granny overheard? More important, did she know anything that might help Noverta?

"Morning, Granny," he said, standing briefly. He didn't know her first name. Everyone had called her Granny as long as he could remember.

Granny Gardner looked over her glasses at him—glasses Cal was sure she didn't need because no one had ever seen her look through the lenses.

"Mornin' to you, too, Sheriff Cal. I'd ask you to stay for breakfast but poor Ernest has been stricken with the p-monia. I'm sure Grace told you that." Granny flashed Grace a look that made Cal want to cover his privates. "Boy of mine has been abed for nigh a week now and I've been looking after him night and day. I haven't even been able to cook."

He glanced quickly at Grace. She'd said Ernest was gone.

Her eyes widened for just a second. The old woman glared at her too. Who was lying? And why? Were both of them covering for Ernest?

"So Ernest is here?" he asked, avoiding eye contact with Grace.

Granny made a clicking noise with her tongue. "Of course he is. Where else would he be? We done had to miss church Sunday when we never miss church, didn't we Grace? Ernest was in such a bad way he plum near died. Me and Grace been so worried. We thank the Lord Jesus he pulled though the worst of that mess."

So Grace lied. Or had Granny told the whopper? Didn't take a genius to see the older woman goaded Grace. He couldn't believe Grace would lie outright—not to him. Only what he knew didn't seem to amount to much lately.

He wasn't ready to turn over that rock. "I must go," he said, reaching for his hat. "I know a lot of people have been taken with the flu, Granny, but I had no idea Ernest was down. Pneumonia, you say?"

He flashed a look at Grace, hoping for some hint. She stared at the sugar bowl, her face flushed.

"That's what I said." Granny popped an arm over her grayish apron. Why wear an apron when she never cooked?

He nodded again. "Please tell Ernest I hope he recovers soon." He hoped the man sniveled for days.

Grace stiffened. "If you have more questions, Sheriff, I can come by your office."

Interesting. She didn't want to talk in front of Granny? Or maybe she'd been caught in a lie and wanted to explain why she hadn't told the truth?

Hell. He'd come for answers and all he had were more questions. "If I'd known Ernest was ill, I wouldn't have bothered you ladies at home." He turned to Grace. "Mrs. Gardner, perhaps you could come by the office later. Bring Granny with you. I have questions for her too."

Granny clutched at the shawl around her shoulders. "Me? Why would you have questions for me? I'm an old woman, I was sound asleep Saturday night. Didna hear nothin'. Didna see nothin'." She clutched her shawl even tighter. "If you have any more questions for me, ask 'em now."

"I think you've cleared things up." He couldn't resist adding, "For now."

He placed a hand on Grace's shoulder. Her blue eyes widened.

"Thanks for the coffee, Grace. If you think of anything that might help Vertie, please let me know." He ambled toward the front door.

As he opened his car door, Grace rushed toward him. "Cal. Wait."

He waited. She stopped a couple yards from his car. The front door she'd slammed edged open.

"Was there something else, Grace?"

"Ernest isn't here. That's the truth."

He glanced at the house. "Okay, where is he?"

Grace shook her head. She opened her mouth, only to close it again. She turned and walked back inside.

"That went well." Cal got inside his Packard and slammed the door. Hard.

# CHAPTER 7

Grace peeked from behind the living room curtain, willing Cal to drive away. When the car finally pulled onto the gravel road, she went outside to sit on the porch swing, desperate for fresh air.

Granny followed. Naturally.

The old woman pulled her old green shawl tight around her shoulders. "Cal Henderson is right handsome, don't you think?"

She knew Granny eavesdropped, but normally the old woman tried to pretend she didn't. A spike of pain shot through Grace's temples. "You should go back inside. It's cold."

"I know it's cold. I don't need no bossin' though." Granny clasped her food-laden hand to

her breast, smearing a line of purple on the snarled
fringe of her shawl. Holy bibles. Had the old
woman eaten the peanut butter and jelly sandwich
Grace made for lunch?

"I'm not *bossin'*, Granny. Just didn't want you
to get *p-monia*."

"Don't get smart with me, missy."

Grace sighed, longing for the days of long
ago—for the time before she'd become a sarcastic
shrew. Granny had picked a bad day for her
goading. Grace had put up with the woman's
insults for ten years, listened to her taunts, tried to
please her when pleasing the woman was harder
than wearing a scarlet letter.

"I'm not getting smart, Granny. You shouldn't
have said Ernest had pneumonia."

"I had to cover for you just now, didna I?"

Granny loved a reaction. Grace took a deep
breath, forcing a calmness she didn't feel. "No."

"Yes, I did. I could'a told that handsome sheriff
what you done."

Grace took another breath, determined she
wouldn't react. "I'm going to school."

"You make arrangements to meet that man?
Don't do something you oughtna."

"I have no intention of doing anything. Your
son is the cheater, not me." Granny had no right to
treat her like the harlot.

The woman cackled. "You keep giving me lip,
young lady, and maybe I *will* have a little talk with
your lawman friend. Tell him what really

happened Saturday night. Does he know about your gun?"

How dare the old woman threaten her? If Granny talked to Cal, everything would fall apart and things would be even worse. For everyone, Granny included. The woman must know that. She wouldn't really go to Cal, would she?

Once, Grace believed she deserved the strikes life had thrown at her. She'd made the bed and all that, so she tried to make it up to Ernest by being nice to his mother. She'd struck out. In return for her efforts, Granny reminded her every single day how she'd ruined Ernest's life. Grace had messed up all Granny's plans for her son, according to Granny anyway.

Seeing Cal again changed her perspective. Now, Grace saw the past through his eyes, remembered Ernest had always been directionless. Heck, her husband would probably be a grifter if she didn't cover his debts. Granny didn't give a fig about a Lincoln or a sawbuck, but the old woman wouldn't have a place to live if Grace didn't put a roof over her head.

It was time for a change. "Granny, I want you out of here at the end of the month."

The woman's mouth dropped open, but like all talkers, she recovered. "Grace Randolph Gardner, what will people say? You kicking an old woman to the street."

If Granny's response hadn't been so expected, it might have hurt. "They'll probably say I've finally come to my senses. I mean it, Mrs. Gardner. I want you gone."

Granny flapped her gums again. "And I mean it, too, Gracie. I'll talk. Tell folks what you done."

Grace stared back at her, refusing for the first time to look away. "You do that. Make sure you tell your bible study group how much Ernest enjoys sleeping with a different woman every night, too." Not willing to give the woman a chance to respond, she walked away.

After grabbing her purse, Grace took the extra cash she kept hidden beneath the frying pans. Granny would never cook, but once the woman realized Grace was serious, Granny would scavenge the entire house for anything she could steal before moving out.

*If* she moved out.

Grace resisted the urge to slam the door. After all, it was her door. She'd have to figure out what she was going to do about lunch.

# CHAPTER 8

The Senator's house rivaled any of the antebellum homes in Nashville or Natchez. Huge and immaculately white, it looked like Tara must have looked, pristine and welcoming. The warm invitation was an illusion. With John Randolph in residence, the mansion was a giant rattrap, waiting to spring and strangle.

Cal parked his car on one side of the circular driveway, not looking forward to his interview. You'd think a man trying to keep his son out of the electric chair would be cooperative, but Cal had no such expectation of John Randolph. Still, he had questions—hard questions—and he'd demand answers.

John hurried down the steps leading to a wraparound porch. At age sixty, the senator had the vigor of a man twenty years' younger. "Calvin, good to see you, boy. I trust you've found out who killed Noverta's wife and my boy's already out of jail."

"I'm sorry, Senator. Vertie is still behind bars."

John frowned. The charismatic senator had been an abusive father, but he wouldn't allow anyone else to mistreat his offspring. "So why are you wastin' time out here. I want my son out of jail. *Now.*"

The man's fervor surprised Cal. Although, maybe he should have expected the passion. John had once hit Noverta with a golf club for missing a par. The same week, the senator fired an aide for telling his son to get his feet off the desk. They might be a dysfunctional family, but the Randolphs stuck together when faced with an outside threat.

"Could we speak privately, sir?" Cal glanced first at the Randolph's driver, then at a man shaping an arborvitae into some spiral-shaped thing.

The senator nodded. "Sure thing, son. Come on in. We'll talk in my study."

Cal hated the senator's study. The room forever reeked of cigar smoke, a scent he couldn't separate from the beatings Noverta endured as a boy. Cal had stood outside the door, wishing he could tell someone, but Noverta begged him to keep quiet.

Over the years, John Randolph mellowed, but Cal still regretted his silence.

He followed the senator past the frescos in the front parlor, and into the large mahogany-walled study just off the main hallway. To Cal's surprise, the senator shut the door, sat down at his desk and put his head into his hands.

"You feeling all right, sir?"

"I'm a mess, Cal. I'm a mess."

Cal stared at the brim of his hat, wondering what he should say. To the best of his recollection, the senator had never shown any emotion. On the campaign trail, the man acted appropriately upbeat or dismayed, depending on the situation, but in private, John Randolph seemed a little short of human. Or had in the past. His current display of distress seemed a little convenient.

The senator raised his head and swiped at his cheek. "Tell me, sheriff, what happened?"

Cal gave him a brief summary of the events—at least the one's he'd personally observed. Then, he went right to the hard questions, determined not to maintain his boyhood silence. Cal would lead the interview, the senator would follow. He owed Noverta nothing less. "I have to ask for an account of your actions on that evening and morning."

"I was at my Nashville house. You know I stay there when congress is in session. I got a call from Grace around six o'clock on Sunday. What an awful morning. Gracie told me Noverta had gone to jail."

Cal blinked. Grace called her father? He'd heard they weren't talking and had assumed Noverta called the senator. Another thing Grace hadn't mentioned.

"It's bad, huh?" John asked. No judgments, no laments of how Noverta shouldn't have married Lily. Maybe the senator had changed.

"It's not good," Cal admitted.

"Noverta didn't do this." The senator frowned, bringing his bushy brows into a continuous line. "Boy doesn't even own a gun. God knows I've told him to get one. Living in the middle of nowhere like he does." The man gripped his unlit cigar, so tight it flattened in his fingers. Another chink in the armor of John Randolph? "I'll testify he doesn't own a gun. That should be good enough for anyone."

Cal said nothing. Once the senator thought about what he'd said, he'd know that wouldn't help.

"What the hell was Noverta doing at home anyway?" the senator asked, shaking his head. "He was supposed to be at that cattlemen's convention until Monday."

Cal's neck hairs stood at attention. How did the senator know his son's whereabouts? Had the old man been involved in Lily's death? "You knew Noverta was out of town?"

"Of course I did. Just because the pigheaded moron doesn't talk to me, doesn't mean I don't keep track of him. I watch out for my children, you know that."

Cal did, but he wouldn't want anyone *watching out* for him like that. He said a silent thanks his father hadn't been anything like the senator. "Did you know about Lily's indiscretion?"

"Hell, boy, everybody knew about 'em. I told Noverta not to marry that…that woman." The senator sucked in more than his share of air. "And I was right about her. Thank God Noverta was finally going to divorce her."

"Who told you that?" Cal asked.

"I hear things, son."

Probably from a lawyer violating client-attorney privilege. "What kind of things did you hear, sir?"

"I heard Lily took one lover too many. And I got Noverta proof."

Cal took another long breath, sensing things were going to get worse for Noverta. "Proof? What kind of proof?"

The older man ignored his question. "I'll simply tell Jackson he can't prosecute. That'll be the end of this."

"Senator," he said gently, "you can't do that."

The man snorted. "Don't be naïve, Calvin. I can and I will."

No one argued with the senator, but that didn't mean they obeyed his commands. John Randolph needed to understand how bad things were. "Your influence won't help this time, sir. We have to find a way to clear Noverta."

The senator raised his massive arms into the air, fists curled, his eyelids clenched. For a brief moment, Cal feared the man who couldn't be ruffled might break something. Just as quickly, the senator faded like a sinkerball and slumped into his chair. Noverta thought his old man didn't give a damn, but he clearly was wrong. The senator did care.

*Enough to get rid of his cheating daughter-in-law?* That would be bad news for Noverta. If John Randolph commissioned the murder, proving anyone other than Noverta had committed the crime would be next-to-impossible. The senator didn't make mistakes and Cal had no other suspects. Unless he counted Grace.

"So what do we do, Cal?" The man who *never* asked for advice was asking him?

Cal cleared his throat. "This proof you mentioned, sir. I need it." He hoped the senator would just give him the information without launching into a filibuster.

The older man sank even lower in his chair. "Damn woman was a disgrace to the Carleton name."

Cal's head reeled from the implications. "About that proof, sir…"

The senator nodded. "I hired an investigator."

Damn. "And he got concrete evidence Lily had a lover?"

The senator nodded. "Yes. I'm sure the gal had more men at her beck and call, but I only got one photograph. Once the flashbulb went off, Lily knew about the private eye."

A photograph? Cal felt sick. The senator had supplied Noverta's motive. "Did Vertie know?"

The senator nodded. "I told him about the photograph."

Hell. "What did Vertie say when you told him?"

John snorted. "He smarted off saying I shouldn't have hired an investigator without telling him."

Cal looked down at his feet. He couldn't disagree with Noverta's reasoning.

"You think I done the wrong thing, too. I can see it on your face, Calvin, but I had to do something. That woman was making a laughing stock of us."

Noverta had been trying to get out from under his father's control for as long as Cal could remember. Marrying Lily was his first real act of defiance. That had been an unforced error—in many ways. Still, it couldn't have set well with Noverta to have his father interfering again.

"What did Vertie say when you showed him the photograph?" he asked. "Did he know Lily's...partner?"

"Didn't show him. I talked to the boy on the horn while he was in Memphis." The senator gave him a look—practiced patience. Cal had seen the same look when a voter voiced an unfriendly question.

"And?" Cal prompted.

"Noverta told me to go to hell." The senator sounded detached. He could have been saying "good morning" to the housekeeper. "Said he didn't need my damn photograph. Can you believe that? After I spent all that money. Said he'd catch her in the act. I told him to just give the damned photograph to the lawyer and be done with it. Hardheaded boy wouldn't listen. If only he'd listened, Calvin."

Damn. The senator had thrown another strike at Noverta's defense.

And once again, Cal had to choose between doing the *right thing* or saving his friend. Protecting Noverta won. "Sir, you can't tell anyone else about the photograph."

The senator's pinkish face turned even ruddier. "Why the hell not?"

"Because the photograph will give Vertie a concrete motive."

"Hell." The senator leaned back in his chair, tossing the squashed cigar toward the trashcan. It missed.

Just because they couldn't mention the photograph didn't mean it couldn't help identify the real killer. "Sir, who was with Lily?"

"I don't know."

"Didn't you look at the photograph?" Cal asked.

The senator opened his humidor and took out another cigar. "Course I did. Only I couldn't see the asshole's face. Just Lily's. Damn girl was a jaybird."

Maybe things weren't as bad as they seemed. "Then it doesn't prove she was having an affair, sir. The man could have been Noverta."

The senator snorted. "Man in the photograph couldn't have been Noverta. There's a tattoo on his arm. Vertie doesn't have a tattoo."

"What kind of tattoo?" Cal's lungs seemed to turn to concrete.

"That rodent—the one on y'all's baseball caps. Holding a United States flag."

Cal feared he'd be sick. He'd never touched Lily, never even considered it, but the senator had just described his tattoo.

"I need to get busy and get my son out of jail. Do you have any more questions?"

The man's dismissive words barely registered with Cal. He swallowed, calling on his D.C. training to maintain his professionalism. "Not right now, Senator, but I will probably need to talk to you again. I also need that photograph."

"Hell, I'll get it for you now." The senator shuffled out of the study but returned after a few seconds with a large manila envelope. "Here."

Cal took the packet and mumbled the perfunctory goodbye. He managed to navigate the circular staircase without stumbling, not an easy feat with his mind churning. He couldn't shake the notion he'd just sealed Noverta's fate.

"Calvin."

He turned toward the voice. The man stood at the hallway entrance, looking ten years' older than he had earlier.

"Find something that will save my son. Please." Maybe John Randolph was human after all.

Cal nodded and headed out. He had to find a killer before his friend went on trial. Maybe then, the blackness would leave.

Or maybe not. Right now he had three suspects. All of them Randolphs.

# CHAPTER 9

Cal stared at the empty cell. He'd been pleasantly surprised when Judge Sparks granted Noverta bail. Maybe the feud between the judge and the senator had finally fizzled or maybe Sparks knew Noverta was no murderer.

Only Cal had hoped to have a chat with Noverta while they were alone. That wouldn't happen now.

The fancy Memphis lawyer who'd stopped by earlier made that quite clear. "My client will not be answering any questions. Do not contact him."

That was that. Cal had only one new lead—the envelope the senator had given him. So why didn't he just rip the thing open?

Maybe because he didn't want to know which former teammate could be slimy enough to have a ring-a-ding-ding with Lily. Every member of the 1928 Leeton Mudcats had gotten the same tattoo inked on his bicep, with the exception of Noverta, who had a phobia about needles.

Cal picked up the envelope, letting it dangle from his thumb and forefinger. Identifying the cheater would probably do more harm than good. If one of Noverta's friends had been playing footsie with Lily, Noverta's motive would be hard to dispute.

Nope. Better if he didn't know.

Still, if he hoped to help Noverta, he needed to start somewhere. He propped his legs on the desk and tugged at the glue keeping the envelope sealed.

Cal re-tasted his coffee. He should have been prepared since the senator described the photograph, but seeing so much of Noverta's wife in the arms of another man made him feel downright sick. Lily's image was clear, but the picture only showed the back and right arm of her partner.

Fighting off his nausea, Cal forced his brain to concentrate. Not much he could do with a blurry arm with a blurrier tattoo .

*Son of a bitch.*

"Sorry to interrupt, boss. Heard you wanted to talk to me?" Rodney stood at the door, still wearing his hat.

Cal yanked his feet off the desk. He wanted to shove the photograph in a drawer, but that would draw Rodney's attention. He didn't want his deputy to have to testify about the envelope's contents, especially since Cal wasn't sure the evidence should see the light of day.

"I know you're mimicking Herb, but stop with the *boss* stuff," Cal said, having no illusions about being Rodney's *boss*. The deputy did as he pleased and Cal thanked the stars it *pleased* Rodney to adhere to his supervision. The deputy had earned several accommodations during his tenure with the MPD and had only come back to the country because Cal asked. Rodney could get his city job back at any time. Unlike Herb.

And Herb *did* have a tattoo. He'd been cut midway through the Mudcats first—and only— season, but the junior deputy had gotten a uniform. And inked.

Cal shook his head. Lily had been a bit loose, but he doubted she'd give her favors to the likes of Herbert Smith.

"Cal?" Rodney asked. "You okay?"

"Yeah. I'm fine." Only he hadn't been fine since the murder, maybe even before that. Didn't matter. Bellyaching never made anything better. "Did you know Lily was having an affair?"

The deputy took off his hat and leaned against the doorjamb. "Hell, Cal, everyone in the county knew that." Rodney made a clicking sound. "Well, maybe everyone except Vertie. If he'd known, I'm sure he would have…" The deputy wisely stopped talking.

Cal wished he didn't know what Rodney meant. Probably ranked as some sort of miracle Lily's shenanigans hadn't fueled Noverta's temper sooner. Noverta didn't rile easily but once something set him off, his temper blazed hotter than Jimmie Foxx's bat. Everyone in the county knew that, too. And those same people would make up the jury pool.

Cal stared at his deputy. "You don't really think…"

Rodney took off his hat and tapped it against his thigh. "Don't know what to think."

Hell's bells. Even Noverta's cousin was convinced of his guilt?

"You know who Lily was seeing?" Cal asked.

Rodney shrugged. "I heard some rumors, but given the poor dish is dead, doesn't seem respectable to name names."

Cal chewed on his piece of toothpick, wishing he could give up the damn habit. "Might need to cough up those names. One of them could have killed her."

"I think you're graspin' at those straws you keep chomping on, but I hope you're right, Cal. If not… Can't say as I blame Vertie for losing his head. Hell, if I'd caught my babe making whoopee with another Joe, I might be tempted to drill someone, too."

*Too*? "Hold on, there, Rod. We're still investigating. Don't be jumping to conclusions."

"I'm trying not to, but..." Rodney shook his head.

"But what?"

"I read the report. Hard to point the finger at anyone else."

"Doesn't matter. As officers of the law, we deal with facts and only facts."

Rodney scoffed. "Don't you sound all proper? Don't worry none, though. You know I'll do everything I can to clear Vertie's name. Proper or not."

Cal ignored the implication. He supposed he couldn't blame Rodney for not believing in Noverta's innocence. The deputy hadn't seen the prime suspect at the crime scene. "Vertie just didn't act guilty."

Rodney nodded. Only another lawman would know what it meant to *not act guilty*.

"I know he has motive, Rod, but we also know he's never even fired a pistol."

Rodney leaned back against the wall, crossing his arms over his chest. "Not that we know of. He did buy that little gun for Lily, so he must've known where she kept it."

Cal yanked his head away from the window to stare directly at his deputy. "Noverta bought the snub-nose?"

Rodney nodded again. "And if Vertie heard about her latest..."

"Heard about her latest what?"

Rodney shook his head. "Forget it. Probably just people bumping gums."

"What did you hear? Tell me."

"You won't like it," Rodney said.

Cal frowned. "I don't like anything about this entire matter. Tell me anyway."

"Fine. Lily was spotted at the Charleston Club with Ernest Gardner."

Cal blinked. "Ernest? Grace's Ernest?"

"Yeah."

Hell's bells. No wonder Noverta called Grace.

Cal grasped for some reasonable explanation. "That might not mean anything. Maybe Lily just needed someone to show her a good time. Everyone knows she liked to jolly up. Hell, the woman lives for the foxtrot and Vertie's a dead hoofer on the dance floor." Cal winced at his word choice.

"Don't blow your wig," Rodney said, patting him on the back. "I'm sure it's just booshwa."

Cal nodded, not quite as positive. If he were a betting man, he had a Lincoln that said the rumor was true. "Maybe it's time we paid Ernest a little visit."

"Past time," Rodney replied.

# CHAPTER 10

*Wednesday, November 9*

Cal waited with Rodney at the entrance of the Gardner residence, figuring Ernest would still be sleeping. "Maybe he isn't home," Cal said.

He took a step backward, regretting his decision to bring Rodney along. Even if Ernest admitted he and Lily had partaken of forbidden fruit, that confession would only make things worse for Noverta. Might even signal the bottom of the ninth for Grace.

Rodney stepped around him and banged harder on the door. "Even if Ernest isn't here, Granny should be home. That old cow never goes anywhere. She can tell us where Ernest is."

The old cow wouldn't tell Cal anything. He didn't need the Hindenburg crashing on his head to know that. "Let's go," he insisted, backing down the steps. "Without a warrant, we can't force her to open the door."

Just as he reached the bottom step, the subtle click of a latch echoed. "What you boys want?" Granny slurred, a telltale track of snuff on her cheek.

"Need to talk to Ernest," Rodney's voice boomed, his breath visible in the morning chill. He didn't have to talk so loud. Cal knew the woman's hearing was as good as her eyesight.

"Done told the sheriff yesterday my boy's got the p-monia. Why ya'll here messing up his restin' time?"

Rodney opened the screen. "Just got a couple questions, Granny. Won't take long."

The old woman made a quick shift, blocking the deputy's entrance. "Not today."

"Come on, Granny." Rodney shifted from one foot to the other, switching from authoritarian to cajoling in the same motion. "Just two minutes."

The old woman shook her head.

"We can get a warrant," Cal said, moving so he could peer into the whitewashed shed next to the house where Grace parked her automobile. He didn't see Ernest's cabriolet, but he spotted something totally unexpected.

"Get all the fancy papers y'all want," Granny said, still slurring. "Doc Strange done said Ernest can't be disturbed." She stuck her arm inside the house. When her pudgy hands became visible again, she held a Browning rifle. Granny took a step forward, staring at Cal. "Right now, y'all need to get off my property so my boy can rest."

Her property? Cal forced a smile as he tipped his hat.

"Tell Ernest to come see me if he's able," he replied. "Otherwise, we'll be back tomorrow. With that warrant."

No point in hanging around. Damn woman probably would shoot at something and Cal had no intentions of being a target.

Besides, he had something more important to check out. "Let's go, Rod."

The deputy hesitated, but after a second backed away and followed him to the car. Rodney's posture mirrored Cal's frustration. The deputy slammed the passenger door. "Bitch is lying. I bet Ernest isn't even sick."

"I know. But I don't think he's here," Cal replied.

Rodney looked at his watch. "Yeah, probably at some gin joint. Man doesn't have *p-monia*." He mimicked Granny's snuff-laden drawl. "He's got liquor-monia. Should I go looking for him?"

"Probably a good idea." Cal shifted into reverse. "But this trip isn't a complete rainout. I just spotted Vertie's dog." After he confirmed his theory, he intended to ask Grace why she hadn't mentioned the hound.

"Where?" Rodney's head turned sharply.

"In the car shed. I'm fairly sure it was Tanner. When we get back to the stationhouse, I'm coming back for the dog while you look for Ernest."

Rodney shook his head. "If you come back without a warrant, Granny *will* shoot you, Cal. Hell, that mean old bitch will shoot you even if you do get a warrant. Besides, that's not Noverta's dog."

"I'll get Grace to let me in." Cal frowned. "Hold on. What do you mean it's not Noverta's dog? Looked like Tanner to me."

"Ernest has a dog, too, Cal. He and Vertie got their pups from the same litter."

"Two dogs? Both of them have blueticks?"

Rodney nodded.

"Well, hell." Yet another dead end.

# CHAPTER 11

*Thursday, November 17*

Jackson McKinney didn't deliver on his promise.

Instead of having two full weeks to clear Noverta, Cal had been involuntarily benched. He joined the rest of the county packed into the brick courthouse. The overflow crowd wasn't exactly a surprise. Nothing as exciting as a murder trial had happened in Leeton since old man Sweeney set his barn on fire after the stock market crashed. The same people who packed into the junior college gymnasium on Saturday night to cheer the high school basketball team—last year's District champions—sat shoulder-to-shoulder on the hard pews.

Cal wiped at his brow, wondering if he should give up his seat and join the masses standing in the back. The temperature outside might be forty degrees, but even the giant fans whirling overhead didn't diminish the stifling heat inside. One of the town's two factories made church pews, thus the courthouse had the same uncomfortable seats as the First Baptist Church.

Or maybe it was just him. He shifted in his third row seat, trying to find a spot that didn't rub against overtired muscles.

Giving up on comfort, Cal searched the crowd for Ernest Gardner, not really surprised when he didn't find the man's mug in the masses. Cal huffed out a breath. Seemed as if he'd been looking for Ernest every waking hour since Sunday morning. With no luck. Cal had questioned all Ernest's cronies, he'd visited all the places Ernest was rumored to frequent, and he'd watched the house, hoping to catch the man leaving or arriving.

Nothing. The man had simply disappeared.

Cal did everything possible to convince Jackson McKinney the disappearance couldn't be a coincidence. He'd insisted Ernest's vanishing act created a lot of reasonable doubt about Noverta's guild. The DA wouldn't listen to reason.

Now, Cal was out of time. The judge would make sure the trial didn't interfere with the start of the annual Turkey Tournament—in one week. Leeton basketball was far more important than any pilgrims or events at Plymouth Rock. Sparks probably also wanted to get the proceedings started before Senator Randolph used his political clout, although the judge had no cause to worry. Governor Browning wasn't a Randolph fan and Roosevelt had bigger worries than the small-town trial of a senator's son.

"Here they come." Cal didn't recognize the man's voice, but the excitement in his tone was hard to miss.

He did recognize all of the jurors as they marched in with the pomp of kids on the last day of Vacation Bible School. Damn people didn't even try to conceal their eagerness. Rebecca Hill, who'd once dated Noverta, ran a tongue over very red lips. Stanton Cagle, the county mailman, rubbed his skinny hands together. The jurors' anticipation seemed to seep through the courthouse and infect the crowd. The mood should have been pro-Vertie but the atmosphere seemed pro-blood. Noverta's blood.

Perhaps his senses were just off. He hadn't seen much of his pillow during the past week, having spent every waking hour trying to find anything that might help clear Noverta. He'd uncovered nothing.

"All rise." He stood while Judge Sparks scuttled toward the dais, swiping at the long strand of hair half-covering his balding head. The man actually smiled as he took his seat.

Cal reluctantly sat back down on the torturous wood. He'd give anything to be far away from the coliseum and the gladiators. Only he had to testify—for the prosecution, then for the defense.

"Call your first witness," the judge barked at Jackson.

"Prosecution calls Sheriff Calvin Henderson to the stand." The words he'd dreaded for days echoed throughout the building.

He thought he'd been smart to sit on the end of a row, but since he'd chosen the side closest to the windows, he had to pass by the defense table on his way to the hot seat. He glanced at Noverta, hoping his friend understood just how much he'd sacrifice to avoid testifying for Jackson.

Noverta didn't even raise his gaze. The accused just stared at his hands, his fingers motionless on the scarred wood table. He looked like a man resigned to his fate.

"Raise your right hand, sheriff."

He did as Fern Anderson, the bailiff, asked and placed his hand on the bible. As he swore an oath he hoped he could keep, he spotted the Mudcat tattoo almost completely hidden on Fern's arm— another reminder he'd failed Noverta. Not that he hadn't checked out the bailiff. Fern had been at the county hospital when Lily was murdered, welcoming the arrival of his fourth son. With about twenty witnesses. Thus far, every member of the Mudcats team he'd investigated had a solid alibi.

Cal sat down. A sense of doom, almost a physical thing, descended over him.

"Permission to treat this man as a hostile witness, Your Honor," Jackson said, pausing to place a finger on the side of his chin.

Judge Sparks hooted. "You've let all that schooling go to your head, boy. He's our sheriff. There's nothing hostile about him."

Everything echoed in the pre-Civil War building, especially the sniggers and chuckles in response to the judge's jab. You'd think folks had gathered for a broadcast of the *Chase and Sanborn Hour* instead of possibly condemning one of their own.

Jackson McKinney dallied, taking forever in a pretense of reviewing his notes. Cal scanned the crowd. Hadn't he read somewhere that the guilty sometimes attended trials? Or was that the crime scene?

His eyes locked on Grace, her beautiful face and dark brown hair, mostly covered by a green hat. The thing on her head didn't hide her grim expression. Hell, it looked as if she'd given up, too. Same as Rodney. Only Rodney didn't have Grace's intuition, an insight that had always frightened Cal.

She raised her head, almost as if she'd sensed his stare. He gave a little nod in her direction, but she looked down, seeming suddenly fascinated with her purse.

Cal wasn't surprised at her reaction, or lack of reaction, but the cut still bit at his gut. He'd been a fool to believe Noverta's misfortune might change anything between them.

The banging of the gavel made him flinch. He turned his gaze toward the district attorney, saying a little prayer to the legal gods, begging that he not do too much damage.

Jackson looked up from his stenographer's pad. "Good morning, Sheriff Henderson."

Nothing good about it. Still, Cal tipped his head in a greeting.

Jackson turned toward the jury. "Sheriff, walk us through the events of the morning of November 5th."

Cal paused. "Don't you mean November 6th?"

More sniggers and chuckles erupted. Good. Jackson had earned his first error.

He'd rehearsed the response to that question. Cal tried to remember the words Noverta's lawyer had asked him to repeat, only his mind went blank. He mumbled, recounting the events as he remembered them, doing his best to skip over the incriminating facts. The DA interrupted. Often. Every question forced Cal to further implicate Noverta.

"You asked for a…" Jackson stared down at his pad, clearly grandstanding. The DA probably knew exactly what he planned to ask since he was clearly better at memorizing than Cal was. "Ballistic report?"

"Yes. A *ballistics* report." If he could go back in time, he wouldn't have ordered that. The report definitively identified the bullet in the victim's head as being fired from the snub-nose Noverta had held the night Lily died.

"So why don't you explain to the jury what this test is and what the results mean."

After Cal explained, Jackson made him admit, several times, that Noverta had been holding the murder weapon in his hands. Somehow, Cal managed to get through his narration. He waited for Jackson to excuse him. Only the DA looked at the jury, making sure he had everyone's attention.

Jackson turned toward Cal. "Tell me, Sheriff, did the defendant, while his poor wife lay dead in his bed, ask you to find his dog?"

Hell. That made Noverta look bad. Really bad.

Exactly how did Jackson know about the missing hound? Herb wasn't even at the scene when Noverta asked about Tanner. Or had he and Noverta talked about the dog later? They must have since Herb was the only one who could have given Jackson McKinney that tidbit.

Unless someone else had been at the scene. Maybe the same someone who'd driven away without turning on his lights?

Nah, he was swinging at a ball in the dirt. Herb knew Cal had looked for the dog. The deputy had told Jackson and the DA had twisted the information.

"Objection!" The lawyer John Randolph hired from Memphis jumped to his feet. "Hearsay."

About time the man got out of the dugout. Cal really hoped the lawyer would earn his fee. Maybe a good cross-examination by Noverta's attorney would undo some of the damage he'd done— having sworn to tell the truth.

"I'll rephrase." Jackson tugged at the lapels of his suit coat. "Was Noverta Randolph more concerned about his dog than he was about his dead wife?"

"Objection!"

Judge Sparks held up his hand, glaring at Jackson. "Sustained."

Cal huffed a breath, thinking he'd dodged an inside fastball aimed at his head. Jackson shrugged.

The DA put his hands into his suit coat, smiling. Then he asked, "On the night of the murder, before the victim was removed from the crime scene, did Noverta Randolph ask you to find his dog?"

*Hell.* Cal swallowed, debating who could challenge him if he said "no."

"We don't have all day," the judge drawled. "Cal, just tell this fool man if Noverta asked you to find his dog."

He'd been beaned after all. And there was his tell-the-truth oath. "Yes."

Instead of releasing him, Jackson asked the same questions about the murder scene in a variety of ways. Man probably wanted to ensure Cal's damning testimony would be permanently imprinted on the jurors' minds.

Cal shifted in his seat. Christ Almighty, how much longer? He glanced at the jury box. The juror's expressions had changed. Rebecca examined her fingernails. Did Cal dare hope the other jurors were also bored? Jackson should have quit while he was ahead.

"Jack." The judge interrupted, "Unless you have something new, excuse this witness."

Instead of accepting his reprimand and acting accordingly, Jackson held up his hand. "One final question, Your Honor." The district attorney turned to face him, looking smug. "Do you have any concrete evidence of any kind that would suggest Noverta Randolph did *not* kill his wife?"

Why the hell didn't the Memphis guy object?

Cal stared at the suddenly re-interested faces. He had to say something. Even if it meant blowing his best lead prematurely. "Yes. There was a bloodstain on the wall that did not match either Lily or Noverta's blood type."

A simultaneous intake of breath echoed throughout the courtroom. The whispering ceased for the first time.

Jackson's face turned beet red. He clearly hadn't read all of Cal's report. Good.

"But there was no sign of forced entry, no—" The DA back-pedaled.

The judge interrupted, "Jack, you don't get to testify. That's the witness's job. And don't you dare try to rephrase. You've asked that question at least three times. Do you have anything new?"

Cal experienced a flicker of hope. The judge might be impatient, but he would be fair.

Jackson's already beet red face darkened. "No sir."

"Then the court will recess until after lunch."

Jackson launched into an objection, but the judge got up and walked away while the Yale man yammered on. The district attorney fumed. He clearly didn't want the bloodstain to be the last impression of Cal's testimony.

"Cal, you didn't tell me about the bloodstain."

"Was in my report."

Cal ignored the DA and studied the twelve jurors as they filed out of the courtroom. He feared Jackson had no cause to worry.

# CHAPTER 12

Rodney folded his newspaper as Cal approached the office, but not before Cal read the *Leeton Herald* headline:

**Guilty Verdict Likely**.

"Hey Cal. Let's head over to the diner and get something to eat. You look like you could use a good meal."

"Not hungry," Cal replied.

His deputy lifted a brow. "You? Not hungry."

Some of the tension left his body. "Yeah, hard to believe, huh? You go ahead. I need to get away from town for a while."

Cal didn't wait for a response, he headed down Main Street, feeling restless and out of sorts. He might have been one of the golden boys, but he'd never felt at home in his hometown. He again cursed himself for his boneheaded idea to move back to Leeton. What had he been thinking? Coming back to a place he'd rather forget? Where the woman he loved was married to another man?

On the other hand, if he hadn't returned, he wouldn't be able to help Noverta. Not that he'd exactly hit any home runs for the defense.

"Cal. Wait."

Had he imagined Grace's voice? He turned, spotting her green hat as she headed toward him, her stride no less purposeful in high heels than in the sensible shoes she wore when teaching school or the rubber boots she wore at her farm.

*Damn.* "Grace? I'm sorry. You know I did the best I could."

She nodded. "I know."

He nodded back, feeling the familiar ache that never seemed to go away. Why hadn't she waited for him all those years ago? The woman might be stubborn as a mule crossed with a mountain lion, but fickle? He didn't think so. So why had she dumped him as if the special bond they shared never existed? Every letter he had written went unanswered.

When September rolled around and the Buffaloes hadn't made the playoffs, he'd returned to Leeton for the winter. Only to find Grace married.

His hangover lasted for most of the four days he'd been home. Noverta asked him to stay, but the moment Cal sobered up, he'd gotten on a train and headed back to Houston.

Memories only brought more pain. He needed to focus on the present, on making sure Noverta stayed out of prison. "I'll keep searching, Grace. I promise. There has to be something to clear Vertie's name."

She nodded again. "So you don't believe he killed her?"

Why would she doubt that? "No."

"Good. But, Cal, what if there's nothing to find?"

He studied her face, wondering if she'd truly given up on her brother's freedom. Maybe she'd heard the rumors about Ernest and Lily. Maybe she thought her brother really had killed his wife for making woo with his brother-in-law—Grace's husband.

"Grace, where is your husband? It's essential that I talk to him."

"I don't know where he is. I'd tell you if I did."

Did he believe that? Maybe. From his investigation, Cal determined the man pretty much did as he pleased.

He should ask the logical follow up questions: Did she know about Lily and Ernest? Did she think her husband was involved in Lily's murder?

Only the timing was all wrong. With the way the trial had gone, he wouldn't embarrass her further. Not today.

"Don't give up, Grace."

She shrugged. "From what I've seen, Noverta's already as good as convicted."

He couldn't argue. Look what happened to Bruno Hauptmann. "Can I buy you lunch?"

She stared directly at him, something in her expression he couldn't read. Yearning? That was probably *his* wishful thinking.

She looked away, staring at something down the street. Was the past coming between them, or did she know something she wasn't telling?

"Thanks, Cal, but I'm looking for Kenny. I saw him in the upper balcony when I was leaving the courthouse, but by the time I got outside, there was no sign of him. Have you seen him?"

"Burton let Kenny watch Noverta's trial?" Cal couldn't remember exactly how old Grace's young cousin was now. Probably fifteen or sixteen, but the teen had the mental capacity of a five-year-old. Why in the name of everything sacred had they let that boy go to the courthouse? Especially alone.

Grace actually met his gaze. "I'm guessing Burton doesn't know Kenny's here."

Burton, John Randolph's younger brother, had contracted polio as a youngster and couldn't walk without a cane. The man had married late in life and the new wife had delivered a baby exactly eight months after the wedding festivities. Shortly after Kenny's birth, the mother left a note saying she couldn't deal with a handicapped child. No one heard from her again.

Everyone in the county knew Burton couldn't look after a youngster—especially one with special needs, but the man loved the boy to distraction and refused to put him in a home. Everyone pitched in to help the new father. Even now, the townsfolk did what they could to keep Kenny safe—no easy task.

"Kenny walked here all by himself?" Cal asked, knowing that's exactly what the boy had done. Burton would have tried to keep Noverta's situation from Kenny because the boy idolized his cousin. Seeing Noverta in handcuffs would distress Kenny to no end. Even so, Kenny was brighter than most people knew. He would have heard about Noverta's problems and would want to know what was going on.

Grace shrugged. "You know how he is. Just takes off whenever he sees a butterfly or anything the least bit interesting. That boy is too much for Burton to handle."

"Did you call, Burton? Maybe Kenny went home."

She shook her head. "Burton doesn't have a phone."

"Still?" Cal squinted into the midday sun, surprisingly bright for November.

Of course, Burton wouldn't have a phone. The man wouldn't be able to put food on the table if the ladies at First United Presbyterian didn't drop off a casserole or basket of fried chicken each week. Burton suffered while his older brother, the big shot senator, sat in his enormous white house and refused to help. In contrast, Grace did everything she could without compromising Burton's pride.

"Kenny shouldn't be hard to find, Grace. Is he still carrying that stick everywhere he goes? There's pirates everywhere, you know?"

Her lips curved into an almost smile. That smile used to light up Cal's world, but he hadn't seen it since he returned to Leeton, not that he'd seen her much in the last fourteen months.

"That's your fault, Cal. I hear you're the one who read <u>Treasure Island</u> to him. Ever since, Kenny has insisted he's a pirate and that stupid stick is his sword."

Who knew? Kenny hadn't even been able to talk in those days. Hard to believe a story would impact a boy who'd never be able to read. Cal grinned, feeling some of the heaviness of the last few days lift. The reprieve would be temporary, but he'd take what he could get. "Come on, I'll help you find him."

Grace shook her head again. "Thank you, but I'm sure you have things to do. Even if I don't find him, I'm sure he'll wander home sooner or later." She turned and hurried away before Cal could say otherwise, the click-clack of her heels on the sidewalk seeming to mock him.

He watched until she turned onto First Street and disappeared from his view. "Well, damn."

Cal glanced at his watch. The trial had recessed until two. He headed back to his office. If he could locate the name of the company that made the Leeton Mudcat uniforms, maybe the manufacturer could tell him who'd ordered a size 7 cap. That might narrow down the list of suspected lovers. Especially if one Ernest Gardner wore that size.

Cal stopped short. Kenny sat on the concrete steps.

He squatted down in front of the boy. "Hello Kenny. Grace is looking for you, son. What do you say we go tell her where you are and then head over to the Tastee Freeze and have a corn dog?"

"Uh-uh, Sheriff Cal." Kenny kicked his high top boots making the leather straps wrap around the legs of his pants. The laces fascinated the boy and he kept kicking. The leather kept swinging.

"Kenny?" Cal prompted.

The boy shook his head—in sync with the swinging laces. "I need to tell you some'un, Sheriff Cal. This is real, real, real..." His head kept going from side to side. The boy stopped moving, his eyes wide. "Im-por-tant."

Kenny seemed pleased to have gotten the word correct but his look of satisfaction disappeared. His face became haunted. "But it's bad, Sheriff Cal. Real bad."

Shit. He obviously meant Noverta's situation. Best to keep the boy calm. Or try to. His afternoon was shot to hell anyway. Baseball cap sizes could wait one more day. "Can I help?"

The boy started shaking his boot again. "It's about Cousin Vert." Kenny seemed to lose his train of thought.

Poor kid. "What about Vertie?"

The boy stopped moving again. "I know he don't kill Lily. I know. I know." He paused. "I know."

Could Kenny actually know something? Or did he just think his cousin would never do anything bad? Crazy thought. Cal knew he really grasped at a limp straw if he expected Kenny to help.

The logic didn't stop his racing brain. Could Kenny have killed Lily? Cal dismissed the thought as quickly as it flashed in him mind. Kenny might be strong as a charging elephant, but he wouldn't hurt a flea, especially Lily. Noverta's wife hadn't had many unselfish moments, but the few she'd had were usually reserved for Kenny. She'd actually taught the boy, who had trouble walking, to dance a credible waltz.

"Kenny, how do you know Vertie didn't kill…eh, hurt Miss Lily?"

"Cause I know who did, and it wasn't Vert. Wasn't Vert."

The boy had his full attention. With Noverta's neck on the line, Cal would swing at any pitch near the plate. "Kenny. This is very important, son. Who hurt Miss Lily?"

"Can't tell you," the boy replied, crossing his arms. He began to shuffle his feet back and forth on the ground.

Cal squashed his flash of hope. At 2:00 a.m. Kenny would have asleep. The boy hadn't seen anything.

"Why can't you tell me?" he asked anyway.

"Cause, Sheriff Cal Henderson, I can't." The feet shuffling continued. "Just wanted to tell you wasn't Vert."

After a series of "Why not?" and "Cause," Kenny jumped up, his shoelaces swinging. "I ain't no tattle-tale." The boy raced down the sidewalk.

Did Kenny have the mental capacity to make up that story? If his tale had some truth to it, that meant Kenny liked the person he thought killed Lily. Otherwise the boy would have told. Cal imagined the only person Kenny liked more than Noverta was his father. Or Grace.

Cal wanted to go after the boy, but he'd only be chasing smoke. Too late anyway. Kenny had already covered a couple hundred yards. Cal watched him shuffle-race down the street until he disappeared from sight.

He needed to let Grace know Kenny was okay, but he didn't know where she'd gone. He'd have to find her at the courthouse.

\* \* \* \*

Cal couldn't find Grace. He scanned the entire courthouse but didn't see her. Maybe she'd taken Kenny home.

The DA called him back to the witness box. Cal's fingers weren't as clammy as they'd been in the morning. Surely the worst was over.

Jackson meandered toward the stand, the smug look back on his face.

Judge Sparks tapped a pencil against the wood surface. "Get a move on, Jack. Lunch is over. Are you ready to rest?"

"No, Your Honor."

*Hell.*

The DA stared at Cal, but quickly averted his gaze. "I have a few more questions."

The judge huffed a breath. "Then get to it."

"Sheriff Henderson, did you give Noverta Randolph a handkerchief so he could clean his prints off the murder weapon?"

"Objection!" Noverta's fancy lawyer bellowed. "Question is leading."

"I'll rephrase," Jackson said. "On the night or morning Lily Randolph was murdered, did you hand a handkerchief to the defendant?"

Cal glared at Jackson, trying to compose a sentence that might undo some of the damage. Who'd suggested he'd given Noverta a handkerchief anyway? Or had the DA laid down a bunt since he had no real firepower. Cheap hit, but the man had planted the image of Noverta's hands on the murder weapon in every juror's mind. An image that would remain even after Cal set the record straight. He'd underestimated Jackson's ambition.

"I did not," Cal replied. "I did not even have a *handkerchief* on my person. Being awakened at two in the morning, I didn't have time to think of a handkerchief. I certainly didn't allow Noverta to remove fingerprints. With anything."

The DA seemed to understand he'd made a mistake. He swallowed twice, his Adams apple visible beneath his jowls. "Understood. Yet you arrested Noverta Randolph, did you not?"

Damn Jackson. He'd ordered Cal to arrest Noverta, only Cal wouldn't be allowed to say that. Jackson had sucked him in. Cal waited for the fancy pants lawyer to object, but the DA held up his hand.

"Withdrawn. The prosecution is done with this witness."

Thank God. Cal got to his feet, intent on getting out of the courthouse, the faster the better. Noverta's attorney stood, his shiny cufflinks glittering in the harsh lighting. "Not so fast, Sheriff." He turned toward the judge. "I'll cross now, Yo' Honor. If that's okay."

The judge nodded. "By all means."

Noverta's lawyer might have given him some warning. He'd expected to testify during the defense, but didn't know about the cross-examination.

The man ambled to his feet and turned to smile at the jury. The lawyer glanced back at Cal, an odd expression on his normally passive face. "Tell me, sheriff. Do you think Noverta Randolph killed his wife?"

"Objection." Jackson screamed. "Hearsay."

"Your Honor," the fancy defense lawyer whined, "the sheriff is a seasoned law enforcement officer. I'm asking his opinion as an expert witness." The last two words sounded like "exxpart wittt-nas."

The lawyer was up to something and Cal suspected John Randolph was behind the scheme, whatever it was. The senator sat in the second row, looking far too content for a man whose son sat in the defendant seat.

"Expert?" Jackson smirked. "Our good sheriff has made no arrest more serious than disturbin' the peace."

"Nonsense," the judge replied, still looking bored. "Cal Henderson is a decorated policeman. I'm sure his experiences in that God-forsaken District of Columbia subjected him to horrors you can't even imagine." Judge Sparks exhaled loudly making his cheeks puff out. "You can answer the question, sheriff."

Cal swallowed once to ensure his voice would resonate. "No, I do not think Noverta killed his wife."

"That's all," the lawyer said, twisting his shiny cufflink.

Judge Sparks nodded before turning his bored expression in the direction of the defense attorney. "Jackson, do you have a redirect?"

"I do." The DA jumped up, glancing at the jury before he whirled and smiled at Cal. "You have stated that *you* do not believe Noverta Randolph killed his wife, Lily Carleton Randolph. Is that correct?"

"It is."

"Then please tell the court, who did kill Mrs. Randolph?"

Cal glared at Jackson, for all the good it did. "I don't know."

The district attorney turned to the jury and smiled, imitating the defense attorney's earlier gesture. A young woman in the front row giggled.

"Thank you, Sheriff Henderson," Jackson drawled, not seeming the least bit sincere. "I do appreciate your *expert* opinion."

# CHAPTER 13

*Monday, November 21*

Cal straightened his tie, thanking everything holy that he could finally testify for the defense. He hadn't been able to return to the courtroom after being questioned by the prosecutor on Thursday, but Rodney had kept him up-to-date on the proceedings. His deputy didn't think any of the new testimony had swayed the jury one way or the other. Maybe he could tip the scales in Noverta's favor with round two.

The Memphis defense lawyer fired his first question, a question Cal had already answered during his previous time in the witness box. "Do you think Noverta Randolph killed Lily Carleton Randolph?"

"No, sir. I do not," Cal replied.

Surprisingly, Jackson posed no objection. That worried Cal.

"Then why did you arrest Mr. Randolph?" the lawyer asked.

"I didn't arrest him." Cal crossed his arms, doing his best to hide a smirk as the courtroom began to buzz.

"Pardon me," the lawyer said, scratching his head. "Then why was the defendant in the jail?"

"I brought Noverta to the jail for questioning," Cal said, glad he finally had an opportunity to explain. "I planned to let him go afterward, but the district attorney filed charges." Cal didn't add that he never got to question Noverta because the lawyer arrived and refused to let his friend speak to anyone. The attorney had insisted on keeping that under wraps.

"The district attorney?" the Memphis hotshot frowned, sounding like a Shakespearian actor Cal had seen in a D.C. show.

"Yes sir," he replied.

The lawyer nodded. "Did the *district attorney…*" the man paused, a pinched look on his face. "Did the district attorney review the evidence with you?"

"He did not." Cal made eye contact with Jackson.

While the DA glared back, the buzz in the courtroom grew louder, echoing from the chambers. Noverta's lawyer scratched his head again. "So the district attorney filed charges without even knowing what was going on?"

"Objection!" Jackson jumped up, looking like a street brawler with his hands curled into fists.

The judge snorted. "Sustained. Go ahead and *re-phrase*, counselor."

The Memphis man, smiled. "To your knowledge, did the district attorney have any evidence when he filed charges?"

"Objection! That's prejudicial, Your Honor."

"Overruled," Sparks said, swiping at one of the strands of hair remaining on his balding head. "Sit down, Jackson. Answer the question, Sheriff."

"No sir." Cal experienced a flutter of hope. Real hope.

The defense lawyer smiled again. There was something sinister about the man. Thank God he was on Noverta's side. "In your *expert* opinion, Sheriff…" The lawyer paused to glance at the jury. "Was Noverta railroaded?"

"Objection!"

The judge no longer looked amused.

"Withdrawn," Noverta's attorney drawled in a sing-song voice. He turned toward the jury with a dramatic flair. "There is simply no case here, so the defense rests, Your Honor."

*The defense rests?* Son of a… What the hell kind of defense was that?

"He can't do that!" Cal glanced at the crowd, most of the faces reflected his expression. Shock.

"The witness will refrain from outburst," the judge admonished.

"But Your Honor…"

"Shut up, Cal." The judge banged his gavel. "The witness is excused."

Cal didn't know what else to do, so he rushed from the witness stand. Did the damned lawyer actually think that strategy would work? Think Leeton folks were that dumb? Just saying there was no reason to defend Noverta wouldn't convince anyone of that truth.

*Hell's bells.* He had to find something before sentencing. In Cal's mind the verdict was a done deal, and Noverta was down to his last strike.

Cal managed to reach his friend before the bailiff handcuffed him. "I'll find a way to get you out of this, Vertie."

"What?" Noverta looked dazed.

A little old lady in the second row covered her mouth with a lace handkerchief and shook her head. Cal forced a smile. The elderly woman looked away. What was wrong with everyone? The town loved Noverta. Didn't they?

The turkey tournament would start in four days. Maybe the basketball games would serve as a reminder: Noverta was a hero. He'd been part of the state championship teams in 1927 and 1928. Only the blasted attorney had just ensured the verdict would come in before the reminder.

Even so… Surely the folks who cheered so loud then wouldn't turn on one of their own now.

Cal caught Jackson's gaze. The DA still glared as if he'd been wronged, probably ticked that he hadn't had more time in the limelight. Damn man. In high school, Noverta had spent hours with Jackson working on his free throws. Jackson clearly didn't remember that.

Cal couldn't think about all that. Not now. If Noverta hadn't already been publicly convicted of a murder, he'd been labeled a cuckold. Cal had to find the real killer—just in case the town's poor wanted revenge on the town's richest family. Whatever the verdict, Cal decided he sure as hell wasn't running for reelection.

He made a beeline for his Packard. After waiting for the crazies to clear, Cal shifted into first gear but held in the clutch. He should wait for the Memphis lawyer and convince the man he needed to talk to Noverta. The judge would probably ask for the verdict tomorrow. Cal leaned against his steering wheel, rubbing his temples. The slamming of his passenger door made him sit up straight.

"Grace?"

"Just drive." She studied his face with an intensity only she possessed. No tears, no fear—just determination with a hint of resignation.

Had he ever seen Grace cry? Cal didn't think so. Even as a kid, she'd been tough. At age ten, she'd barely whimpered when she broke her arm. They told her dad she'd tripped over a log, but Grace had climbed up to visit Cal's treehouse, even though he and Noverta had pulled the rope ladder inside. Fifteen feet in the air, Grace fell when Noverta yelled, "Get out!"

Cal pinched the bridge of his nose. "Grace, I'll find—"

She pressed a gloved hand on his bicep. "You did what you could. You're a good friend, but I need to get out of here. Just drive. Please."

He complied. Not knowing what to say, he stared at the road. She moved her hand to his shoulder. Cal fought to keep from swerving at the contact.

"Vertie will be okay," she whispered.

"You don't understand," Cal replied. "If he's convicted, new evidence won't automatically get him out of prison." Cal had run into that legal nightmare in D.C. after he and his partner arrested a man for robbing a grocery. Two days after the man's conviction, the storeowner caught his wife in a hotel with his butcher and shot the woman dead. She had a wad of cash in her bag, almost the same sum the storeowner reported stolen. The falsely convicted robber spent another eighteen months in jail.

Cal glanced at Grace, hoping she understood how serious a guilty verdict would be. His front wheel hit a rut on the narrow street. "Damn. Eh, sorry."

Grace didn't respond.

"He won't be okay, Grace. Vertie won't last a day in prison. Hell, they may send him to Alcatraz like Machine Gun Kelly."

When the road looked smooth for a few yards, Cal glanced at her again. She didn't seem appropriately alarmed. Couldn't she see her brother was going up river?

"Take it easy, Cal. He'll be all right." She was calm. Far too calm. *Why*?

"You don't think Vertie's guilty, do you?" he asked.

She withdrew her hand. "I know he's not guilty."

How could she know that for sure? Unless she knew who actually killed Lily.

"Tell me how you know, Grace. We can get that smarmy lawyer to…do something. How do you know Vertie's innocent?"

"My brother said he didn't kill her, Cal. If he were lying, I'd know."

"Yeah, let's tell that to the jury." He needed to stop his negative thoughts. One more day remained. He could still find some evidence that would prove Noverta's innocence.

Grace's house came into view. He barely remembered the drive, wasn't even sure why he'd decided to take her home. He shifted his car into neutral.

"Would you like to come in for some coffee?" she asked.

"Eh…" He had no time. Only, he couldn't truthfully say he was busy because he didn't have his next move planned yet, other than looking at baseball cap sizes. Time with Grace sounded like a balm for a dreadful day. Maybe a break would allow him to refocus.

"Eh—you sure it's okay?"

Grace flashed a sad little smile. "Relax. I won't put cream in your coffee again."

He didn't want coffee. God help him, he wanted Grace. Still.

Might as well address the fat goat in the cow barn. "What about Ernest? Where is he, Grace?"

Cal desperately needed to have a chat with Ernest—find out what he knew, why he'd disappeared. Too bad the man's presence would turn the balm Grace offered into a bed of fire ants.

She frowned. One might think she'd forgotten she had a husband. No, that was most likely more wishful thinking on his part. "He's not here, but maybe we should go to your house."

"Oh." He should follow his plan—demand an answer about Ernest's whereabouts. After all, no one had seen the man since Lily's murder.

Hold on. Grace had said *his house*? Did that mean…? "My house?"

She sighed. "It was probably a dumb idea. I just don't want to be alone right now."

"I feel the same." He shifted into gear and backed out of the driveway before she could change her mind. He'd waited ten long years for some quality time with Grace. He'd put his suspicions aside for another hour or two. He'd demand his answers about Ernest when he brought her home.

Neither spoke as the car motored down the country road. He pulled into his driveway, got out, opened her door. After he escorted her inside, he didn't know what to do.

"Can I get you—I'm sorry, Grace. I don't have any tea."

"Water will be fine." She sat down in the chair with the attached telephone table he'd inherited from his aunt. Grace once told him the seat-thing was Rococo-style—whatever the devil that meant. Why he remembered that, he didn't know. Maybe because he'd made love to Grace on the thing one Saturday night while his guardian had visited a sick friend in Knoxville. The memory loomed vivid—Grace, practically nude and so beautiful he swore his heart stopped beating for a moment. Then she banged her knee.

Cal handed her the glass of water, the movement enhancing rather than jarring his memory. She'd asked for water then too. Grace rubbed her hand over the arm of the chair. Did she remember, too? She turned to face him, blinking once when his fingers touched hers.

Somehow, the glass ended up on the little table. Then *somehow,* he was kissing her. Or she was kissing him. Didn't matter. Fire was fire. No amount of water could quench the flame.

He touched her face, her hair, her shoulder. She didn't resist. That was the important thing. His hand slid beneath her dark green jacket. Then the pristine white blouse. Pure heaven.

He shouldn't. He knew he shouldn't, but it had been far too long since he'd experienced anything close to pleasure. Cal did everything he could to prolong the moment, wrapping his arms around her, pulling her slim body tighter against his chest. He delighted in the feel of her.

Why had she married that lowlife Ernest? He'd ask later. At the moment, he'd just kiss her and be content.

Then he kissed her again.

He wasn't sure who pulled away, but just as suddenly as they'd started their lip lock, they were kissing no more.

"Eh…" Grace swiped at her dark hair in a futile attempt to restore the escaped tendrils. "What was… We shouldn't."

Cal swallowed, trying to slow his hammering heart—and the parts of him that shouldn't be hammering over a married woman. "I know."

"I'm still married."

He nodded. "I know." Of course, he knew. Too damn bad that knowledge didn't reduce one ounce of his desire. "We should probably go."

Grace nodded, still looking at her feet. "Probably best."

Damn. Angry wasps seemed like a pleasant thing compared to his disappointment. Probably the punishment he deserved, given his lack of honor. "Forgive me, Grace. I shouldn't have…" He turned, needing desperately to get her out of his house.

As he reached for the doorknob, Grace placed a hand on his bicep.

*Keep going. Walk directly to the car.*

Only he couldn't. He turned to face her. One glance at her brown eyes, her lips—movie star lips—and he had to stay.

"Cal…"

He swallowed. He didn't dare speak.

"We *should* go." Grace said, biting at her lower lip, the same lip that had his libido topsy-turvy. "But I want to stay."

Hell.

And hallelujah.

# Robin Weaver

# CHAPTER 14

Dear, sweet Lord. What had she done?

Grace crawled out of Cal's bed, being careful not to let the oversized wooden headboard bang against the wall. The bed had belonged to his mother and Grace had always loved the bright blue color. Mrs. Henderson would chase the worms out of her coffin and come back from the grave to reprimand her if the lady knew what had happened beneath the brightly colored headboard.

Grace reached for her blouse and headed for the kitchen. Only four in the morning and already a massive headache had formed behind her temples. Tea. She needed tea. Only Cal didn't have any tea. Not that it mattered. What she really needed was a confessional.

Sleeping with Cal ranked as the very worst thing she could have done. Only the afternoon—and the night—had been divine. A momentary reprieve from the hell that had become her life. Being with him equated to sweet, sweet pleasure—even better than their lovemaking when they were together ten long years ago. Things had been so good then.

Of course, that bloom of young love had landed her in her current mess in the first place. She didn't know if her one slip would provide her with a precious memory or become a reminder of what she could never have. Probably both.

If only she could tell Cal the truth. Maybe then, they could go forward. She planned to divorce Ernest anyway. After ten years of misery, mostly self-inflicted, she had finally reached the conclusion that she must leave her husband. She'd made that decision even before her father forced the legal issue. Without meaning to, she'd punished Ernest as much as she'd punished herself. That wasn't right, no matter what Ernest had done.

Coffee would have to do. Grace searched for the beans, not surprised to find them in the same place Mrs. Henderson had stored them so many years ago. In those days, she and Cal hadn't been allowed to have coffee.

She really should go home, but she wasn't quite ready to face her world again. Instead, she put the kettle on the stove. Soon, the title of divorcee would belong to her, a label the people in Leeton considered worse than death. A fate she'd done everything possible to avoid. Grace Randolph did not fail, thus her marriage could not fail.

She'd been so stupid.

\* \* \* \*

Cal sat up, adrenaline raging through his body. Where was he?

*Grace.* Grace was in his bed. Or had been. He leaned against the wooden headboard.

Shit. He hadn't meant to fall asleep. What if Ernest finally came home and discovered Grace hadn't returned? What time was it anyway? He glanced at the clock as he hopped out of bed.

If only he could stay buried in the downy mattress with Grace. Forever.

He couldn't. Noverta needed him and Grace didn't belong to him.

Cal yanked on his pants and found her in his kitchen, her posture reminding him of a picture he'd seen of George VI's wife, Elizabeth. She was far lovelier than the queen of England, lovelier than any royalty. Only their fairytale had to end. "I should probably take you home," he said.

"I know," she replied without turning to face him.

Neither moved. Neither spoke. Cal poured a cup of the coffee, knowing it would be awful. Of all the things Grace could do, brewing a good cup of Joe wasn't one of them.

Grace whispered something, but her words were too soft.

"I didn't hear you," he said, sensing he needed to know what she'd said.

"This can't happen again."

He'd had the same thought a minute early, but hearing the words spoken aloud packed a bigger punch than the caffeine. *This can't happen again.* As in never. He realized in an instant that he'd held on to hope, a flicker of *maybe someday* that he'd have to relinquish. He'd lost Noverta. He couldn't bear losing Grace forever.

"I suppose you're right," he replied, believing her on an intellectual level.

"At least not until…"

"Until?" He turned on the overhead light so he could study her expression. Her eyes flashed, just once, then all emotion seemed to drain from her face. "Until what?"

She shook her head. "Never mind."

With those two little words, hope died.

# CHAPTER 15

*Tuesday, November 22*

Cal removed his hat and hurried into the courtroom. He slipped into the back row, wondering what he'd missed.

"Mr. Foreman, has the jury reached a verdict?" Judge Sparks asked.

Son of a gun. He'd missed closing arguments completely. When had the judge asked for a decision? The jury couldn't possibly have reached a verdict already. Not possible, right?

"Yes, Your Honor," the jury foreman replied.

Cal searched for Grace, finding her sitting behind Noverta, her hands folded, her head facing the judge. He offered a silent prayer to a God he seldom consulted, hoping for a miracle. He feared

Noverta was being railroaded, he just didn't know why.

"What say ye?" Sparks asked.

"We find the defendant guilty of murder in the first degree."

*Damn.* Everything blurred. Cal grabbed the armrest, thankful he'd sat down at the end of the pew. Noverta couldn't be guilty. Son of a bitch, he couldn't be guilty.

His vision funneled to Grace. He couldn't see anything else, only her face surrounded by haze. She dabbed at her eye with a gloved hand. Otherwise she didn't move.

People shouted. The judge called for a bailiff. Cal couldn't move. He managed to shake his head, hoping for some clarity, hoping something would make sense.

The procession of bailiff and prisoner reached his row. Cal jumped up. What could he possibly offer in lieu of evidence, but he had to say something, show his support. "Vertie, I'll—"

Noverta grabbed his arms, the cuffs on his wrists clanging. "Just find Tanner, Cal. Take care of my dog."

\* \* \* \*

*Thanksgiving day.* What a joke.

Cal put his feet on his desk, wishing he could get his head back into the investigation. He had received several dinner invitations, but he was mad at everyone in Leeton. To his way of thinking, the townsfolk had deserted Noverta. Besides,

Thanksgiving was a family holiday. With his parents gone, Noverta and Grace were all the family he had left. Now they were gone too. Hell, he'd never liked turkey anyway.

He yanked his feet down and tapped his desktop with his fist, trying to propel his brain to think of something he'd missed. He'd been doing the same thing for two days, with the same results. Hadn't that Einstein fellow said doing that was insanity?

His office door flew open. Melvin Thompson barged toward him, his salt and pepper hair wild, his expression wilder still. "Did you have anything to do with it?"

*What the devil?* Cal leaned back in his chair. "Afternoon, Mel. I thought you'd be stuffing your craw with your wife's famous cornbread stuffing. Why are you here exactly?"

Melvin pressed an arm against the doorjamb, his large stomach sucking in and out. "You know. Why else would you be in your office on Thanksgiving Day?"

Cal stood, consciously using his height to intimidate the owner of the *Leeton Herald.* "All I know right now, *Mel*, is that only a story would drag you away from the table. Why don't you tell me what it is I *know* and save us both some time."

The editor took a step back, his eyes narrowing. Cal had no clue why the man was so agitated. Melvin wasn't a bad guy and usually not so rude, but like Jackson McKinney, Noverta's trial had elevated his status.

The furrows in Melvin's brow relaxed. "You really don't know, do you?" Then the man started to laugh.

Cal started to get annoyed. He stifled the rude words dancing on his tongue and forced a smile. "I'll play along, Mel. What is it I don't know?"

Deputy Herbert Smith rushed in, seemingly from nowhere. He almost knocked into Melvin. "Boss, did you hear?"

The editor held up a hand. "Let me tell him, Herbie."

Cal waited, hoping to God someone would tell him soon or get the hell out of his office. "Tell me what?"

Melvin straightened, taking in a deep breath. The man enjoying keeping him in suspense. He huffed another breath, probably anxious to spill the beans.

"Noverta escaped!" Herb shouted

"What?" Cal jumped to his feet, his annoyance replaced with something much worse—dread.

"Why didn't you let me tell him?" Melvin whined.

Herb ignored the editor and grinned at Cal. The deputy crossed his arms over his chest, a big grin on his face. Surely the deputy couldn't be happy Noverta had escaped.

"I told you he was guilty," Herb proclaimed. "Why else would he run?"

# CHAPTER 16

*Thanksgiving, November 24*

Grace peeked through the window and let the curtain fall. "Criminy." She'd been expecting Cal, had been yearning for him actually, even knowing seeing him again wouldn't be wise.

"I know you're there, Grace. Open the door."

She hadn't intended to hide like some pea-hen, but she couldn't breathe. Being with Cal had brought the feelings she'd stuffed into the trunk of her mind back to the surface. She'd never fooled herself, had always known she'd never get over him, but she'd learned to exist without him. Now, that existence was questionable.

"Grace!"

onlySucking in all the air she could get, she squared her shoulders. She might not be able to function emotionally, but she was no coward.

The second the door opened, Cal pushed her hand away from the jamb and barged past her into the foyer. She planted a hand on her hip, watching him as he walked to the living room door and looked inside. Then made his way to the main bedroom.

What the heck? "Well, good afternoon, Cal. Why don't you come on in?"

The sheriff made a one-eighty, his expression hard as granite. He looked nothing like the lover who'd stroked her face with so much tenderness she almost cried. And she never cried.

"Where is he, Grace? No one has seen him. And I mean *no* one. "

She frowned. Was he *still* looking for Ernest? Maybe she'd better just tell him that sordid story. Only why did he still want to question her husband with Noverta already convicted.

Because Cal would never give up.

"Ernest isn't here," she said, hoping her voice sounded calm, reasonable, soothing even.

He slammed his fist against the oak door. "Don't play games. You know I'm talking about Vertie." He shook his head, and then stormed into the second bedroom.

Apparently her voice hadn't been soothing at all. "Vertie?" she asked, following Cal into her bedroom. He shocked her when he opened her chifferobe. "What are you looking for?"

"Vertie."

She blinked. "In the chifferobe? You're looking for my brother in the chifferobe?" She leaned against the wall, her head swimming.

Cal stopped his search and turned to face her, his granite features now downright scary. His fists curled and uncurled. "Stop, Grace. Just stop. You and Vertie might be my closest friends, but friends don't make you the town laughing stock."

She sucked in some air, only it wasn't enough. Cal still considered her his closest friend?

He snapped his fingers in her face. "I'm going to ask one more time. Where is Vertie?"

What the devil was he asking? He'd been there for the verdict. "Why are you being cruel? You know Vertie's in a holding facility. Waiting to be…" She couldn't even say it, wouldn't even think about it. She'd find a way to keep her brother from going to the penitentiary. For a crime he hadn't committed.

Cal studied her, his gaze feeling like a spotlight. Even with years of bearing her father's scrutiny, she found it difficult to endure Cal's inspection without squirming. Even so, she refused to move.

After a few seconds, his shoulders drooped. The wind seemed to have dropped out of his rage sail. "You don't even know about the escape, do you?"

Escape? There was no escape. She shook her head, desperate for a normal breath. What did Cal mean? Had Ernest said something?

"I don't know what you're talking about," she said. That much was true, if not exactly an answer to the question he'd asked.

He chewed his lip, clearly unsure about her response, maybe even unsure about her. With good reason. "Your brother escaped."

"Holy bibles." She slumped down on her bed, not like the conclusions her brain had made.

"He's gone, Grace. Where are Ernest and Granny?"

She shook her head, still trying to wrap her brain around Noverta's escape. "With Gardner relatives, I suppose. It is Thanksgiving."

Cal took off his hat, running a hand over his head. "If you know where they are, Grace, you need—"

Dear Lord. She should tell Cal why they'd left, but she needed to deal with Noverta's escape. Why would he do a fool thing like that? Especially after they'd planned an appeal. Running made him look guilty. "I don't know where Ernest is, Cal. I swear, but if you're thinking Vertie is with Ernest, or that my husband helped with the escape, I can tell you Ernest doesn't have enough ambition to get out of the bars before they close. He couldn't arrange a jail escape if his life depended on it."

Cal nodded, seeming to see the truth in her assessment. "You're right."

"How?"

He raised his head. "How what?"

"How did my brother escape?"

Cal huffed out a breath and then sat beside her. "I was hoping you could tell me. Someone let him out of the state holding facility."

"Let him out?" She blinked, then blinked again, but still couldn't make her vision focus. "You mean Vertie just walked away. You don't think…" Her father could certainly arrange something like that. Had escape been the plan all along? Didn't those idiots know Rodney would be blamed?

Cal waited, his eyes narrowing. "Think what, Grace?"

"I know Rodney's the obvious suspect, but he didn't… I know he and Vertie are close, but Rodney wouldn't do that."

Cal shook his head. "I never even considered Rodney, Grace. Maybe I should have, but Rod couldn't have been involved. He was looking for…" Cal stopped talking, clearly having said more than he intended. "I sent him out of town. Conflict of interest and all. I suppose he could have paid someone, but that just doesn't feel right."

Thank the Lord. The breath she'd held whooshed out. She couldn't bear it if her brother and her cousin were both in trouble. The only thing that would make matters worse would be if…

No. She had to stop thinking awful thoughts. Nothing was going to happen to Cal. She might never be with him, but he'd be safe. He had to be.

"If not Rodney, who helped him, Cal? Noverta would never run on his own."

Cal nodded. "You're right. But Grace... Swear to me you really don't know anything about the escape?"

She didn't hesitate. "I swear."

Grace didn't know anything about the escape, but that didn't stop other thoughts from bombarding her mind. Had her father been involved? The old man might not like his son and daughter, but he wouldn't let one of his offspring stay in jail.

Cal would make the same leap of logic. She didn't dare look at him. He'd be analyzing every movement she made.

"I don't know anything about the escape, Cal. I swear."

"How about your father?"

She shrugged. "A real possibility."

"Did he say anything? If not directly, has the senator said anything that would indicate he's...involved?"

Grace shook her head, glad she could tell him the truth, the whole truth. "No. Before Vertie's arrest, we hadn't spoken in a year."

"A year?"

She lifted her head to face him, seeing the scowl she expected. She'd loved that scowl once. Still loved the man behind it. Although he'd hate her if the full truth ever came out. "My father and I still don't see eye-to-eye on many things. We tolerate each other, but my *dad* really hasn't changed much."

Cal's expression turned from annoyed to sympathetic. "I'm sorry, Grace."

She preferred annoyed. "Don't be. I've come to terms with the situation. My father's not a nice man. I don't like him and he doesn't like me."

Cal ran a finger over his chin. "I don't think that's true, Grace. Your father acts very proud of you."

"When I'm not around."

Cal shrugged. Even he couldn't deny the truth about her father. "I think he cares about you and Vertie—in his own way."

"Yeah," she said, unable to keep *that tone* out of her voice. "As long as he can control us. Now that Vertie's in trouble, the senator is our umpire again." Grace knew she sounded whiny, but she also knew Cal might be the one person who understood. She loved him for that, too.

Cal wrapped an arm around her shoulder. "There may be a reason he's like he is, Grace. Best to let go of the anger. For your own sake."

She pulled out of his comforting embrace. "Have you let go of yours?" Criminy. Why had she asked that?

Cal blinked, the mask covering his emotions dropping for a mere second. Grace didn't like what she saw. Pain. Pain she'd caused. Pain that caused self-hatred. Only she couldn't change the past and she wouldn't do anything different if she could.

"I've never been angry at you Grace. You know that."

She looked away, unable to return his gaze, unable to regurgitate a hurt that would never really go away. "I know."

He didn't reply, just waited. Grace bit at her lip, refusing to say anything. Any words coming out of her mouth would likely cause more regret.

"Grace… Does Vertie get along with the senator now? I mean, they seem fine on the surface, but what's really going on between them?"

She shook her head, finally able to blink back unfamiliar tears. "He and Vertie are polite, but they don't really talk. Vertie likes things peaceful, so he rarely speaks out, but he doesn't have any more love for the senator than…" Uh-oh. She needed to stop her waterfall mouth.

"Even so…" Cal's voice was so soft, Grace had to hold her breath to hear him. "You think your father is behind Noverta's escape, don't you."

"Yes. The jailbreak reeks of my father." Grace finally chanced a look at Cal's face. "The senator will never admit anything, though. And you won't find any evidence."

"I know. But Grace…" He had her full attention. Why did he hesitate?

"Yes?"

"If you know anything, about anything, you'd better tell me. You brother may be out of jail, but they'll shoot him if they find him before I do."

That wasn't what he planned to say. She knew every nuance of Cal's expressions, and the little twitch in his jaw meant he'd changed his mind. Part of her was glad. More of her wanted to tell him everything.

Only she couldn't.

If her father was involved, Noverta would be safe. Only she'd never see him again. Her world had gone from hell to worse.

# CHAPTER 17

*Monday, November 28*

Cal ran his palm along the edge of his desk, needing to do something with his hands. Noverta's guilty verdict had made his world stand still, but after Thursday's prison break, Cal's brain had turned into lead. What was he supposed to do now? Even if he found something to prove Noverta's innocence, he'd have to find him to free him.

Still, Noverta wasn't capable of murder. The fancy lawyer insisted he could get Noverta a retrial. After all, there'd been no real evidence against him.

Perhaps he thought anything was better than the penitentiary. There had to be some reason, because Noverta sure as hell was innocent.

*So why did he run?*

Cal couldn't answer that question, so he grabbed some paper. Making lists usually helped him create a game plan, no matter how much manure cluttered his mind. After doodling for more than an hour, the two pages in front of him only added to his frustration. He stared at the rows of names, hoping for some clarity, some clue as to where to best apply his energy. He wasn't looking for a miracle, just a tiny lead.

The first page had a long list. *Persons who could have killed Lily*. He'd jotted down more than twenty names. Cal studied the page and then struck a line through Deputy Smith's name, not because he didn't think the deputy could be the murderer, but because Herb wasn't smart enough to act as dumb as he'd acted at the crime scene.

Or was he? Herb had managed to find Lily's parents without aid and he did hate Noverta. For an idiot, he had moments of pure brilliance. Cal re-added the deputy's name at the bottom of the list.

Writing Herb's name again changed nothing. So what had he missed? Cal resisted the urge to crumple the page into a wad, and pushed the list to the side of his desk instead. With any luck, the second sheet might jar something in his mind.

*Persons with motive*. At least that list was much shorter, more manageable.

Cal studied the first three names, wishing he didn't have to consider any of them suspects. Being well trained, he'd written them anyway: *Noverta Randolph, John Randolph, GRACE*. He'd made a fourth entry and that's where he intended to expend his time—investigating anyone who'd had an affair with Lily or anyone related to those men.

Lily had been killed with a snubnose, Lily's snubnose. A jealous wife or girlfriend could easily have fired the gun—a woman's weapon. Only thus far, all the men associated with Lily Carleton Randolph had been single. With alibis.

Maybe he should have another chat with Kenny. Buy the boy some hot chocolate and see if he really did know something. Kenny might be simple, but the boy didn't lie. Cal's mind began to free itself from the leaden prison. Who was friendly with Kenny and also had a motive to murder Lily?

*Grace.*

Damn.

No. He wouldn't believe that. True, she'd do anything to protect her brother, had been protecting him since their mother died when Grace and Noverta were only ten. Still, Lily posed no real threat. At the worst, Grace would have convinced Noverta to simply divorce the woman.

He grabbed his hat and shoved his lists into the desk. Grace's name caught his eye as he closed the drawer. Why had he written her name in capital letters? He hadn't done that with any other names.

Kenny could wait. Time for a long overdue heart-to-heart with Grace. This time, he'd act like a lawman and not some lovesick fool, still pining over his high school sweetheart. He *would* find out what she was hiding. And while he was at it, he'd talk to that no-good husband of hers, too. Hell, maybe he'd talk to Ernest first.

The ringing phone almost made him fall out of his chair. Every time his phone rang, his life took a nose dive into hell. He was in so deep now, he doubted he'd ever see the light again.

"Calvin Henderson?" a voice asked.

"Yes."

"Hold on, Sheriff. The governor wants to speak to you."

The governor? Hell. Cal had expected chastisement, but he thought it would come from the mayor. Not the governor.

"Sheriff Calvin Henderson?"

"Yes sir," Cal replied, trying to remember if he'd ever heard the governor's voice before.

"I'm guessing you know why I'm calling, son?"

Cal took a ragged breath. "No sir, can't say as I do."

"I'm calling because I don't like people breaking outta my jails, son."

Cal didn't see how he could be responsible for that. Noverta had been taken to the holding facility in Memphis. "I can understand that, sir. Just not sure why you'd call me."

"We gotta fix this, Sheriff Henderson."

*We*? "How can I help, sir?"

"I'm sending one of my investigators to talk to Senator Randolph. In the past, the senator has been…rather uncooperative. I'd appreciate it if you would accompany my man. If the senator is *uncooperative* again, you are to arrest him. Do I make myself clear?"

Damn. "Yes sir."

"Good. The investigator will meet you at the senator's house. Man should be there within the hour."

"You want me to go to Nashville?" Cal asked, wondering what the repercussions were for disobeying the governor.

"We have it on good authority the senator is in his Leeton residence. Agent Arnold will meet you there."

Cal nodded, wondering if he'd ever feel any semblance of control again. "Yes sir," he replied but the governor had already hung up.

What the devil? The phone definitely wasn't his friend. He sat back down, trying to make sense of the call. He'd definitely landed in the no man's land between the governor and Senator Randolph? And he'd thought things couldn't get worse.

The senator wouldn't be happy. Best if he left now. Cal could warn John, maybe negate some of the damage caused by him accompanying someone from the governor's office.

Twenty minutes later, he pulled into the circular drive. A tall lanky man waited, wearing a grey-striped suit that made him look more criminal than federal. Cal didn't see a car.

As Cal got out of the car, the man walked toward him with his hand out. "Sheriff Henderson? I'm Agent Arnold. Did the governor call?"

The agent was early. *Damn.*

Cal shook hands, trying to remember where he'd met the man. The voice sounded familiar.

"He called," Cal replied.

"Are you ready? To accompany me inside the senator's house?" the agent asked. Or maybe he demanded.

"Not sure why you need me. I'm sure you can interview the senator without my help."

The agent shook his head. "Probably not. We don't have a warrant, so he doesn't have to let me inside."

Cal frowned, not keen on being used as a pawn. Still, probably wouldn't help anyone if the governor decided Leeton's sheriff was uncooperative. Against his better judgment, Cal knocked on the massive door, wondering if he should try one of those antacid mints he'd seen on a Memphis billboard. He should definitely have called the senator before just showing up on his doorstep.

Senator Randolph's maid opened the door. "Sheriff Calvin." The woman nodded at the G-man. "Sir. How can I help you gentlemen?"

"Need to see the senator," Cal replied.

The maid smiled. "I'm terribly sorry, but the senator is away."

*An out and out lie.* Cal sucked in his lip, working hard to contain his temper. He couldn't target his anger at the woman and her overly-starched apron. The maid was just following orders.

"I don't think so," he said, forcing a smile. "I saw the senator's Alfa Romeo in the garage. And his driver is hitting golf balls in the backyard. So please tell the senator, who isn't in, that if he doesn't get his congressional butt down here in three minutes, I'll execute a warrant for his arrest."

"One moment." The maid closed the door.

"Well played, sheriff," the agent said, grinning like an overfed opossum.

A few seconds later, the senator opened the front door, fiddling with his cufflink. When had the man gotten so old?

"Damn you, Cal..." The senator raised his head.

Cal tried to signal with his eyes. Only the senator wasn't looking at him. John Randolph glared at the G-man.

"What is the meaning of this, Sheriff Henderson?" The senator asked, without so much as a glance in Cal's direction. The senator glared at the G-man. "And you. How dare you strong-arm a member of the U.S. Senate."

Cal smiled. Good thing he and the senator had an *understanding*.

The agent cleared his throat. "That would be the governor's strong-arming, sir. If I could have a few minutes of your time."

"Do you have a warrant?" the senator demanded.

The special agent flashed his opossum smile again. "That would imply I need one," he said, his pleasant tone holding a hint of snake venom.

Cal swallowed, wishing he could melt into the welcome mat. "Sir, if we have to get—"

"Fine," the senator interrupted, making it clear nothing was fine. "I'll do it for you, Calvin." He glared at the G-man. "I'll answer your questions, *Special Agent*, but I will not provide upholstered furniture to cushion your ass. Make it quick."

Cal choked. The governor might be able to pull strings, but the G-man holding onto the loose end had no idea he'd just crawled into a noose.

"Speak, man," the senator barked.

"Eh…" The agent licked at his lip. "How exactly did your son escape…sir?"

"You don't know?" John Randolph laughed. "Surely the gov'ner isn't trying to blame me for his poorly run holding facility. Son, that jail is not my responsibility. I have no earthly idea why things are so shoddy a man can escape from a supposedly secure cell."

Cal winced. The senator shouldn't know Noverta's cell status.

"We have evidence that you bribed one of the guards, sir."

"Now you listen to me, son." The senator moved closer. His six-foot-three frame might have a few years on its chassis and several extra pounds in places a man didn't want weight, but he still cut an intimidating figure.

The agent took a step backward, banging his leg on a plant stand. To the G-man's credit, he didn't even wince. "I'm listening, sir. Are you saying you *didn't* bribe the guard?"

"Which guard did I *supposedly* bribe?"

The agent almost kept his face free of expression, but Cal detected a tiny tic in the man's jaw. He'd be damned. The agent was lying about a guard being bribed. He'd just tossed out a knuckle ball, hoping the senator would swing. The man was clearly a rookie.

"I'm not at liberty to say," the agent replied.

"You are not at liberty?" The senator made a "haw" sound. "Then you shouldn't be stomping on my life and *pu-suit* of happiness. Unless you got something more, you best get off my property." The senator's face had turned an alarming shade of red.

The agent cleared his throat and focused his gaze on Cal. Shit. He definitely stood in no-man's land. And was about to get his gonads fried.

"Excuse me, Senator," Cal said, trying not to swallow too much air.

The senator blinked, his face losing some of the ruby coloring. "What is it, Cal? You paying close attention to this conversation, son? You might need to be a witness at this boy's trial when I sue him for libel."

The agent's face took on some of the senator's red coloring. "It's not libel if—"

Cal placed an arm on the agent's shoulder, needing to defuse the situation. "What the senator means, agent, is he's in a hurry." He turned to the senator, saying a silent prayer that Noverta was right and the man did consider him family. "Sir, we understand how busy you are, but as a personal favor *to me*, could you just answer the agent's questions."

Nobody spoke for several seconds. Cal didn't breathe.

"Very well," the senator said, his shoulders drooping. "Come on in. But I don't have all day."

After twenty minutes of *standing* in the main hallway, the special agent cleared his throat. "That's all the questions I have for now. Thank your time for your time, Senator. We'll be in touch."

They'd learned nothing. The senator basically filibustered every question. Cal expected a tirade from the agent, but when the door closed, the G-man jangled the change in his pocket. "Thank you for your assistance, sheriff."

"That's it?"

The agent nodded. "For now."

Cal looked around for a car. "You need a ride someplace?" he asked.

"Nah. Left my car over by the park. I'll just be on my way. Have a ways to go and want to be in Nashville before dark."

Cal scratched his brow as he watched the man walk down the oak canopied street. People just made no sense. The interrogation made no sense. What the hell had the governor hoped to accomplish? Probably just wanted to piss off Senator Randolph. Wouldn't be the first—or even the most powerful—man to try that.

Cal headed toward his car, glancing down the street once more before getting inside. The G-man was nowhere to be seen.

"Son of a bitch." Cal knew where he'd heard the G-man's voice.

Robin Weaver

# CHAPTER 18

Cal didn't know what game the so-called agent played, or if he was even an agent. The man who'd gone to the senator's house was the same man who'd pretended to be the governor. He'd been played a fool. But why?

Maybe someone just wanted him out of his office.

He rushed back to his building. When the door didn't budge, he pulled out his key. "Damn." The key didn't work. Had someone jammed the lock?

Cal put his shoulder into the wood and shoved. The door opened with minimal resistance. He hurriedly looked around. Nothing seemed out of place. Maybe he'd made a gully out of a pothole.

He sat down in his chair, scratching his brow. Where was Herb? He'd sent Rodney to Booneville, Mississippi, hoping to find Noverta. A long shot, but Noverta had a great aunt living there.

Herb should be covering the desk, though. Damn deputy was probably in Della's Bakery, jawboning about what a fine lawman he was.

Thirty seconds later, Cal grabbed his hat and headed for the bakery. He spotted Herb through the glass of the large front window, chewing on a honey-glazed donut.

"Hey, Boss Man," Herb called when Cal walked inside.

Several heads turned in Cal's direction. Someone snickered. Cal ignored everything but his deputy. "What are you doing, Herb?"

The deputy gestured at the checkerboard and at Della's husband, as though playing games was a perfectly logical thing for a county lawman to do on duty. Damn. Herbert better not be betting on the game.

"How long you been here, Herb?"

The deputy blinked. "Eh, not long. Something wrong, Boss?"

"Besides playing checkers when you should be working?"

"Hey, I'm entitled to eat lunch." The deputy leaned back to tuck his shirt tighter into his pants.

Cal let his gaze stray to the bakery clock. Three p.m. He'd deal with the deputy's long lunch later. "You see anyone go into the office?"

"Hell, Boss. You know I can't see the office from here."

Cal nodded. "That's the point, Herb."

He turned and walked toward the door. No sense in losing his temper. Besides, his jawboning was no more productive than Herb's.

"Hold up, Cal," Herb said

Cal glanced back. Herb had gotten up and reached in his pockets. The deputy slammed some money on the table. "I forfeit," he said to his game partner.

Cal turned and started walking. Herb caught up to him before he reached the office.

"Is something wrong?"

"Not sure." Cal replied. No sense biting Herb's head off when he was the one who followed the agent without verifying the man's credentials. He gave Herb an overview of his visit to the Randolph Place.

"Maybe the man really was an agent," Herb mused. "You said the governor called, right?"

"I don't think so, Herb." Nothing to be gained by telling Herb the same man who'd posed as an agent also posed as the governor. "Call the governor's office. See if anyone really did call our office."

Herb scratched his nose. "How do I…"

"Just get Adeline on the switchboard, Herb. She can connect you."

Ten minutes later, the deputy stuck his head into the door. "The lady in the governor's office says Governor Browning is in Jackson, Mississippi, for some farm convention."

No real surprise there. "Thanks, Herb."

"Eh… What you want me to do now?"

"Go make rounds," Cal replied.

"Dang, Boss. It's Rodney's turn."

"And he's not here. Do the rounds, Herb."

Cal pretended to study his list, waiting until Herb left before he leaned back in his chair. The entire afternoon made no sense. Hell, the past month made no sense. Why would anyone send him on a goose chase to the senator's house? He could think of only two reasons. First, someone wanted to question the senator. Only they wouldn't need him for that. No, his second idea made more sense, the same idea he'd had earlier. Someone wanted him out of the office.

Only there was nothing of value in his office. Unless… Cal opened his desk drawer.

"Son of a bitch."

The Mudcats cap he'd found outside Lily's window was gone. The picture the senator had given him was missing, too.

# CHAPTER 19

Cal went thru every possible scenario. The thief must have been after the photograph, only no one knew he'd taken the Mudcat's hat. Did that mean the killer had taken the picture and then recognized his cap? Or had Grace seen him take the hat the night of the murder? Ernest *had* been a Mudcat. The headgear could have belonged to Grace's husband.

All the more reason to talk to Mr. and Mrs. Gardner. Damn, but Grace's last name still made him gag.

Cal headed to Grace's house. Her car wasn't in the driveway. She should be teaching school, but why take the automobile when she normally walked?

Thinking of Grace and her sensible shoes always made him smile. Today was no exception, despite the dire circumstances that brought Cal to her house. Grace had gotten a lot of grief for her *sporting* behavior, but after her mother died she'd grown up surrounded by males. She could keep up with any guy but Cal didn't know anyone more womanly. Not only did she have the body of a pin-up girl, she never went anywhere without her pearls—he'd even caught her wearing them in the barn on occasion. Probably because Grace remembered her mother never went anywhere without the heirloom jewels. Even with the pearls, Grace had grown up tougher than her younger brother. She just looked a lot better in heels. A lot better.

He'd best concentrate on the case. He'd come to the farm to talk to Ernest. He had questions for the S.O.B. Tough questions.

The swings hanging on each end of the porch rocked slightly in the chilly breeze, giving a lonely feel to the normally vibrant house. Cal suspected the structure would come alive when Grace returned. He wasn't sure how she maintained the big house, the yard, and the dairy while still managing to teach twenty-five third and fourth graders. Maybe she didn't sleep.

Cal knocked on the green door, freshly painted and decorated with dried hydrangeas. He counted to ten and knocked again.

No answer. Damn. He should have insisted on talking to Ernest last week. He'd been afraid of the disease, even though he knew you couldn't *catch* pneumonia. Something about other people's mucus scared him more than facing a double-barreled shotgun.

*Assuming Ernest actually had pneumonia.*

Grace said Ernest had pneumonia but maybe her crumb husband lied to her. Man probably lounged at the pool hall or maybe he'd gone to check on some chickens. Rumor had it Ernest kept fighting cocks.

Cal waited and knocked a third time. He wasn't surprised Ernest was out—once a bum, always a bum—but Granny and her shotgun should be home. The woman rarely left the house for anything. Except church.

He banged harder. Still no answer. He stared at the red metal chair beside the doorway as he listened, letting his inner lawman absorb the scene. The yard had turned brown since his last visit and the roses had shriveled. Grace inherited the house and farm from her maternal grandmother, but she'd turned the ramshackle farm back into a viable business all by herself.

Cal had good memories of the big farmhouse, having spent a lot of his youth in the place, exploring the acreage with Grace and Noverta. As an adult, he now understood why they'd loved being at Mammie Bumpass's house. Even if the place hadn't been magical, it provided a sanctuary from John Randolph's temper. And his belt.

Shortly after John won his senatorial seat, the man built his fancy house in Nashville. At seventeen, Grace refused to move with her family. By then, Mammie Bumpass had gone to join the heavenly choir, so Grace packed her bags and moved into the house she'd inherit when she turned eighteen.

"Fine," the senator had decreed. He was as unflappable as Grace was stubborn. "She'll come to her senses when she runs out of money."

Only Grace hadn't run out of money. She'd worked every odd job she could find—before, during, and after school. She used every spare penny to make improvements on the dairy barn. In hindsight, Cal could see he'd been a heel, complaining Grace never had any time for him.

John Randolph knew he'd been bested, but he couldn't have his teenage daughter living alone. After all, he was a politician and propriety was paramount. He'd sent Marie, his Nashville housekeeper, to live with Grace. The senator actually pretended it was his idea to let his daughter live in Mammie Bumpass's house so she could finish high school in Leeton.

Cal banged on the door one more time. No human sounds other than his own breathing. He was alone. Might as well take a look at the bluetick in the barn. Make certain the dog wasn't Tanner.

He zig-zagged as he walked toward the shed, listening for any sound. He wouldn't put it past Granny to pretend she wasn't home and then threaten to shoot him for nosing around. When he finally reached the shed, he took a step back. Someone had pulled the roll-down door closed. And locked it. Who locked doors in Leeton?

Damn. He listened, but knew he wouldn't hear anything. Even a person as mean as Granny wouldn't shut the door if an animal were inside.

Well, hell. He might as well have that chat with Grace so the morning wouldn't be a complete waste. He got in his vehicle and headed toward the school. When he arrived, he didn't see Grace's car.

Principal Sweeney wasn't in his office, but his wife Connie, who taught second grade, sat behind the man's desk. "Need to see Grace Randolph."

"Sorry, Cal." Connie gave him a lop-sided smile. "Mrs. *Gardner* is not here today." Her grin evaporated as quickly as it had materialized. "Can you believe she sent that boy to tell us she's sick?" Connie exclaimed, dramatic as ever. "Grace has *never* called in sick. *Ever*. I don't think she was sick even when we were in school. That woman is healthier than those cows of hers. You can't imagine how hard it's been trying to keep three classes of bratty kids in line. Awful, I tell you. Just awful."

Cal took a step back. Grace was sick? Connie was right The idea staggered his mind. Grace had the constitution of Old Ironsides.

"Eh… What boy?" he asked.

"You know, the slow one. Her cousin."

Grace sent Kenny with her message? And Kenny thought he knew who killed Lily? What the heck did Grace know? Cal gave his head a little shake, hoping to clear his mind. Surely if she knew who killed Lily, she'd tell him. Right?

Connie kept talking, but he had no idea what she said. She seemed to be bellyaching about some class, so his inattentiveness probably didn't matter. The teacher clearly couldn't help him. Nodding, he tried to bid the woman "good day," but she kept talking.

A little girl came skipping into the office and Cal used the opportunity to escape. "Thank you, ma'am."

Outside, he surveyed the grounds, unchanged since his own schooldays. Only he didn't care about the old ballfield or the rusted swing set. He stared at nothing, hoping for some clarity. There was none.

The sinking feeling in his stomach had returned.

* * * *

Determined to talk to Grace, Cal got out of bed at four a.m. Probably overkill since he could have waited and tried to see her at the school again—surely she wouldn't miss teaching two days in a row. He wouldn't take the chance. Grace lied and he needed to know why. Not as if he could sleep anyway.

When he arrived at the farm, he headed for the barn. Mr. Hess, who helped with the milking, herded Holsteins inside for the morning milking.

Cal nodded at the man. "Morning. Looking for Miss...eh, Mrs. Gardner."

Hess tapped the brim of his John Deere cap. "Sorry, sheriff. Haven't seen her this mornin'."

Cal frowned. "How about Ernest? Seen him? Or Granny Gardner?"

Hess paused for a second before turning to hit the flank of another cow to move her along. "Can't say as I have. Now that ye mention it, ain't seen any of 'em since Saturday. Not like Miss Grace to not show for the milking three days in a row. Didn't think much of it afore, just done the milking by my lonesome. Can sure use the extra money."

Well, hell. "Grace hasn't been here since Saturday?"

The man nodded. "Not that I recall."

"Thanks." Cal turned to leave.

"Eh, Sheriff," Mr. Hess said. "Any reason I should be worried?"

Cal shook his head, but didn't stop walking. "I don't think so. Just tell Grace I'm looking for her when she shows up."

Inside his Packard, he banged his palms against the steering wheel. Grace would show up soon. She had to.

Her car was missing, but would she leave town? Surely she wouldn't leave her farm. The place was her life. Always had been. The house had been more important than him.

Hell, would he ever get over the woman? Grace's fear of having to abandon her precious house if she married a baseball player had probably ended things between them ten years ago. Only he would never have asked her to leave her home.

He glanced at his watch. Barely four-thirty. Still far too early, but he doubted he'd be able to go back to sleep. Might as well go into the office. Making more futile lists at his desk would be just as productive as watching the clock at home and waiting for eight. He'd count every torturous second until he could go to the school and look for Grace.

When he reached his office, he tossed his hat toward the filing cabinet, missing his target, but not really caring. After he started a pot of coffee, he pulled out some paper to start a new list, only he didn't write anything.

Son of a bitch. He was doing exactly the same thing in his office he'd wanted to avoid at home. He watched the clock, counting every second as he waited for eight a.m.

# CHAPTER 20

*Tuesday, November 29*

"I have to see Cal. Right now!"

Cal blinked, thinking he'd imagined Burton Randolph's voice. An entire pot of coffee tended to put a man on edge.

"Not sure he's here, Burt." Rodney's voice. "I just clocked in for my shift a few minutes ago and Cal doesn't come in until eight."

When had the deputy gotten to the office? Cal glanced at the clock. 6:15. Hell, he'd dozed off. He stared down at his list, seeing he'd written *Grace Randolph* ten times. "Damn."

Rodney stuck his head into the doorway. "I thought I heard... I sure am glad it's you." The deputy grinned, but the smile quickly faded. "Burton's here. He's wheezing like a lunger."

Cal nodded, shoving the paper into his top drawer. "I'll be right—"

Before he could say more, Burton limped in behind Rodney and leaned against the doorjamb, holding his mid-section. "You gotta...gotta help." The raspy words were hard to understand. The man's asthma had obviously flared up again. "It's Kenny. Oh God, Cal. Kenny's gone." The older man made a half-groaning, half-crying noise. An animal in pain.

Cal got an odd stinging sensation in his stomach, but tried to ignore the ache. Kenny was just fine. Boy had to be—Cal had enough on his platter.

Burton leaned forward, resting one elbow on the desk as he wheezed again. "You gotta find him, Cal. Afore they hurt him." *Wheeze.* "Someone..." *Wheeze.* "Took 'im. Took Kenny."

"Take it easy, Burt. Kenny probably woke up early and went exploring. He'll be back." The boy wandered off all the time. Hell, the incident at Noverta's trial was nothing new.

Burton shook his head, prompting another round of gasps. Cal waited.

"Not this time. Window..." *Wheeze, wheeze.*

"Here, sit down." Cal stood. He half-led, half-pushed the older man toward his vacated chair. "Take it easy. We can't help Kenny if you pass out on us."

Burton wheezed for several seconds. Cal stooped in front of him, hoping the gesture didn't make it harder for Burton to breathe. His own gut burned with the fires of hell. If something really had happened to Kenny…

"What were you saying about the window?" Cal asked.

Burton finally managed a complete breath without a wheeze. "Kenny's window. Broken. Glass everywhere."

Some of the tension in Cal's neck relaxed. "Kenny probably hit the glass with that stick of his, Burt. You know, the one he pretends is a pirate sword. Hell, he was waving that thing at everything last time I saw him."

Burton tapped a fist against his chest. The man had completely lost his composure. Or maybe his heart was about to give out. Cal wondered if he should call an ambulance.

"Nu-uh. Crash woke me up. A loud crash." The older man stopped talking and coughed. "The glass was inside the room, Cal. All over Kenny's bed. Means window was broken from outside, right? After I heard the noise, I went to…" *Wheeze.* "To check on Kenny. He was…gone. Just gone." *Wheeze.*

The pain in Cal's midsection stabbed him again, with greater intensity this time. He could no longer assume Kenny just wandered off. "You sure the boy didn't break it? Maybe he woke up early and was playing outside."

Burton shook his head. "Don't think so. Broken glass was…all over the bed. Kenny would have told me if he'd done that." The man raised his head, his pupils huge—a small animal looking into the jaws of a gator. "Kenny's gone. He wouldn't break the window and then run away."

Hell. Cal glanced at Rodney, feeling a tad better. He could tell from the deputy's expression, Rodney was thinking the same thing. That breaking and running is exactly what Kenny *would* do.

"Get Burton some water, Rod. If his wheezing doesn't stop, get him to the doctor. I'll go to his house and check it out. Don't worry, Burt. We'll find him."

"Whose house? Find who?" Herbert Smith asked, letting the door to Cal's office bang into the outer wall.

Damn. Why did Herb have to pick today to be on time?

"Where you going?" Herb asked.

"Kenny's not in his bed." Cal unlocked his bottom drawer and took out his .38, praying he wouldn't need the weapon. Only he had a bad feeling. He reached for his hat but it had fallen behind the filing cabinet. *Damn.*

"You can come with me, Herb," Cal said. The deputy would be a pain in his backside, but leaving him with Burton would only make the old man feel worse. "We're going to Burton's house to check on Kenny."

"But—" Burton wheezed again.

"We?" Herb scowled. "Why is finding that boy our business?"

Cal held up his hand, hoping Burton wouldn't say more. "You're coming with me, Herb. No arguments. Let's go."

Herb crossed his arms over his mid-section. "You want me to go with you to check on a runaway boy? Hell, Cal, I ain't no babysitter. I haven't even had any coffee yet."

"Rodney, when you can, drive over to Grace's house. If she's not home, find her. She may have seen Kenny." And maybe she'd answer the door if Rodney knocked instead of him. Assuming Grace was at home. "Herb, let's go." He walked from the room, knowing Herb would follow. To argue if for no other reason.

"Boss, why do I have to go?" Herb asked, following Cal to the street.

Cal wanted to ram his fist into the windshield of his car, but he'd only have broken glass. And no satisfaction, because he really wanted to ram his fist into one Herbert Smith. Why couldn't the damn man cooperate? Just once. "Because I *said* so."

"Fine." Herb's tone indicated things were far from fine.

So be it. "Let's move," he ordered.

"I gotta get my hat out of my car," Herb whined. He didn't wait for a response, just marched toward his automobile.

Cal got in his car and pressed his forefingers against his temple, willing his head to stop spinning. He didn't know why he bothered. The world had already spun out of control. First Noverta gone, then Grace. Now Kenny? If something happened to that boy…

He took a deep breath, and then turned the key. The minute Herb slammed the passenger-side door, Cal turned on his siren and released the clutch. He'd never used the siren for official business, only for the Christmas parade. Maybe because he'd never had anything more serious than kids sneaking moonshine into the gymnasium.

He sped down the lonely country road, driving the short distance as fast as he could, all the while working to control his temper. Too bad he couldn't take the shortcut through the woods Burton had probably taken. The path couldn't be much worse than the road. Navigating the gravel surface required frequent swerving to avoid ruts and foot-deep potholes. Herb, who normally liked speed, turned green and gripped the door handle.

The dismal bungalow finally came into view and Cal slammed on his brakes. Herb jumped out and leaned over the hood of the car.

Good, the deputy's vertigo would give Cal a chance to survey the scene from inside the car. The sun had risen, but the house remained in darkness, hiding in the canopy created by ancient oaks with brown leaves still clinging stubbornly to the branches. Burton's place looked peaceful, a little shabby perhaps with the peeling white paint. Okay, a lot shabby. One shutter hung haphazardly to the clapboard siding, but nothing about the abode said "kidnapping here."

The trees might not be bare, but leaves covered the entire yard, a testament to Burton's degenerating health. The man never had money, but in days gone by, Burton maintained a showpiece yard. Too bad he lived off the main road and folks rarely had an opportunity to appreciate his efforts.

Those days were gone and Burton's lack of raking effectively eliminated any footprints—either Kenny's if he'd meandered away, or someone more sinister if the boy had indeed been abducted.

Cal stared at the old well, wondering why Burton hadn't put a covering over the open cistern. Then he turned to look at the concrete porch, crumbling into cement dust in more than one place. Plenty of hazards, but nothing to indicate a crime had occurred.

Abruptly, Herb stood. The deputy yanked his gun belt straight, and then made a beeline for the house.

"Damn." Cal banged his knee getting out of the car. "Herb! Don't go in there."

The deputy had already yanked the door open and disappeared inside the bungalow. Cal rushed after him, banging his knee again when the front door recoiled. Once things calmed down, he'd fire Herb.

Cal found Herb just inside Kenny's room. Cal couldn't remember the deputy ever being in Burton's house before, but he'd gone straight to the back of the house? As if he knew which room was Kenny's.

"Hot damn!" Herb exclaimed, all of the bluster gone from his tone.

Cal glanced over the deputy's shoulder, into the bedroom. Hot damn, indeed.

Burton accurately described the glass—shards covered the painted floor. The lone chair in the room had been overturned and a pillow lay on scarred wood next to Kenny's stick. Weird that there wasn't much glass on the bed—maybe because Kenny's lanky body had covered most of the small mattress.

Nothing made sense. Who would kidnap the boy? Burton had no money and anyone who knew anything about Senator Randolph knew the man wouldn't give two cents for his nephew's release. So why take Kenny?

Unless… *Was it possible*? Did Kenny actually know who killed Lily? Is that why he was missing?

Herb picked up the pillow and tossed it on the bed. "What do you think happened?"

"Damn, Herb. I told you not to touch anything." Good thing the deputy hadn't called him *boss*. That might have pushed Cal right past his pretense of control.

He leaned against the wall, determined to maintain his composure. Wouldn't help Kenny if he were behind bars for punching Herb in the throat.

What on earth made him think he could be sheriff anyway? He had a dead body with no suspects, a friend convicted of a murder he didn't commit, and now a missing kid who'd already been sucker punched by life too often. Worse, he was in love with the woman who was somehow in the middle of everything.

He needed some air, solitude. "I've seen everything I need to see, Herb. When you're through...looking around, wait in the car." If the deputy valued his life, he'd do as he was told. For once.

Cal went out the backdoor, breathing in the cold morning air. Just after seven a.m. and his day had already been shot to hell. Nothing to indicate anyone had walked behind the house during the night. No prints, no broken bushes, nothing that didn't fit in the overgrown area.

Cal followed the little path past Burton's scraggly arborvitaes, his feet making a crunching sound on the frost-covered leaves. Once upon a time, Burton had carved those bushes into the shapes of animals. Back then, the evergreen creatures gave Cal the creeps.

He rounded the corner, happy to see the little pond created by the beaver damn still remained. The pool was small, only thirty feet at the widest point. A thin layer of ice covered the water's edges, a reminder of the unusually cold Tennessee weather. A chill that mirrored his state of mind.

Cal picked up a rock and skipped it across the icy water, desperate to clear his mind. He needed to *not think* before he could analyze. Grabbing another rock, Cal lifted his arm to repeat his brain-numbing exercise, only something caught his eye. He lowered his arm, trying to figure out what seemed out of place.

The sun had risen higher, giving a pinkish-gray hue to his surroundings and enabling a clearer view. Hollies, scrub pines, poplars, and oaks. An assortment of trees but nothing that should have jarred his concentration. Hell, even the broken branch was normal in the natural regeneration of the forest.

*Hold on.*

Cal looked at the poplar tree on the other side of the pond. A limb was missing, clearly a new break given the color of the splintered wood. Nothing extraordinary about that—branches broke all the time, especially in the cold of winter.

*So why's there no branch on the ground?*

Well, hell. He walked uphill, to the spot where the stream split and formed the pond so he could cross to the other side and examine the tree. Sure enough, the branch that should be laying on the ground was nowhere to be found. But what did it mean?

"Boss?"

Damn Herb. Cal needed to look for the branch and he didn't need the deputy hovering. He'd have to come back later. He wasn't sure why the branch was important, but he knew in his gut, he had to find it.

# CHAPTER 21

Locating Grace moved to the top of the list. Cal pulled into his parking place and waited for Herb to get out of the car.

"Aren't you coming in?" the deputy asked.

Cal shook his head. "I need to head home for a bit. I'll be back soon." Not exactly a lie, he just had a stop to make before he went back to his place.

"What are we supposed to tell Burton, Boss Man?"

*Damn.* He really should talk to Burton, but he had to go. "Tell Rodney to drive Burton home and stay with him. I'll drop by with an update as soon as I can."

"But—"

"Call the sheriff's offices in Fayette, Tipton, and Shelby counties. Tell each of them to be on the lookout for Kenny. Notify the radio station, too. Can you handle that?"

Herb blinked, but nodded. To Cal's surprise, he closed the door without argument.

Cal hurried to the school. This time, Principal Sweeney was in the main office. The man jumped up and grabbed his hand.

"Cal. Good to see you, son. Thanks again for that autographed picture of Dizzy Dean. Got it hanging over my mantel. Right next to yours."

Cal tried to extract his hand, attempted to concentrate on Sweeney's words, but failed at both tasks. He really wanted to tell the man to be quiet, but the principal rambled on about Cal's baseball days, not even pausing for breath. Cal let him talk. When the principal finally paused, Cal's mind was exhausted. He opened his mouth to ask about Grace, but Sweeney started again. Just when he thought he'd have to be rude, the principal gave his head a little shake.

"Listen to me, would you? Going on and on about stuff you already know. I'm sure you're not here to reminisce about the good ole' days. Still, makes me downright sad when I think about you messing up your leg. Sad about your buddy, Vertie, too. Sad thing. Sad, sad thing."

"About that." Cal spoke quickly, not about to give the man time to launch into another oration.

"I'm looking for Noverta's sister. Is she here today?"

"Grace? You and her used to date, right? Back in the day. Sad about her marrying that Ernest fellow. We all wondered about that."

"Mr. *Sweeney*."

The principal's eyes widened. Cal experienced a little twinge over his interruption, but he couldn't let the man start talking again.

"Apologies for the interruption," Cal said, hurrying his words, "but I'm here in an official capacity. Is Grace in her classroom?"

"Official?" Sweeney's eyes seemed to grow even larger. "You should have just said so. I haven't seen her today. Connie's madder than a Bannie hen sittin' on a dozen eggs."

"Thanks. Did Grace let you know she wouldn't be in?"

The principal scratched his chin. "Can't say as she did. I do believe that boy might have said something yesterday. You know, that Grace might be out more than one day."

"Thanks again." Cal hurried outside, no longer concerned about his manners.

Where the hell was Grace?

# CHAPTER 22

*Wednesday, November 30*

Twenty-four hours. Kenny had been missing for a full day.

Grace had been missing longer. And Cal still had no hint of where Noverta had run.

He removed his hat and rubbed his head. He'd searched every place Kenny might have gone, had even sent Rodney and Herb door-to-door asking if anyone had seen the boy.

Nada.

Maybe if he found Noverta's dog, the bluetick could help him track the boy. Maybe not. The hounds the penitentiary guards used to search for Noverta had yielded nothing.

Cal wasn't convinced the trackers had tried all that hard. Except for the ranting mayor, the newspaper editor, and him, no one else seemed the least bit concerned about Noverta's escape.

Still, Cal needed to find the dog—dead or alive. Tanner's disappearance nagged at his subconscious, had bothered him since that dreadful night he'd gone to Noverta's house. And Noverta had twice asked him to look after the dog—an odd request from a man whose freedom was on the line. Was the request a hint?

On an ancient, instinctual level, Cal knew the dog was the key. Besides, looking for Tanner would be doing *something*. He hadn't given up on finding Kenny, but he was down to his last strike.

He picked up the phone but returned the receiver to its cradle. If he asked the operator to connect him with Ida Simmons, the operator would likely listen in to the conversation. Why he cared who overheard, he didn't know. Still, probably better if he trusted no one, not even Grace. Maybe especially not Grace. She hadn't been exactly forthcoming and best he could tell, she'd lied about Ernest's pneumonia. And she'd disappeared.

He got into his car and drove to Ida's house. The older lady met him at the door, rubbing her hand over the hip of her checked dress.

"Sheriff Henderson. How nice to see you." The woman smiled, but the gesture seemed forced. She looked up and down the street before motioning inside. "Come on in."

What the devil was she hiding?

Cal took off his hat, trying to shake off his suspicious nature. The damn case had gotten to him if he was distrustful of sweet old Ida Simmons. Poor woman probably wanted to make sure Herb wasn't in tow.

"Afternoon, ma'am." He forced himself to go through the usual pleasantries, not really giving a damn if it hadn't rained in almost a month—not since the day Lily died to be precise. He lasted as long as he could, but when Ida asked if he missed playing baseball, his patience snapped like a bat making contact with a Lefty Grove fastball.

"Ida, I need your help. Have you seen Tanner?"

She blinked, clearly surprised—hopefully not offended. "No. I didn't really think about the dog before. I guess I should have. Surely someone took the animal in after… Well, you know."

"After the murder you called in."

Her head snapped back, her lips pursed. Not the reaction he'd expected, but then he had been rude.

"Eh… Yes. Only I didn't know there was a murder then, *Calvin*."

Using his given name might have made him ashamed of his bad manners a month ago, but the last three weeks had changed him. For the first time in his life, he didn't care what anyone thought.

"I need you to think, Ida, think back to that night. You said you didn't hear the dog barking? Are you sure?"

He could almost hear her brain working. "No, I don't believe I did. I should have, though, shouldn't I? That dog barks at any car that comes around these parts, unless it's Noverta's car. Dog doesn't bark then. You don't think all those cars I heard were Noverta?"

"All four of them?" Cal asked, feeling the annoyance that had never completely left rise to the surface again.

Ida didn't seem to notice. She frowned, causing a multitude of lines in her forehead. "That can't be right. The cars didn't sound the same, you know what I mean, right?"

"I think so, but tell me in your own words." And just why hadn't she mentioned that before?

"The engines sounded different. One kind of purred—you know, a continuous sound. Another one sounded a bit clunky. More like a tractor. I don't remember what the others sounded like—it's been a while." She shook her head. "But, all those cars couldn't have been Noverta, so I guess the dog wasn't there."

Or she'd gotten used to the barking and just didn't remember. The barking gave him an idea, though. He hurried his goodbye.

Cal went by his house and whistled for his half-beagle, half-whatever. If Tanner was anywhere in the area, Lucky would find him. Why hadn't he thought of that before?

Lucky had gotten his name when Noverta joked, "That animal is lucky he strayed into the yard of the one man in Leeton with no dog-sense. That critter couldn't track a rabbit if you tied it to his leash. Nobody but you would keep the mutt."

Noverta called that one correctly. Lucky wouldn't track a squirrel or a quail. But let another dog within a square mile and his mutt would sniff him out.

He coaxed the dog into his automobile and when they reached the Randolph driveway, Cal let him loose. Lucky ran excitedly around the house and then found a patch of clover. The dog settled down and closed his eyes.

*So much for my dumb idea.*

"C'mere, Lucky." Cal whistled, low and soft.

Lucky's eyes opened wide and he came loping back, tail wagging. Cal pushed the animal's hindquarters toward the front seat, but the dog's ears flared back. Lucky pointed his nose down the road, in the opposite direction of Ida Simmons' house.

Without warning, Lucky broke out of Cal's hold and shot off. Cal thought he'd seen a hare in the distance.

*Now he decides to chase rabbits?*

Cal jumped into his automobile and took off after his dog. If he remembered correctly, the old road ended in less than a half-mile. He'd have to search on foot and he didn't have time to play hide-and-seek with his mutt.

He didn't make it far. An old tree had fallen across the road.

Cal cursed as he got out, grabbing the shotgun in case of snakes. Might be November, but he'd take no chances. He *hated* snakes. He walked a couple hundred yards, seeing nothing, hearing nothing. Then he heard a bark. Lucky's bark.

Cal rounded the road, now little more than a path, only to discover what appeared to be an old smokehouse. He thought there might have been a house with the structure when he was a kid, but now, only the shed remained. The building was large for a smokehouse, and must have held many a ham in its day.

He looked around, suddenly wishing he wasn't so exposed. No need to blow his wig though. Nobody would be interested in an old smokehouse.

Lucky dug furiously at the door, whimpering with every scratch. As Cal got closer, he saw a chain secured the door—a shiny chain with a brand new lock. Maybe somebody did care about the old building.

Cal walked to the window and looked inside. He rubbed his eyes and looked again, not convinced he'd seen what he thought he'd seen.

*Tanner?*

He shielded his eyes for a better view through the narrow glass panels. Poor dog had a mussel on his snout. Cal experienced simultaneously outrage and confusion. Who would do that to the dog? And why?

He tried to see more, but dirt coated the yellowish glass, inside and out. Only thing Cal could make out was a bowl on the floor, make that two. Dog food and water?

Had someone simply stolen the valuable dog? Or was there another reason Tanner remained captive in the middle of nowhere? The smokehouse window was too narrow to permit entry of his large frame, so Cal looked for something to break the chain on the door.

He changed his mind. If Tanner's capture was something more than dog nabbing, maybe he shouldn't reveal his hand.

Cal tried the second window in the back of the shed, thinking he might be able to get through the larger frame. The fit would be tight and he'd have to break the glass. If he did that, whoever took Tanner would know he'd found the place.

Couldn't be helped. He wouldn't leave Tanner.

Maybe one more look at the perimeter of the building—just to be sure there was no other way. He spotted loose boards, just below a small window. Cal gave a yank and heard splintering. Damn. Pulling the plank with his bare hands would break the wood.

Cal grabbed Lucky by the leash and half-dragged, half-followed the dog back to his car. As he moved, he studied the surrounding to ensure no one watched, not an easy thing with Lucky yanking on his leash.

When they reached the Packard, he put Lucky into the car and backed into a woody area, hoping his tire tracks weren't obvious. With any luck,

Lucky wouldn't pick today to have a barking spell. Maybe his stealth bordered on paranoia, but he'd take no chances.

Cal cracked the window so Lucky would have air and then grabbed the crowbar from his automobile. He returned to the smokehouse and removed a couple of loose boards, being careful to preserve the rusty nails. He squeezed through, barely.

"Tanner." He rubbed the dog behind the ears, looking for signs of abuse. Other than the muzzle, the dog seemed fine—a bit on edge perhaps. Cal wanted to remove the nasty muzzle, but he wasn't sure if he wanted his discovery known. Not just yet.

Tanner's abduction had to be related to Lily's murder. If he could set a trap—maybe wait for the abductor to return to the shed, he'd have a suspect.

His mind worked on a plan, one that would probably mean leaving the poor dog. In the same condition Cal had found him. Seemed cruel to remove the bit of leather from Tanner's mouth only to put it back.

Cal turned away, afraid he wouldn't be able to leave Tanner behind if the dog kept staring at him with those sad brown eyes. He had to leave the dog. If the plan had a chance in Hades, no one could know Cal discovered the shed.

He scanned the entire smokehouse, trying to determine if the building was just a hiding spot for Tanner, or if something else was going on. He

didn't see much. Some old canning jars, rusty lids
and a couple of old shaker chairs. Tanner was tied
to a bolt on the wall, obviously recently installed.
Peanut plants and shells covered the floor. Once-
upon-a-time, the smokehouse had been a drying
bed for peanuts, but not recently.

Cal could make no sense of the scene. Maybe he
should just take the dog and forget his damn plan.
He reached for the bolt to see if he could pry it
open with his crowbar, noticing some of the shells
looked out-of-place. As though they'd been moved.

He moved just enough debris to clear the floor.
And discovered a hinged trapdoor.

"I'll be damned."

Cal stared at the opening for several seconds.
He had a sick feeling about opening that door,
mainly because he had a loathing for cellars. Dark
holes were favorite spots for snakes.

He got up and checked both windows, stalling
as much as making sure no one watched. Tanner
gave up on being rescued and lay his head on the
floor, his big sad eyes condemning Cal. Maybe he
should at least remove the muzzle for a bit. The
dog could give warning if anyone came into the
shed.

No. No way could he put that thing back over
the dog's mouth.

He'd stalled long enough. After a ragged
breath, Cal dropped to his knees and lifted the
concealed door. Staring into the darkness, he saw

nothing. A musty smell emanated, causing a gagging sensation in his throat.

"A dark hole doesn't necessarily mean snakes." His motivational speech didn't stop his imagination from conjuring up a couple dozen slithering critters lying in wait.

*A dark hole and no lantern.* There was definitely no sane reason to crawl into the gorge. Maybe he'd just take a look. Cal lay flat on his stomach for a better look. The peanut shells and dust weren't exactly uniform-friendly but compared to a snake…

He couldn't see much. Why hadn't he brought his flashlight?

Dumb question. Who carries a flashlight at midday? He contemplated walking back to his car again—he kept a flashlight in his automobile.

"Ah, hell," he said aloud, causing the dog to lift his head. He didn't have time for another half-mile walk and a light would just let him see the snake. Or snakes.

He took a deep breath and crawled through the small opening.

# CHAPTER 23

Something hit Cal's forehead, too firm for a spider web. He yelped like a toddler and reached for the trapdoor opening.

The thing hit him again. Panic battled with common sense. Whatever had whacked him was too small to be a snake.

Just because the thing wasn't a snake, didn't mean there *weren't* snakes below. Cal remained still, willing his panic to subside.

Then he saw it. A cord hung in front of him, just beyond the hinged door. He waited, letting his pupils become accustomed to the darkness. The hanging string looked like a light cord. Not possible in an old shed, right?

Cal tugged on the string anyway. A dim light illuminated the hole. "Well, hell."

With the light shining, he saw the ladder. Had he walked into some type of trap? Once he climbed down, would someone shut the door, locking him inside. Possibly with snakes?

He huffed a breath, realizing his thoughts were ridiculous. "It's winter," he said aloud. Even so, he kept one arm outside the door as he climbed down a couple rungs. The hole didn't lead to a big room, but he saw rows and rows of shelves. All containing liquor bottles. Not old bottles, new ones full of liquid.

*Son of a bitch*. He had stumbled onto a bootlegger's warehouse.

He climbed back into the smokehouse and pulled the cord, darkening the hole again. Rushing, he closed the trapdoor and tried to push the peanut shells back as they were.

He sat down by Tanner, stroking the dog's back as he tried to think. Assuming the bootlegger didn't know he'd opened the door, he might be able to catch him transporting the illegal hooch. Didn't make sense that bootleg liquor could be related to Lily's death, but Cal's gut said otherwise.

Not that it mattered. Illegal booze was a crime in his county. Damn, bad enough he'd agreed to be sheriff. Why in hell had he done so in a dry county?

If he hoped to find out who hoarded the booze, he needed a plan. First he had to get out of the smokehouse without being seen. If the owner learned Cal had discovered the hooch, the bootlegger might abandon the goods and disappear. If that happened and the hoard was somehow related to Lily's death, he'd lose his only real lead. His best option was to stakeout the place, see who showed up with a key.

Like he had time for that with Kenny missing and Lily's killer still free to walk the roads. No, he needed a better plan.

He squeezed through the boards he'd pried open. Tanner's big eyes haunted him as he pressed the nails to secure the lumber. He'd made a mistake when he let Kenny leave without telling him who killed Noverta. Was it another mistake to leave the dog?

He *had* to leave the dog. "I'm sorry, boy. I'll get you out soon."

The dog whimpered. Couldn't be helped.

Cal rushed to his car and started the engine. When he reached the gravel road, he relaxed enough to analyze what he'd found. A bootlegger stash would explain all the cars Ida had heard, but people wouldn't walk half-a-mile off the main road to get a bottle of gin. Maybe Lily had sold the booze from the house? Cal hadn't seen any evidence of that, no bottles in the house, no pile of cash. Still, Lily could easily walk to the smokehouse and take out the number of bottles she needed for one evening. The next morning, there'd be no alcohol.

Or Maybe Lily had stumbled upon the hoard. A beautiful restless woman would naturally be curious about any car driving by her house, especially since the road went nowhere. Had she discovered the smokehouse and been killed because of her knowledge?

That didn't make sense either. The bootlegger had to have a way to sell his wares—unless he just used the smokehouse for a centralized storage.

Cal reached across and scratched his little beagle behind his ear. "Good, job, Lucky."

He needed to catch the bootlegger, but Lily's death was still top priority. If only he knew for sure the booze was related, then he'd stake out the smokehouse and find out who came for the alcohol.

Hell, it might be weeks before anyone came to the shed and Cal couldn't watch the place round the clock. Nor could he involve his deputies. Herb couldn't be trusted to keep quiet. Rodney was completely reliable, but if the seasoned deputy and Cal were never in the office at the same time, Herb would ask questions. No. The fewer people who knew, the better.

A plan started to take shape. His idea didn't preclude a stakeout, but would prove, once and for all, whether Lily's murderer and the bootlegger were one and the same.

\* \* \* \*

Cal wished he'd stayed in the smokehouse. At least he could think there. Since he'd come back to his office, he hadn't had a minute to himself.

"Burton stopped by," Rodney said, his face grim. "He's not doing so well. His wheezing got worse, so I took him to county hospital. They're keeping him overnight for observation. I promised I'd let him know as soon as…" The deputy paused, twisting his mouth in an awkward expression.

"Damn." Cal sucked in a breath. "Did you find Grace?"

The deputy shook his head. "Nah, dropped by the school after I left Burt at the hospital. Sweeney said she was out, so I drove by her place. She wasn't there either. You don't think…"

"That Kenny is with her?" Cal shrugged. "Can't believe she'd leave a broken window. Any idea where she might be?"

"Did you check her dad's house?"

Cal frowned. "The senator. I thought…" Maybe what he thought was wrong. He hadn't *really* talked to Grace in ten years. Still, she said she didn't talk to the Senator.

"You thought her old man's house would be the last place she'd go?" Rodney asked.

Cal nodded.

"Normally, you'd be correct," Rodney stated, "but the old man is in Washington."

"So?"

"So Marie is the one person Grace would go to if she needed a shoulder. You know Marie went to work for Randolph after Grace…eh, married."

Cal frowned. "Why would Grace need a shoulder?" Did Rodney think Grace had something to do with Lily's murder, too? And why the hell had he thought, "too?" He did not believe—would not believe—Grace was involved, but he did fear she wasn't telling him everything.

"You're kidding, right?" From Rodney's expression, Cal wondered if he'd stepped in some bad turnips. "Who wouldn't need a shoulder in Grace's situation. Her brother has been convicted, gone to prison and escaped. Grace may act like she's strong as an Angus bull, but Vertie's all she's got."

He wanted to ask, *what about Ernest*? Only he didn't dare.

No, he wouldn't ask about Ernest. "Isn't Marie the housekeeper who stayed with Grace while she finished high school?"

Rodney nodded. "The very one. I'm not sure how much housework she does these days. Woman's pretty old but the senator doesn't use his house here in Leeton all that much, so maybe there's not much cleaning to do."

"Thanks." Cal's head spun. Could Grace actually be at her father's house? Why wouldn't Marie go to Grace's house?

He picked up the phone, clicking twice for the operator. "John Randolph's residence, please. The one in Leeton."

After the operator connected him, a woman answered, "Randolph residence."

"I'm looking for Marie Cox," Cal replied.

"Speaking," the woman replied.

Cal didn't recognize the woman's voice, but he hadn't spoken to her in over a decade. "Hello, Marie. This is Sheriff Henderson. I'm actually looking for Ernest or Grace Rand…Gardner."

"Of course, sir. Miss Grace is here," Marie replied. "Poor thing is so sick."

*Grace, a poor thing?* And sick? Maybe Marie was confused and Grace wasn't there after all.

"Mr. Ernest left town though," the housekeeper continued. "Nowhere to be found. Now if you ask me, and nobody does, mind you, that's what's wrong with Miss Grace. She's sick with embarrassment. She doesn't want anyone to know, so pretend I didn't tell you."

Cal opened and closed his mouth, waiting for the swell of relief to pass. But what did she mean, "sick with embarrassment?" Was Rodney correct? Did Ernest have an affair with Lily? Did Grace know?

Could Grace have killed Lily?

No. He would *not* think that.

"Did you want me to see if Miss Grace is able to come to the phone, Sheriff?"

Cal started to say "yes," but changed his mind. Maybe he should *see* for himself. He glanced at his father's pocket watch. In half an hour, he was scheduled to meet with Noverta's lawyer. "Thank you, but no. Just tell her I called."

Time to pay Grace another visit. Only it would have to wait until tomorrow.

# CHAPTER 24

*Thursday, December 1*

"Grace?"

The unexpected voice startled her. "Cal?" Oh, God, no. What was he doing at her father's house? Especially in the backyard.

She stood. Too fast, making the rocking chair bang against the back wall of the screened porch—twice. The rocker slowed to a peaceful sway on the gray painted floor but Grace's heart kept thumping. Marie should have warned her.

Dumb thought. Marie didn't know she'd need warning. Grace swallowed hard, placing her shaking hands under her armpits.

"Quite the surprise finding you here," Cal said, no trace of emotion in his voice.

She pulled her coat collar around her face. "I know. It's chilly, but this view of the fields is one of the few things I like about this place."

"I didn't mean outside, Grace. I meant here at your father's house."

"Oh." Criminy. She'd told him she didn't talk to her father, and until Lily's death, that had been true. He'd think she lied. Heck, she *had* been dishonest about too many things.

She swallowed again, praying her voice wouldn't crack. "Are you here to see my father?"

He shook his head. "No. Here to see you."

"Me?" The porch floor seemed downright squishy.

He smiled, but his eyes flashed with anger. "Yes, you."

How did he find her? How much did he know?

Grace flashed her own smile, hoping her mouth didn't look as brittle as it felt. "Well, here I am."

"I've been looking for you all week."

*A week*? "I... Eh..." Probably best to remain silent, plead the fifth if necessary. Cal would never understand. Hell, she didn't understand herself.

He circled around to look at her from the side. She froze in place.

"At first, *Gracie*, I thought you were avoiding me."

He'd only called her Gracie once before. Then, he'd complained that she spent all her time on the farm, complained that she cared more about dirt than him. He didn't understand—his childhood had been normal. He couldn't know that sometimes just watching clover grow kept a person sane. He certainly wouldn't understand how much love scared a person who'd never been the recipient of it.

He pierced her with his intense bluish-gray gaze. She desperately wanted to look away, afraid he could see through her, clear to her deceptive soul. Only she wouldn't. After dealing with her father, she could face Cal.

Cal still loved her, she could tell—he tried to mask his feelings, tried to act all tough and aloof, but the intensity still burned. She knew, because she burned too. They'd probably always have that love. No matter how much pain it caused, no matter how much each of them tried to kill it.

"After I located you, I didn't call, *Grace*. You know why?"

She had a pretty good idea, but shook her head anyway.

"Because I *know* you're avoiding me. Figured you'd try to avoid me again. Question is, why?"

Hell, she wouldn't lie when she didn't have to, though she wasn't avoiding Cal in particular. She was avoiding everyone. "I'm not…"

"Not what?"

"Myself."

Cal blinked. She'd thrown off his interrogation technique. He'd resume though. Man was the sheriff through and through. Their conversation was not to be a cordial chat between former lovers.

"You know what I did yesterday, Grace?"

She did. She'd heard Mr. Hess's story. Not from the man himself, but her father heard it from someone who'd heard it at the diner. "What?"

"I got up at four a.m.. To catch you in the barn."

Grace laughed. She couldn't help it. The idea of Cal going to bed at four wouldn't surprise her, but the idea of him getting up with the cows somehow lightened her mood.

"You think that's funny?" Cal asked, but the tension had gone from his voice.

"A little." She stopped laughing and wrapped her coat tighter around her body, suddenly very cold. All the way to her toes. Looking at his face, thinking of everything lost, she wanted to cry. "Why are you here, Cal?"

He shrugged. The slight grin that never failed to fascinate Grace faded from his expression.

A choked sound escaped Grace's mouth. She covered her lips with her hand.

"Ah, hell," Cal said, walking toward her. He pulled her gently into his arms, his hands shaking a little. "Are you all right?"

She nodded into his chest. In his embrace, everything *was* all right. Being in Cal's arms made her feel like Wallis Warfield Simpson must have felt when Edward VIII abdicated his throne for her. How could something so firm and steely feel so good?

When they were together after the trial, the intimacy had been about sex—well, maybe not *just* about sex, but she'd only focused on that part of the experience. If she compartmentalized, it wouldn't hurt so much later. Today, they were connected. That connection would shatter, but today she would relish him. She'd missed Cal. Too much.

"Shh." His breath tickled her ear. "It's okay."

For the moment, maybe. But she'd take that moment. Might be the last good one she had for a while. Concentrating on his warmth and the strength beneath the muscled arms holding her with such tenderness, she willed her unshed tears away. Clinging to him, loving the feel of his body, she stopped thinking. For a moment.

The moment ended. She moved out of Cal's embrace.

"Are you really okay?" he asked.

"No." She stepped back. She had more to tell him. Only he didn't know that and he clearly hadn't driven to her father's place to comfort her.

"Grace..." he hesitated, his expression hard, but somehow still sympathetic. "What are you hiding? I can't help you if you don't talk to me."

She swallowed hard, determined she wouldn't cry again. She wanted to tell him everything. Only she couldn't. "Why did you need to find me?"

He shook his head, flashing a sad little smile, as if he somehow knew the moment had passed. Even that sad, half-hearted grin did strange things to her insides.

"First," he said, "tell me what you're doing in your father's house. I thought you two weren't speaking? Was that a lie?"

She took a deep breath. "No. It's—"

Cal held up one hand. "Sorry, that can wait. There's more urgent news. Have you talked to Burton?"

"Burton?" She'd prepared her little speech about being at her father's place, planning to tell him the whole story. The whole story about Ernest anyway. She didn't know why he'd mention her uncle. Unless… "Is Burt all right? What about Kenny?"

Cal's Adam's apple did that dancing thing. Not a good sign. "Maybe you'd better sit down."

She shook her head, then shook it again. "No. Just tell me."

"Kenny's missing."

Grace sat down, grateful she hadn't moved far from the rocker. She covered her mouth but the moan echoed anyway. Dear God, what had she done? Kenny had to be okay. If anything happened to him… She was never going to forgive herself anyway. "When?" Maybe he'd just wandered off. He did that all the time.

"Almost a week ago."

"Dear Lord." Grace propped an elbow on her thigh and gulped all the air she could inhale. The only thing she heard was her pulse in her ears. "Do you… Do you have any leads?"

Cal didn't respond. She looked at his face, blinked and took another breath. He still wouldn't come into focus. She knew he studied her. Did he think she had something to do with Kenny's disappearance?

"This can't be happening," she whispered, knowing her words were in vain.

"It happened, Grace." Cal's words sounded harsh as he kneeled down to be at eye level with her.

She couldn't look at him. White dots still marred her vision, but she wouldn't be able to face her former lover anyway. Kenny's disappearance might be her fault. "What happened, Cal?"

She strained to understand as he explained. Not easy with the hammering in her head.

"Burton woke up and the boy was gone. Someone broke his window."

Not good. "Did they ask for ransom?" She lifted her head to look at him, finally able to see his steely gaze without feeling woozy.

Cal didn't say anything.

"Cal..."

He shook his head. "No. What are you hiding, Grace?"

Dear God. She should just tell him. She would. Taking in a deep breath, Grace tried to find the appropriate words. She formed the sentence in her head, but rejected the phrasing and tried again.

"Grace?"

She bit at her lip. Cal had a new energy, she sensed it, so strong she could almost feel his anticipation. Only there was a wariness about him, almost as if he expected any good news to turn sour.

She worked hard to control her voice. "I…" Her entire body begin to shake.

"Ah, hell, Grace. I—"

He reached for her again, but she backed away. If she didn't tell him now, she might never tell him. "I have something to tell you."

"Grace. No." He looked as if he'd been hit with a shovel.

"Kenny might have run away because he thought I shot Lily."

"What?" Cal looked as if he'd been hit with a shovel *and* a pickaxe.

She hurried her words. "The boy saw me with my rifle. That night."

Cal took a step backward, his Adam's apple bobbing. "That night? The night Lily died?"

She nodded.

"Hell." He looked away. Then looked back. "Did you shoot her, Grace? Did you shoot Lily?"

She glared at Cal. "No, of course not. I shot Ernest."

"Ernest?" Cal's voice had risen several octaves. He took a step back and held onto a porch column. "You did what? Why? Is he… Damn, Grace."

She shook her head, not knowing where to start. "Ernest isn't hurt. Nothing a little Epsom salt won't fix."

Cal shook his head—she'd probably do the same thing in his place. "Why on earth would you do a damn fool thing like... Holy hell. You knew about Ernest and Lily?" Cal's voice had softened.

Grace didn't want Cal's sympathy. Not because of her cheating husband, anyway. "Yes, I knew. There have been others. For a long time now. At first, I didn't mind. After all, I practically tricked poor Ernest into marrying me. His cheating was probably my fault.." Even so, she did mind.

Cal squinted. "So Ernest and Lily *were* having an affair? And you knew?"

"Of course I knew, Cal." She took a deep breath. Admitting that to him was more painful than knowing about the cheating.

"How long have you known about the two of them?" he asked.

She shrugged. "I don't know. A while. I looked the other way, thinking it wouldn't last. Lily had other lovers. She never stayed with anyone very long."

"And you did nothing?" Cal leaned forward slightly. "Hell, Grace. What's wrong with you?"

She stiffened her back. "For heaven's sakes, what was I supposed to do? I thought it would blow over. Noverta knew Lily was...unfaithful. He planned on leaving her anyway, so I didn't see any reason to add to my brother's misery. Vertie thought Ernest was his friend. I thought Ernest was his friend. I deserved what I got, but Vertie didn't."

"So you shot Ernest?" Cal looked as if he'd been hit by a line drive.

"It wasn't exactly planned." She hurried her words again, desperate to get the story told. Let Cal judge her and be done with it. "Vertie called me from Memphis and said he was coming home early. He wanted to catch Lily with one of her men so he'd have grounds for a divorce. Only I couldn't exactly let him catch his wife with Ernest, could I? Vertie would hate me for not telling him. Bad enough his wife had betrayed him. I couldn't let him think his twin sister had done the same."

"Ernest rutting around like a pig in heat didn't bother you, but Noverta..." Cal shook his head again. "Did you shoot Lily, too?"

"God, no! I only shot Ernest, Cal. And I barely grazed him."

"Grazed him? That explains the second blood smear."

"What smear?" she asked.

"Never mind that. I don't see why you had to shoot Ernest. Why not just tell him Vertie was on the way home."

She took a deep breath, striving for patience. "You think I didn't do that? I told him. Ernest and Lily were doped up on some kind of opium or something. When I told him he had to get out of there, Ernest just laughed at me. Told me he loved

Lily and he didn't care who knew. Even me. Maybe especially me."

"So you shot him in a jealous rage."

"No! I shot him, but not because I was jealous. When he wouldn't get out of that bed—Noverta's bed—I *threatened* to shoot him. He still wouldn't move, so I had to do something."

"So you *shot* him?" He couldn't have looked more stunned if she'd told him she kidnapped Lindbergh's baby. "Damn Grace."

"I told you I only grazed him. Just as I meant to do—you know my bullets go where I aim. I needed him to get a move on. That's not the same thing as assaulting him. And please lower your voice. I don't want Marie to hear."

"You just tell me you shot someone, and I'm supposed to lower my voice? Dear God in heaven! What I'm supposed to do is arrest you. I *am* the sheriff, you've broken the law."

"Don't be silly. The skin on Ernest's arm was barely scratched. He won't press charges. I gave him the money he wanted—rather my father paid him off—and now he's gone. If I'd given him cash sooner, maybe Noverta wouldn't be in jail."

Cal rubbed both hands over his head. "That's why you're here? In this house? To get the senator to pay off Ernest?"

Grace could feel the anger radiating from him. "Not exactly."

He opened his mouth, closed it, then opened it again. "You better explain."

She nodded, surprised he hadn't already arrested her. Not that the charge would stick.

"After I fired at him that night, Ernest decided I was serious. He came back to the house with me, coddling his silly little flesh wound like his arm was going to fall off. And of course, Granny pampered him as if he were three instead of thirty-five-years-old. All the while they treated me like I was Lizzy Borden. Ernest said he was afraid to be near me. Granny thought she owned me, demanded I give her money or she'd talk. I'd had enough and decided to spend the night at Vertie's. I left. And ran into you. You know what happened after that."

"You left Lily alone? Alive?"

Grace nodded. "She was laughing when we left. Making fun of Ernest for howling like a skunk-sprayed dog."

Cal took off his hat and rubbed a hand over his hair. "So why didn't Granny talk?"

That's what he wanted to know? She might never understand men. "Granny couldn't blackmail me about a secret if everyone knew. I knew she wouldn't say anything."

Cal's face still sported that *swallowed-a-rotten-egg* expression. "Where is Ernest now?"

She shook her head. "I really don't know. When he heard about Lily the next day, Ernest went a little loco. I think he believed he'd be blamed. Ernest packed a bag and walked out the door. Didn't say a word."

Cal grimaced. "So Ernest left. Then why hide out at your father's house?"

Grace huffed out a breath. Cal wouldn't understand—a person needed to live in the same house with Granny Gardner to truly understand. "I couldn't stay in the house with Granny there. She constantly demanded money so she could follow Ernest. I gave her what I had in the house, but that wasn't enough."

"Let me guess," Cal said. "You went to your father and asked for more money."

Her cheeks felt hot, as if she'd been slapped. "I did *not*. Granny went directly to him. I don't know if he paid her off or not. When he found out what happened, Father demanded I divorce Ernest. Even started the proceedings. Didn't ask me if that's what I wanted, but when has he ever?"

"Is it?" Cal asked. "What you wanted?"

Again, not the question she expected. "You mean the divorce?"

He nodded.

"Yes. Just didn't want my father to…" She tried to smile but her teeth seemed glued to her lips. "You know how I am. Wanted it to be *my* idea."

Cal pursed his lips, blowing out enough air to lift the hair off his forehead. He turned away, but spun around quickly. "Grace, no one's seen Granny. Or Ernest? You sure you don't have anything you want to tell me?"

Dear Lord, did he think she'd killed them or something? "I don't know, Cal. I truly don't."

He nodded, but clearly didn't believe her. "And your automobile. Where is it?"

Her car? She'd just told him she was divorcing the husband she'd shot and he wanted to know about her Ford? "Parked at home. My father's driver picked me up. Probably so he could hold me hostage here."

Cal shook his head. "Your car isn't at your house now."

Seriously? Ernest had come back for her car? How could he do that? Sure, she'd practically forced the man to marry her, but she'd paid enough.

The door squeaked and almost banged into her head.

"Excuse me, Miss Grace."

Grace jolted at the sound of Marie's voice. Cal looked none-too-happy about the interruption, and that might be a gross understatement.

"Uh, eh..." Great. Now she sounded illiterate. "Did you need something, Marie?"

"There's a call for Sheriff Henderson," Marie said, a big smile on her face. "Y'all should get inside. It's colder than a well-digger's hinny out here."

Grace glanced at Cal. She didn't hear what he said to Marie.

Cal headed through the back door. What the hell was she supposed to do now? Another chill spread over her, but going inside would make it seem like she wanted to overhear Cal's phone call.

She didn't—too much on her mind. Where was
Kenny? The boy should not be part of the equation.
Was it possible his disappearance was a
coincidence?

She took a deep breath. And another.

When Cal came back, she'd tell him everything
she knew. He'd hate her, but they had to find
Kenny.

Robin Weaver

# CHAPTER 25

Cal hung up the phone, blinking to make the white spots disappear. Hell, he would never again believe things couldn't get worse. He needed to deal with Grace's *situation*, make sure Ernest and Granny were still breathing. Instead, he had more urgent matters.

He hurried out the back. Grace jumped up when he opened the door. He really didn't want to talk to her.

"I have to go, Grace. Make sure you're here when I return."

She nodded, just once.

He hesitated. "You need to find out where Ernest is. I have to talk to him."

Grace bit at her lip. "I'll ask my father. That's all I can do."

He needed to hurry, but for some reason he couldn't move. The thoughts in his head weren't things he wanted to think about. "Swear to me Ernest is still alive."

Grace snorted. "He was alive last time I saw him. That's all I can tell you."

"But Lily is dead." Cal didn't know why he repeated the obvious. Maybe to see Grace's reaction.

"She was very much alive—and, as I said before, laughing—when Ernest and I left her. I haven't always told you everything, Cal, but I've never lied about that night."

He relaxed his arms and dropped them to his side. "You told me Ernest had pneumonia. That was a lie."

She shook her head. "No. I told you he wasn't home. Granny told you he had pneumonia."

"Great, now you've got old ladies lying for you?" Cal didn't like his tone, but he was close to being furious.

"She wasn't lying for me, Cal."

He nodded, grudgingly. "No. She wouldn't do anything for anyone but herself. Or Ernest."

That much was true. "Grace, you sure Ernest didn't shoot Lily? You said he was dopey."

"Ernest went back to the house with me. Lily was alive when we left."

"Yet you returned to Noverta's house?" His tone radiated with accusation, but he didn't care.

"I told you why I went back."

"I heard what you said. I also know you didn't like Lily," he challenged.

She shook her head. "She wasn't my favorite person, but I didn't want anything bad to happen to her. I knew Vertie was on his way home and he was mad."

"Did you bury Ernest's body?" Cal narrowed his eyes.

"Cal. I barely grazed him. Ernest is not dead." Grace seemed more resigned than angry. If someone accused him of burying a body, he'd rip out a jugular.

He really wanted to ask about her divorce. Sick when he should be concentrating on the murder. And Noverta.

*Damn.* He had no time for bumping gums. "I have to go. Do not leave the county and, if you leave this house, let my office know where you can be reached."

He hurried across the lawn.

"Cal," she called.

He stopped, turning his head to look at her. "Yes?"

"Be careful. I couldn't bear it if…" She let the sentence hang.

*Now she decides to act like she cares*? A little late.

He put his hat back on, determined to walk away. Only decency dictated he tell her about the phone call. She had a right to know.

"Grace… That was Herb on the horn. They've spotted Vertie."

"Where?" She held up a hand. "Doesn't matter. Just don't let *them* shoot him, Cal. And don't you get yourself shot either."

He nodded, turning away because he couldn't deal with her concern. Not now, not after he'd basically accused her of murder.

Worse, they really would shoot Noverta unless he did something. He got in his car but couldn't start the engine. Who'd sucked up all the air anyway? He had to get it together, get back to his office and do it fast. He rolled the window down, not caring about the icy blast.

He stared at the senator's house, trying to make sense of anything. Grace had been perfect, or so he'd thought. He'd been wrong, but that didn't change how he felt.

Cal rubbed his hand over his head. Maybe he'd move back to his grandfather's house in Boston. The cold didn't seem so bad now. Hell, up there he'd be the dumb hillbilly. Here he was the damn Yankee. Would he ever fit in?

Didn't seem to matter anymore. He'd find out who killed Lily, he owed Noverta that much. Then he'd resign as sheriff. There was nothing for him in Leeton.

After another exaggerated breath, he found the willpower to start his engine. He pulled onto the road, vowing to forego the self-pity. Noverta was about to get his backside shot.

He didn't remember the drive to his office. His car scarcely came to a halt when Herb climbed into the passenger seat. "Let's go. I've locked up."

"Where's Rodney?" Cal asked, not keen on having a wig-blower like Herb as his only backup.

"I don't know." No surprise there.

When Cal first took Herb's call at the senator's old homestead, he experienced relief—Noverta was alive. That reaction had waned on the way to the office. Now he dreaded the trip. Things weren't likely to work out in Noverta's favor.

"Which way do we go?" he asked Herb.

"South on the main highway. They have him holed up in some shack just outside of Olive Branch."

"In Mississippi?" Damn. Driving to the state line meant a half-hour to imagine all sorts of worst-case scenarios. "Who spotted him?"

"Not sure. Somebody called the Mississippi State Police."

"Damn."

"With that reward…" Herb made a *mm, mm, mmm* sound. "Folks will shoot first and ask questions later. Hate to see ol' Vertie get filled with daylight."

"The reward John Randolph is offering clearly states *alive*," Cal replied. Despite his logic, he didn't feel reassured, not even a little bit. The situation meant adrenaline would be flowing and excited folks tended to react without thinking.

"Doesn't make sense Vertie would be in Mississippi," Cal said, more thinking aloud than talking to his deputy. Anybody with a working brain would know political clout was behind Noverta's prison break. Which pointed straight at John Randolph. Only if the senator was involved in the escape, shouldn't Noverta be long gone?

"Assuming it actually was Noverta," Herb replied.

The deputy had a point. Even so, if Noverta had actually been spotted, they could use some help. "We need somebody who can control the situation, make sure Noverta isn't used as target practice."

"We should'a called the senator before we left, Cal. He could'a called the governor and our governor could'a called the Mississippi one."

"Doubt that would help. The senator isn't on the best terms with Governor Browning. Rumor has it Browning thinks John had something to do with him losing his bid for reelection this year."

"What do you mean?" Herb asked, sounding interested.

"The governor thinks voter fraud was involved."

"Fraud?"

Cal nodded. Clearly Herb didn't follow statewide politics. "Boss Crump, a good friend of

John Randolph, supported Browning's opponent. Rumor has it the mob boss registered over 100,000 voters in our county and in Shelby. The governor thinks he lost because of those votes. Browning also thinks our good senator had a hand registering those voters."

"You saying the thing was rigged?" Herb asked, his voice a little louder.

"I'm not saying anything." One couldn't be too careful around the deputy. Herb had a way of spinning the truth into unrecognizable slander. "Besides, what I say doesn't matter. Just be certain Gordon Weaver Browning will *not* aid our cause."

"Well, shit." Herb made another *mm, mm* sound. "Mind if I take a little nap?"

"No." A non-talking Herb would make Cal's drive infinitely better.

If only Rodney was in the car instead, Cal could use the time to brief his senior deputy. There simply had been no opportunity to chat without Herb hovering. If the bumbling deputy learned of the hoard Cal found in the woods, everyone in the county would know. In that instance, Cal's plan to catch a bootlegging killer would go to hell in a whiskey bottle. Noverta really needed to stay alive long enough for him to put his scheme into play.

Cal opened his mouth, intent on reminding Herb not to fire his weapon unless absolutely necessary, but he hit a rut. People might make fun of Leeton's country roads, but gravel could be fixed a lot quicker than tar. Cal swerved to save his axle, but the pavement didn't improve. The road took all his concentration.

After two or three miles, the surface became smooth again. At last he could talk without having to worry about rolling his automobile. "Herb…"

He glanced at the deputy. Not only was Herb sleeping, a bit of drool had formed at the corner of his mouth. The warning would have to wait.

Then, the deputy started to snore. Damn but the man could snore.

# CHAPTER 26

"Herb, wake up." Cal reached over to tap his deputy's arm, but re-gripped the wheel when he spotted a slew of cars ahead. At least twenty.

Herb slumped forward, bumping his head on the windshield. "What...? Shit, we're here already?"

Cal got out of the car. Herb followed him to the front of the vehicle. Then, Cal spotted a welcome sight—Rodney.

The deputy waved, shook hands with the uniformed Mississippi officer, and then meandered toward Cal and Herb. "About time you fellows got here. I drove up as soon as I got the news."

"What's going on?" Cal asked, not interested in chit-chat.

Rodney pulled out his can of tobacco and started rolling a cigarette. "The DeSoto sheriff says some farmer saw Vertie on the road. The man called the Mississippi State Police."

For the most part, Cal already knew that. "Why is everyone just standing around?"

Six Mississippi State Police cars, numerous civilian vehicles, and a DeSoto County Sheriff's department vehicle surrounded the perimeter of the small farmhouse perched on a giant hill. Judging by the rusted roof and peeling paint, the structure hadn't been inhabited since the stock market crash.

Rodney's expression was part grin, part grimace. "Because the farmer, which no one can find, said Noverta had a gun. Nobody's keen on storming the house, given its location. Local boys are waiting on orders."

Cal glanced at the deputy. Then at the house again.

His lungs stopped working. A car was parked next to the house.

Grace's car.

*Hell's bells.* How had her Ford ended up here?

He stared at Rodney. His senior deputy motioned toward Herb and gave his head a little shake.

"Do me a favor, Herb," Cal drawled. "Go find out who's in charge. Tell him the governor has ordered that Noverta is not to be harmed."

"Me? Say the governor did what? Damnation, Cal, did the governor order that?"

Cal shrugged. Had Herb listened to him in the car?

"You want me to lie to all these cops?" Herb asked.

When did Herb grow a conscience? "No. Tell them Sheriff Cal Henderson asked you to deliver that message. You'll be telling the truth. I'm the one telling the lie." Not exactly honorable, but a necessity. On the odd chance Noverta was in the farmhouse, Cal wanted him to stay alive. "And just so we're clear, Herb, that *was* an order."

Herb didn't move. "You know I do as I'm told, boss, but why don't you do your own talking? Might be more convincing."

Cal twisted his mouth, making one cheek pop out. Couldn't afford to lose his temper. "Why are you still standing here yapping, Herb. I gave you an order."

Herb kicked at the dirt, but after a couple seconds, he looked directly at Cal. "Okay." The deputy headed toward the mob of officers.

Rodney shuffled from one foot to the other, clearly waiting for Herb to get beyond earshot. "You saw Grace's car?"

Cal nodded. Neither spoke for a couple seconds. The quietness loomed with eerie foreboding.

"What the hell we going to do, Cal?"

He'd been working on that. "I doubt it's Vertie in that farmhouse. He'd never use Grace's car for a getaway." Cal needed to find out who *had* taken the car.

The deputy shook his head. "I don't know. Men on the run do whacky things."

Not Noverta. "If it is Vertie, he won't have a gun. Let's offer to negotiate."

Rodney shook his head. "You think I didn't try that already. Guy in charge won't let anyone do anything until he gets direction from his higher-ups."

Cal made a quick decision. "Okay, then. Is that…?" He squinted for a better look. "Is someone in the car?" he asked.

"No one can tell for sure," Rodney replied.

"I'm going to find out. I need you to distract everyone."

"For God's sake, Cal. Why would you do a fool thing like that? Won't help Vertie if these Mississippi boys mow you down."

"Just run interference if they notice me."

Rodney huffed out a breath. "I'll do what I can, but don't take any fool chances. I've already lost one friend."

"Vertie isn't lost," Cal insisted.

Cal circled behind the Packard, stooping low. He needed a route that would get him close to the old house without exposing him. The arborvitaes surrounding the south side were overgrown. Crouching low, he half walked, half ran until he reached the evergreens. He paused, taking stock. If he could just make it up the hill without being spotted, maybe he could get inside the house.

But could he get up the hill? Most of the remaining trees had lost their leaves, leaving little cover.

*What was that?* He'd heard a ping of some kind, an odd sound.

Cal stared at the crowd of lawmen gathered at the bottom of the hill. No alarm had been raised.

The noise didn't matter. He had to get to the car. He recited a little prayer, doubting it would help.

Just then, he saw flames. Grace's car was on fire.

The hell with cover. Cal sprinted up the hill. He had to find out who was in the car. Noverta wouldn't be that stupid. Nope, Noverta was long gone. Which meant the person in the Ford was likely the same person who had killed Lily.

"Don't go near that car!" someone yelled.

Cal didn't recognize the yeller's voice. Not that he would have slowed if he had.

"It's going to blow up!" the same person warned.

The man was probably correct. Cal figured he might be running toward his death. He ran anyway. The flames blazed higher.

He heard footsteps behind him, but didn't look back. In case someone chased him, he ran faster, grateful for all those years he practiced on the track so he could steal second base or even third. Glad he'd broken a wrist all those years ago and not an ankle.

The footsteps behind him ceased. He was the only person stupid enough to get so close to a tin can filled with petroleum.

Shielding his face, he moved toward the car. Someone sat behind the wheel. Who?

Smoke billowed, blocking his view. Every instinct urged him to turn back. Only he couldn't. He had to know. Cal edged closer.

"No way." Covering his mouth with one hand and framing his brow with the other, he peered closer.

*Son of a bitch.*

He reversed direction. And sprinted.

A loud boom rang out. Everything went silent. Then black.

\* \* \* \*

"Cal?" Rodney sounded like an umpire, yelling "You're out."

"I guess I'm alive then," Cal replied, feeling anything but alive. "Surely your face wouldn't be the first one I'd see if this was the hereafter."

Rodney laughed. "Only because you're going to get your stupid ass killed first. Why does the Good Lord always spare you idiots? What in tarnation were you thinking, Cal? Running toward a burning car?"

"Had to see, Rodney. Had to know." A fit of coughing overtook him.

"Take it easy, Cal. Breathe." The deputy leaned closer, whispering, "Did you see who was in the car?"

Cal tried to nod, but someone must have filled his skull with bricks. "Wasn't Noverta. But if anyone asks, I didn't see."

Rodney nodded. No questions.

Good man.

Robin Weaver

# CHAPTER 27

*Friday, December 2*

After being prodded by the doctor and a bevy of nurses, Cal was further prodded by a state police detective. Hours ticked away before he got what he wanted most: a fresh shirt. Well, maybe the shirt was his second choice.

What he'd seen in the burning car had shaken him to the core. And he'd obstructed justice again. Only knowledge was power and keeping silent about what he'd seen might work in his favor.

Cal told the lead investigator a partial truth. "The car exploded before I could get a good look." Only he'd gotten a partial look—enough to see who was in the car. It wasn't Noverta. He thanked

Providence the detective hadn't asked any more questions.

He needed to talk to Rodney about what he'd seen. Only the deputy had to get back to the office and had gotten a ride.

Just as well. Cal had to set his trap for the bootlegger and he needed to do it alone. Getting some answers from Ernest Gardner still topped his list, and talking to Grace ranked as a close second, but those conversations would have to wait. If the identity of the burned corpse became known, all hell would break loose. The person who took Tanner might bolt.

He prayed Grace wasn't involved with the booze. He wasn't quite ready to take off his blinders and admit she might be in a heap of dung. His angel could be involved in a murder, or at the very least, in the cover-up. He needed proof though. His heart still held out hope there was an explanation.

Cal decided to stop by Grace's house before going to the smokehouse. He pulled his Packard into the driveway, on the odd chance Ernest had returned.

He thought he was prepared for anything. Grace standing on her porch shocked him.

Son of a… He forced his body out of the car and closed the door, never letting his gaze leave her face.

"You're here," she said, her smile looking a bit brittle, but beautiful nonetheless. "Are you all right?"

He nodded, but winced when his head hurt.

"No you're not," she said, all matter-of-fact. "Come on in, I'll make some tea." She wasn't making anything easy.

"This isn't a social call, Grace."

Her hand went to her throat. "Is Vertie…"

Cal stopped just short of moving his aching head again. He had to tell her. "Wasn't Vertie. I can't say how I know, but your brother wasn't there. For now, keep that information to yourself."

The tension visibly left her shoulders. Her half-smile faded into a little grimace as she pulled her bulky sweater tighter around her slender frame. She definitely wasn't making anything easy. "Unless you want me to come to the station, maybe we could go inside where it's warm?"

"Sure." He followed her into the house. "Grace, you know I don't like tea."

"Actually, the tea is for me. I have a pot of coffee ready for you."

That brought him up short. "You knew I was coming?"

She studied his face, her expression a mask of concentration. An image that brought back too many memories. "I called your office, Cal. Told Herb I needed to talk to you and wanted to meet you at my house. Isn't that why you're here?"

He shook his head. "I didn't know you called Grace. I'm here about your car."

She frowned slightly. "My car? You found it?"

He nodded, wishing he could just leave. Or better yet, have a repeat of the afternoon he'd shared with her after he'd testified at Noverta's trial. "Yes."

She nodded. "Good. Did Ernest call or just leave it somewhere?"

"Ernest? Ernest took your car?"

Grace looked puzzled. "Well I assumed... Who else would take it?"

"So you don't know for sure that Ernest took it?"

Grace looked more puzzled. "I didn't see him take it, if that's what you mean."

He took a breath. "Grace, your car ended up in Mississippi. Someone set it on fire."

She slumped down on the sofa. "On fire? Why?"

He nodded. "Did you let Vertie take your car?"

She lifted her head to glare at him. "How many times must I repeat myself. I haven't seen Vertie. If I had, I would have given him my car. Or anything else. Without blinking."

"I know. Do you know where he is, Grace?"

"No. Let me say it again, *no*."

"You'd tell me if you did?" He studied her face, needing to believe she'd be honest.

"Probably not. But I don't know where my brother is. I suspect my father may know, but he'll never talk." That was honest enough.

"I suspected the same," he replied. "I sent Herb to talk to him."

Grace choked. "You sent… Poor Herbie." She didn't say anything for several seconds, just stared. "That's not why you're here though, is it?" Grace asked.

He shook his head. "I'm here to find Ernest."

Grace's grimace turned into an all-out frown. "I asked my father, but he swears he doesn't know where Ernest went. The old man did admit he ordered him to stay away from Leeton."

"Any idea where Ernest might go?" Cal asked. "No."

He reached for her arm. "You lived with him for ten years. You don't have *any* idea?"

She shook her head, refusing to look at him. "None. We didn't exactly talk much about hopes and dreams."

Damn. He had to find the man. Should he take Grace to the station?

That wouldn't help. He believed she really didn't know. He scratched his forehead, trying to think.

"You said you called my office, Grace. Why did you want to talk to me?"

She bit at her lower lip. Hell, she was nervous. That couldn't be good.

"Come back to the kitchen. I have a feeling I'm going to need that tea."

*Hell.* Cal wanted to ask for something a lot stronger than coffee, but needed to keep his head clear.

He bumped into the couch as he followed her. What happened to her old sofa? Some boxy thing sat in its place—the color of the men's bathroom down at the filling station and ugly as original sin. What was Grace thinking? The pews at the First Baptist would be more comfortable than that itchy-looking couch.

Grace poured him a cup of coffee and handed it to him, sans cream. She turned her back to him and put the tea kettle on the burner.

Cal didn't know what to say. Maybe he should let her talk first.

She turned, wiping her hands on the apron covering her skirt. "Where do I begin?"

Oh, hell. She was going to confess—about what he wasn't sure, but he knew he wouldn't like the conversation. He wasn't ready, needed more time to prepare his brain, his heart. Just a little more time.

Above all else, he needed to understand what happened ten years ago. Needed a reason for the lost years and the lost life. He needed his answers before she permanently destroyed his memories of a once perfect love.

"Why did you marry Ernest?" he blurted out. "I thought you and I... What did I do?"

"You want to talk about that *now*?" Grace sounded incredulous.

Cal nodded. "I need to know. Did you ever love me?" He waited, never letting his gaze leave her face. Memorizing the way she looked at that moment seemed paramount. He wanted to remember her goodness, her beauty. No matter what she'd done, the goodness was still inside her.

She sat down, toying with the edge of her blouse. "Of course I loved you." She sounded annoyed, as if he had no right to ask that question. "But I needed a husband. And fast."

"Ernest got you pregnant?" Hell, things were even worse than he thought. He'd kill the son of a bitch. The coffee in his mouth tasted like kerosene.

"No, Cal. Ernest wasn't the father."

Realization dawned. He opened his mouth, but couldn't speak. Could he be any more of a lummox?

"Me?" he finally managed to ask. "I was the father? Why didn't you tell me?"

She looked at him, her expression mirroring the anguish he'd endured for the past ten years. "Because you wouldn't have gone to Houston."

"Of course not." He had been thrilled when the Buffaloes offered him a spot in their lineup. The team was the minor league affiliate for the St. Louis Cardinals, whereas the Memphis Chickasaws had no major league connection. Even so, he'd hesitated. Grace insisted the move was the best thing for his career, and had offered to wait. "But that was my decision. God, Grace, how could you not tell me?"

She sucked in her lower lip. Then, got up and tinkered with the teakettle.

"Grace, maybe that noble stuff works in books, but you should have told me. I thought you… Hell, it might have taken longer to get to the big leagues, but I could have played for the Chickasaws. Do you know how miserable I've been without you?"

"You?" Grace's voice rose. "Typical man. You, you, you. I've spent the last ten years with Ernest and Granny Gardner. I was seventeen and pregnant, Cal. What was I supposed to do?"

Cal's anger evaporated. "You were supposed to let me marry you."

"Easy for you to say. Maybe I should have told you. But what if you grew to resent me? Hindsight is so, so simple. It's easy to see *now* that I made the wrong decision *then*."

"Grace, sweetheart…," He probably shouldn't call her sweetheart, but he still thought of her that way. Maybe the endearment would soften what he needed to ask—had wanted to ask when she first mentioned her pregnancy. "What happened to the baby?"

"I lost it. Not long after you left for Houston, I had a miscarriage. I married that… I married Ernest for nothing."

"I'm so sorry." He stood and pulled her in his arms, holding her tight.

She pressed her face into his shoulder. He wasn't sure which one of them was shaking more. Didn't matter.

"Cal." Grace pulled away from his embrace and swiped at her eyes. "There's more."

"Okay." Only nothing was okay.

Could he not have even a single moment? He finally understood what happened ten years ago, but he had no time to mourn the misunderstanding, the lost time. Grace's confession would likely follow. In the recesses of his heart, he still hoped she had nothing to confess. After all, Grace couldn't have driven her car to Olive Branch and set it on fire. Nor could he believe someone else had taken the car with her knowledge. The scene reeked of a setup and it didn't make sense that Grace would point the finger at herself.

"It's about Kenny."

"Kenny?" He wanted to shout for joy. Grace wouldn't hurt Kenny. If she wanted to talk about the boy, maybe she didn't have anything to confess.

She nodded.

He put his hands on her upper arms. "Grace, I'll find him, I promise I will, but right now, I need to find Ernest. Where is he?"

She stared up at him, blinking, her confusion evident. "I told you, I don't know."

"And Granny. Where is Granny?"

Grace blinked again. "I don't know. She doesn't live here anymore."

Damn. All his alarm bells should be going off, only they weren't. "Where *does* she live?"

"I don't know. My father took care of it. If he knows where she and Ernest went, he's saying he doesn't."

John Randolph. The man could arrange anything.

"When you say your father 'took care of it,' Grace, what exactly do you mean?"

She shrugged. "Threatened legal action. Or maybe he just paid them to leave. You know how Granny hoarded money."

That made sense. And he'd gotten his answer—Grace clearly had no clue Granny was dead. Cal suspected the senator didn't know either. While he wouldn't put it past John Randolph to kill the old biddy, the senator would take the most expeditious path—a payoff. The senator certainly wouldn't stuff her body in Grace's car.

So he was at another dead-end. Cornering the bootlegger was now even more crucial. Somehow, the hoard in the smokehouse was related to Lily's death. Cal knew it with a certainty he couldn't explain.

"I've got to go, Grace."

"But I still need to talk to you about Kenny."

He held her shoulders gently. "Grace, do you know where the boy is?"

She shook her head.

"Can the conversation wait then?" he asked. "I need to do something and I'm running out of time. I'll stop by tomorrow, okay?"

She hesitated. "Well, okay."

"One more thing?"

She looked up at him, wearing an expression he'd never seen on her face. She looked…lost. "What?"

"I need to get inside Vertie's shed, Grace. Any chance you have a key?"

She nodded. "I'll get it." She got up and took a ring of keys from inside her cupboard. "These are Vertie's. Not sure which one opens the shed. What are you going to do?"

"Investigate."

"But…"

Maybe he was a fool to abandon even a little of his mistrust. After all, Kenny was still missing and he'd left Tanner in that hole. Only he still loved Grace. Hell, he might as well admit it, if only to himself. Despite his feelings, Cal couldn't imagine her being involved with illegal alcohol. And he needed to know what she or Noverta knew about the hoard near Noverta's house.

"I'm setting a trap for a bootlegger."

"Bootlegger?"

He nodded. "You can't repeat what I'm about to tell you. Not to anyone."

She flashed a sad little smile. "Cross my heart and all that stuff."

He'd forgotten her smart mouth and smiled, in spite of everything. "Did Noverta mention anything about bootleggers to you?"

She shook her head. "Never. What bootleggers?"

He had her full attention. "Ida had said a lot of cars drove to Vertie's house. We all presumed Lily had a lot of…eh, visitors, but what if it was something else? What if all those cars had nothing to do with Lily?"

Grace shook her head again. "Just because there are cars on the road, doesn't mean moonshine. I'm sure Noverta would have noticed if that sort of thing were going on. He would have said something. If not to me, at least to you."

"But he'd been traveling a lot, Grace." Noverta had started a breeding program, hoping to improve the quality of his milk cows. He'd been going all over the country looking at cattle.

She stared at him, her gaze unwavering. "True. But I still don't think a lot of cars equate to moonshine."

Cal prayed he wasn't making a mistake by giving her the details. "Not moonshine, Grace. A small fortune in bottled liquor. I found the bootlegger's storehouse less than a mile from Vertie's place. Unless the alcohol belonged to your brother, I think the hoard is related to Lily's murder."

"Unless it belonged to Vertie?"

Cal didn't believe that, but watched Grace's reaction. For a moment, he feared she'd throw the teakettle at him.

"Vertie would *never* break the law," she insisted.

Her anger was reassuring. Grace knew nothing about the alcohol, Cal was sure of that.

He also tended to agree with Grace about Noverta, but the events of the last month made him question everything he thought he knew. Best to be sure. "Vertie hasn't sold many cows lately, and he told me the senator refused to help with the farm. These are hard times, Grace. Everybody needs money."

Her nose twitched, a sure sign she worked hard to control her temper. "He doesn't need *money*. Mammie left the house to me, but she left her money to both of us."

*Good.* "Do you think he knew about the alcohol? That many cars down this way must have aroused suspicion."

She shook her head. "Vertie and I had several heart-to-hearts in the week before he was…before all that happened. He never mentioned anything about alcohol or bootlegging. I think he would have told me if he'd had suspicions."

"Heart-to-hearts? About?"

She poured her tea and smoothed her skirts as she took a seat. "About Lily. What else?"

Cal stared at the teacup. For some reason, the blue and white checked cup with Dutch windmills didn't suit Grace. He pictured her holding some classy white china, trimmed in gold.

She followed his gaze, and then lifted her cup. "Tacky, isn't it? Granny refused to use my china when she was here. 'We can't be breaking that hoity-toity stuff, girly.' Her imitation of Granny Gardner was spookily accurate. "Guess she's using my good stuff now, though, because she only left me these tacky dishes that belonged to her mother. I'm sorry, but I'm glad the bitch is gone."

Cal spit coffee across the yellow tabletop. Gone as in dead? Grace knew Granny was dead?

"Are you all right?" Grace asked.

He shook his head, wondering how it was possible the earth could still be spinning on its axis. "You're glad she's gone? Are you talking about Granny or Lily?"

"Both, I suppose."

That was perhaps a bit too honest. "Grace, how do you know… How do you know about Granny?"

Her brow furrowed slightly. "My father said they left town. And she's not here."

So Grace didn't know about Granny. Cal could breathe again, having dodged a fastball to his head.

Only he needed to focus. Someone had killed the woman, and based on what he'd uncovered, either the senator or Ernest was the last known person to see Granny alive. Both men had some explaining to do, only Cal had to find them first. *After* his trip to the smokehouse.

"Grace, surely you have some idea where Ernest would go?"

" I don't." She scrunched her nose. "Cal, Ernest and I weren't that talkative, even on the good days. I mean we didn't fight or anything, but we… Well I pretended he wasn't here and he pretty much returned the favor. I tried to do the same with Granny, but she was rather difficult to pretend away. I gave her money for food each week—she asked for more than she needed. It was just easier to give her the cash than to argue with her. She was terribly cheap and hoarded every cent she could. I think she probably had enough money to go anywhere—especially if my father gave her more cash."

Cal shook his head. He was missing something. "Before the divorce talk, was Ernest acting strange in any way?"

"You mean besides messing around with my brother's wife?"

What could he say to that? Nothing. So he waited.

"Now that I think about it," she said. "He did seem a bit jumpy. Once I dropped a fork and he nearly came out of his skin. I wish I could help more."

"Grace, I need you to go out on a 'suppose' limb here. If you were guessing, would you say he was afraid."

She shrugged. "If he was afraid of me, wouldn't he have left sooner? I don't know if he was afraid of anything else."

Another silence. Time to get to the smokehouse.

"I really must go." He got up, but Grace put her hand on his forearm, distracting his thoughts.

"You aren't doing something dangerous, are you?"

"If the bootlegger is Lily's killer, then I'm setting a trap for a murderer. Otherwise, I'm wasting my time." He managed a smile. "Either way, I'll be careful."

# CHAPTER 28

Grace watched Cal pull out of her driveway, fighting the urge to run after him. She still hadn't told him.

He gave her a little wave, but otherwise didn't slow, not even when he backed into the small ditch at the edge of her front lawn. He gunned his engine, spinning the tires until the Packard cleared the indentation. She waited on the porch, watching the dust cloud. Odd that it hadn't rained since Lily died.

Then she slumped against the porch column. She was a fool.

Not just a fool, a colossal fool. Grace rubbed her temples, wondering when she'd last had a headache-free day. And why had she confessed about Ernest? She should have kept her stupid mouth closed, but, God help her, she'd wanted to be honest with Cal. Completely honest.

Why hadn't she just told him?

Every molecule in her body wanted to sit down and have a good cry—the good cry she hadn't succumbed to since Cal had left Leeton, ten years earlier. Only she couldn't wallow. She had to betray Cal's confidence, and find out what was going on in that smokehouse. She really wanted to believe no one had gotten involved in illegal alcohol, but since the awful night Lily died, problems just seemed to come out of nowhere and snowball.

Right now, she had to find out about Kenny. If he'd been harmed…

Grace squared her shoulders and marched back into the house for a heavier coat. No point in stalling. As Granny Gardner would say, "Can't stand around pickin' yer nose."

Would she ever be free of that woman?

* * * *

Cal knew he *shouldn't* feel good.

Noverta was *still* missing, Kenny was *still* missing and Cal *still* hadn't told anyone the identity of the corpse in Grace's car. Even so, relief was a wondrous thing. Grace didn't know about Granny—thus she couldn't have killed the woman. Even better, she would soon be free of Ernest. He had hope, adding to his sense that things might finally work out.

If he could just find out who murdered Lily.

He drove toward Broken Bridge Cliff, letting the details of his sting crystallize. Once, there had been a road with an actual bridge crossing a deep stream with very high banks. No more. A New Deal project created a new highway and the road had been diverted away from the cliffs.

The site would be perfect for his scheme, but Cal needed to see the place first hand. As boys, he and Noverta had played Indians there. They never played cowboys and Indians, only Indians. Cal hoped the terrain hadn't changed much. In those days, there'd been a spot where you could see most of the surrounding area without being seen from below. With any luck, he could find that spot again.

He parked his Packard and trudged up a steep pile of dirt. Next to a massive pine—a tree that had grown tall despite having its top cut off for boyhood arrows—he found the site he needed. Amazing that a twenty-year-old memory remained so vivid.

Cal squatted, tested his view. Perfect. He'd have to hunch down, but he couldn't be seen from below. Attempting to lure the bootlegger to the ravine might be overkill, but Cal couldn't think of any other way to prove the man killed Lily. Getting the murderer to take the bait wouldn't necessarily be admissible, but once the killer's identify became known, Cal would have a critical lead.

He scouted around until he found a second site, near to the road, a place to hide if necessary. A lawman always needed an escape route.

Cal spotted an indentation in the side of the earth, about six-feet below his primary site—one not visible from above. He made his way to the spot, holding on to the tiny shrubs that managed to take root in the hostile landscape. When he reached his destination, he looked down.

"Hell's bells."

The drop measured almost thirty feet. The ground below was likely pure red clay, which would be hard since it hadn't rained in a couple weeks. Even worse, parts of the old bridge had crumbled into the water, littering the landscape with broken concrete and chunks of steel. A fall would be treacherous, maybe even deadly. Good thing he didn't fear heights as much as dark holes.

Cal stared at his father's pocket watch. A reminder of how critical his timing would need to be. Once he set his plan in motion, everything centered around getting to his spot before the bootlegger arrived. Maybe he should camp out.

He also needed a place to hide the car, but leaving his note was priority. He had to be in the bootlegger's storehouse during daylight. If the bootlegger showed up, Cal might not be able to see him in the dark.

And he might be cornered by a killer.

# CHAPTER 29

Cal stared at the lines on the paper. Could someone recognize his handwriting? He left notes on the office door all the time. Wouldn't do to let the bootlegger know the sheriff was after him. Maybe he could cut out letters from the newspaper and paste them on a note.

Damn. He'd have to return to his office. He'd been careful, so why shortchange now? With any luck, he could grab his rifle and get back in this car before either of his deputies noticed he'd returned.

No such luck. Herb met him at the door.

"Where you been, Boss? We've been looking for you."

Cal frowned. "Why? Something happen?"

"They found Kenny."

"Alive?" Cal held his breath until Herb nodded. "Where?"

"Down by Mudcats Field. Rodney's already gone…"

"Did anyone tell Burton?" Cal asked.

The deputy frowned. "No, but—"

"Do it. Go see Burton. Right now. Tell him I'll bring Kenny home as soon as we have the doctor check him out. Then call Grace and let her know we found the boy."

Cal didn't wait for Herb's response. He got to his car in two seconds flat. A moment later, he raced down the dirt road toward the old ballfield.

Why hadn't he checked the spot before? Kenny loved that dirt lot. The boy couldn't have been there all that time though. Hell, it had been four days.

Cal came to a screeching halt a few hundred yards before he reached Mudcats Field, remembering—just in time—about the huge ruts that crisscrossed the road. The park hadn't been used in years, not even by local kids. So what the hell was Kenny doing in the place?

Jumping out of his cruiser, Cal sprinted through the trees to the lot. Kenny sat with Rodney on one of the three benches that once comprised the cheering section. When the boy saw Cal, he jumped up and loped toward him with his unique gait, the left foot never going ahead of the right.

"Hi Sheriff Cal. I'm glad to see you, Sheriff Cal. Really, really, really glad."

"Kenny, where have you been?"

"Don't know. The boogieman took me Cal. It was awful. Real awful. He let me go, though. He let me go."

What the devil? "Take a deep breath, son. Who let you go?"

"The boogieman. It was dark. Hate, hate, hate the dark. And snakes were a crawlin' on me." The boy shuddered. "Don't want to talk 'bout it."

"Okay, Kenny. Take another breath." He glanced at Rodney over the boy's shoulder. The deputy shook his head slightly. The snakes were probably in Kenny's head. A lot of things would be in *his head*. How much of Kenny's account would be factual?

Probably damn little.

The boy wheezed in a breath. Then promptly choked. Probably mimicking his dad, because Kenny didn't look upset at all.

"Take it easy." Cal patted him on the back. "Let's go sit down."

He guided Kenny back to the bleacher bench. After a few seconds, the boy stopped fake-wheezing.

"I'm okay, Sheriff Cal. The boogieman let me go. So I'm okay."

Maybe if he could figure out how Kenny arrived in the ballfield, he could backtrack and find out why the boy had disappeared. "Listen, Kenny. I want you to think really hard. Can you do that?"

The boy nodded.

"How did you get here?" Cal spoke really slow.

Kenny shook his head, several times. "I done told Rodney, the boogieman let me go, Sheriff Cal. He push me down and then here I am. That's all I 'member."

"That's all right." Cal had to be careful. If Kenny got distraught, he might forget what little he did remember. "You said he pushed you? Were you in a car?"

Okay, he'd gone from talking too slow to talking too fast. Kenny shook his head again. And kept shaking it.

"Kenny, be still, son. It's okay."

The boy stopped moving. "Don't 'member no car, Sheriff Cal. I was in that bag."

"Bag?" Cal followed Kenny's gaze to a pile of white cloth on the ground, about thirty feet away. Probably an old sheet. Maybe even the top sheet from Kenny's bed. Cal cursed himself for not noticing it was missing. He'd just assumed Kenny's bed had only the bottom sheet and the quilt.

"Were you tied up?"

Kenny's eyebrows went up. "No. But I had a thing over my eyes. To make it dark."

"Very brave. And you got away. How'd you do that?" Cal smiled, a fake smile, but hopefully the boy wouldn't know.

Kenny nodded with the same enthusiasm he'd used to shake his head. "Yep. I got away. If I had my pirate sword, I woulda hurt that ole boogieman."

The boy started to shake again. His entire body shuddered. "But I didn't. It was so dark, Sheriff Cal."

Cal propped an arm around Kenny's shoulder. "It's all right. You're safe now."

The boy wheezed a breath and then another. Cal drew upon his patience while Kenny choked. After several seconds, he seemed normal again, or as normal as Kenny could be.

"Tell me, Kenny. How'd you get away?"

The boy put a finger on his lip for a second. "Dunno. I went to sleep and I just woke up on this bench."

Cal glanced at Rodney. "You found him?"

Rodney nodded. "Got a call from the farmer who owns this land now. He said there was a vagrant on his property."

Kenny kicked at the end of the bench. "I ain't no grant."

"'Course you aren't." Cal patted the boy on the shoulder. Probably wouldn't get anything useful from the boy. Not with the direct approach. "Did you smell anything funny?"

Kenny leaned back to look at Cal, his eyes squinted and his nose wrinkled. "No. Didn't smell nothing. Except air." At least he'd stopped choking.

"Did you hear anyone talking?"

"Just the boogieman. He talked like this."
Kenny spoke in a weird, raspy voice, making Cal
wonder if his abductor had disguised his voice.

"You hear anyone else? Any cows or dogs?"

The boy shook his head, the back-and-forth,
back-and-forth motion so robust Cal wondered
why Kenny's head didn't hurt. "I didn't hear
nothin', Sheriff Cal. I couldn't hear cause it was so
dark. It was sooooo dark."

"I'm sure you were very brave." Cal doubted
the truth of his statement. Whatever happened had
clearly terrified the boy. Seemed a shame to scare
him further when Kenny clearly didn't know
anything.

Cal stared at the bed sheet, trying to make sense
of the abduction. No request for ransom, no known
reason anyone would want to hurt Burton or his
boy. So why would anyone take Kenny, hold him
for a few days, and then just release him?

The sheet was white. Unless the abductor kept
Kenny in some kind of cellar, the boy should have
seen light through the fabric.

Cal nudged at the sheet with his foot. A thin
dark strip of fabric, nondescript and nothing to go
on, lay under the cotton sheet. Kenny had been
blindfolded.

Nothing made sense. And another dead end.

At least they had Kenny back. Safe. Cal turned
to face him. The boy's shoulders hunched.

"You ready to go home, Kenny?"

The boy nodded, as rapidly as he'd shaken his head. Abruptly he stopped nodding, a big grin on his face. "Can I get hot chocolate 'fore I go?"

\* \* \* \*

Cal hurried home. Finding Kenny had been the best thing to happen in weeks, but now he needed to hurry. With no time to eat, he got some jerky from his refrigerator, stuffing his mouth as he grabbed his small duffle bag. He packed his binoculars, grateful he'd kept them even though his scouting-the-opposing-pitcher days were over. For good measure, he unlocked his gun chest and took out his .38. After loading the pistol, he wrapped the weapon in a towel and dropped it into the duffle. He might be facing a killer—an extra gun couldn't hurt.

Cal rolled his shoulder blades, trying to shake off his apprehension. He'd started thinking of the bootlegger as a killer. More specifically as *the* killer. Haunting. Especially when Cal remembered that the same person had probably abducted Kenny. The why of the kidnapping still bothered him.

He glanced at the clock. No time to brush his teeth since it was almost five o'clock. Hell, wasn't like fresh breath would be his main concern when he spotted the bootlegger—potential killer.

Ignoring the jerky taste in his mouth, he hurried to his car. Everything hinged on getting the note planted before the bootlegger returned to the smokehouse.

Robin Weaver

# CHAPTER 30

Cal was exhilarated by his own caution. He drove past Holly Creek Road three times to ensure no one watched. Once convinced he wasn't followed, he turned onto the gravel and pulled into Noverta's driveway. He fumbled with the keys Grace had given him until he found the one that opened the shed. Then, he pulled his Packard into the structure and locked the door. He walked-ran toward the smokehouse, staying near the tree line for cover.

The sun had disappeared when he reached the old smokehouse. Best if he hurried.

He scanned the area for any sign of human movement. Seeing nothing, he still waited a full five minutes before he entered the smokehouse.

Once committed, Cal calculated he had to be in and out in less than two minutes. If the bootlegger arrived while he was inside, the guy might get spooked and abandon everything—and Cal might lose his only hope of clearing Noverta. Or worse, the person might come in shooting.

Cal put on his work gloves and pried open the boards. Inside, he pulled the note out and placed the paper on the old table, reading the block letters one more time.

**I KNOW YOU KILLED LILY**
**I HAVE PROOF**
**MEET ME AT THE BROKEN BRIDGE CLIFF**
**NOON TOMORROW**

A bit melodramatic, perhaps, but with any luck the note would draw out the booze mastermind. It had to. Cal had exhausted all other leads. He wondered again if he should just watch the smokehouse to see who arrived.

He discarded that idea a second time. Since Cal couldn't watch the place around the clock, catching someone entering the smokehouse could take weeks—weeks Cal didn't have. The bootlegger could also send a lackey to the smokehouse.

More important, catching someone entering the smokehouse would prove nothing. At best, Cal could only get them for illegal possession, but even that would be hard to prove. Person could just say he wandered into the place.

No, his note was the only way. He had to get his suspect to another location—one in which Cal had the advantage. Reacting to the message would show the booze was connected with Lily's murder.

Cal hoped so anyway.

At least he could finally get Noverta's dog out of the damn smokehouse. He took Lucky's leash from his pocket. Tanner jumped into pointing position.

"Ready to get out of here, aren't you, boy."

Cal grabbed the leash, but hesitated. He really should take a couple bottles of the liquor with him, too. If something went wrong, the bottles might be all the evidence he had.

The dog dropped to the floor, putting his head over his paws and staring at Cal with pitiful eyes.

"Just one more minute, boy." The dog didn't move.

Neither did Cal. He really didn't want to crawl down in the hole again. Damn, but he hated dark places.

"Ah, hell..." Might as well get it done. Cal closed his eyes and climbed down the ladder. At the bottom rung, he took a deep breath, memorizing the scene. He grabbed a bottle of Blue Hills bourbon and a pint of Mr. Boston rum. He stuffed each bottle into a separate pocket. Last thing he needed was glass clanking at an inopportune time. Then, he scurried out of the hell pit, faster than he'd ever run to first base after a bunt.

He scratched Tanner behind his ears. "Sorry I can't remove your muzzle just yet, big fella." Best to make sure Tanner didn't bark and signal his identity. If the villain, or villains, discovered the sheriff was the blackmailer, they'd know he bluffed. After all, if he had any proof, he'd have already made an arrest.

When he and Tanner reached the edge of the tree line, a bit over a hundred yards from the smokehouse, Cal unrolled his sleeping bag and sat down to wait. No reason to be at Broken Bridge Cliff tomorrow if no one retrieved his note tonight. With any luck, the bootlegger would pass close enough so Cal could get a good look at him. He wouldn't react tonight—he needed the bootlegger to go to the broken bridge to be convinced he was also a murderer. But maybe, just maybe, he'd have a face to put with the crime.

Tanner wanted to run.

"Stay," Cal ordered. The dog sat. Noverta had trained the animal well.

After a third "Stay," Tanner put his head on his paws. No mournful eyes this time. The dog closed his eyes and promptly went to sleep.

"Aren't you the lucky one?" Cal whispered.

He settled in for a long boring evening. After an hour, he couldn't stifle a yawn and began to second guess his plan. What was he thinking? At best, any connection between the bootlegger and Lily's murder was a long shot—the odds probably a hundred-to-one.

The temperature conspired against him; too many days with too little sleep threatened to send him to the dugout. In the silent darkness, he could hear his pocket watch ticking—every second a reminder of the time he wasted. He stayed put, determined to follow through on his plan, even if his time yielded nothing.

He made it another ninety minutes. Enough was enough. Before he moved, Tanner's head shot up. Instinctively, Cal grabbed the dog, afraid Tanner would bolt.

"Heel," Cal whispered, fully alert. He hung onto the animal, but searched the area, looking for the thing that had Tanner agitated.

He spotted a light. Near the smokehouse. "Son of a…" he whispered.

He hadn't counted on the man coming from the opposite direction. There was no road.

* * * *

Grace stared at Nana Randolph's grandfather clock, rubbing her palms together. Already 8:30 a.m.

Where the devil was her ride? Grace had called, but couldn't explain over the phone, not with Adeline on the switchboard. She didn't think the person on the other end of the line got her message.

She lifted the side of the curtain and looked out the window again. She hadn't heard an automobile but looked anyway.

"Hurry. Up," she whispered, knowing her words wouldn't help.

Cal had probably gone to the ravine already. If she didn't do something fast, he would know everything. She'd almost confessed yesterday— almost told him the entire story. Only Cal had been in a hurry and she had the night to re-think her decision. She'd changed her mind. If Cal found out now, everything she'd done would be for naught. Worse, Cal would hate her. Really hate her. Then, she truly would have nothing.

That was a problem for tomorrow. If she didn't do something *today*, people might die.

She heard the chug-chug of an engine. *Finally.*

Rushing to the door, she stopped short. With her hand on the handle, she hesitated. Grace couldn't put her finger on the specific problem, but something was wrong.

She ducked back inside and lifted the curtain, just to be sure. No harm in being cautious, right?

"Criminy."

The driver wasn't who she expected. The car belonged to her father. The jerk wasn't due back from Nashville until Monday. What the devil was she going to do now?

\* \* \* \*

If only he'd camped out closer to the smokehouse last night. After seeing the light, Cal tried to get close enough to see who'd entered the bootlegger's lair, but the man disappeared into the trees before he and Tanner could edge nearer for a good look. At least the dog hadn't barked, alerting the man to Cal's presence.

Cal glanced at his watch again. Three hours before the scheduled rendezvous. Exactly two hours before he expected the killer to show and nothing for him to do but wait.

He hoped like hell his theory proved correct, hoped the person who'd taken Tanner and accumulated the hoard of alcohol was the same person who'd murdered Lily. If not, Noverta was screwed.

"Hell." He might be screwed, too, if the booze had nothing to do with Lily. What would he do if he'd stumbled onto a mob-run booze ring? That sort of organization would snuff him out faster than Bob Feller could hum a fastball.

The mob theory was hogwash. The syndicate didn't operate in the south, right?

"Right." Speaking aloud didn't banish any of Cal's doubts. Hadn't he accepted the sheriff's job believing *drunk and disorderly* would be the only type of crime he'd have to address?

He shook his head, mentally willing his plan to work. His gut said the bootlegger was small time— someone in the town making some extra cabbage. The alcohol was related to Lily's murder-- somehow. Cal's gut kept him alive in D.C. Might as well trust it in Leeton.

He scanned the area as he replayed the expected scenario in his mind. If his plan worked, the bootlegger would come from the road—directly into his trap. After his mistake at the smokehouse, he would be watching the dirt path, too, even though he didn't expect anyone to arrive on foot. He'd taken a few extra minutes to check out the terrain on the opposite side of the steep hill. No road access for at least two miles. No matter how the thug approached, he had to walk into the clearing.

Cal wouldn't be making an arrest today either, not without backup. There was a good chance the bootlegger/murderer wouldn't show up alone either. Best to play it safe. He couldn't help Noverta if he was dead.

Thus his entire plan hinged on getting a good look at the man—or even better, identifying the villain. Once Cal saw a face, he'd head back to his office and start the arrest process. Going on the theory most people were killed by people they knew, he expected to have a name to put on his warrant. On the odd chance the bootlegger was a stranger, Cal would follow him to his car, get enough information to set up statewide road blocks.

He studied the area where he intended to hide, checking out the line of vision from each angle. He lay prone, testing his movements to make sure he cast no shadows. The concealed position had one blind spot. Couldn't be helped.

Cal picked up his rifle, holstered his .38, and draped the binoculars around his neck before he moved cautiously to the edge of the ravine for a better look. He stood to make sure he had an escape route. Before he could reposition himself,

Cal heard a noise. Someone walked toward him — through the woods.

*Hell.* At least he'd prepared this time. One problem: if Cal didn't know the person, he wouldn't be able to give a description of the vehicle.

The man was early — way early. In all his D.C. experience, thugs always showed up early, hoping for an advantage. But *never* three hours early.

Cal scanned the foliage and saw movement but no human form. He aimed his binoculars at the spot where the evergreen branches moved.

*Come on. Show yourself.*

He waited. Nothing.

Where had the man gone?

He started to second-guess his plan. He should have risked bringing one of his deputies. Or at least told someone he'd be at Broken Bridge.

The sound of screeching brakes echoed from his side of the cliff, as if his trepidation conjured up the automobile.

"Son of a bitch," he whispered. Two of them?

He couldn't see the automobile. Not yet.

A car door opened. Cal heard a faint click. A shell being chambered?

Double son of a bitch. If anyone spotted him, he'd be a sitting duck.

He sucked in a breath, determined to remain calm. He hunched lower, being careful not to dislodge any dirt. He needed to remain motionless.

He waited, continuously scanning the trees and ground cover without moving his head. A noise from the non-road side of the fallen bridge captured his attention. A horse snorting?

He saw something. Sunlight glinting off metal. Hell. Probably a rifle barrel, a far-away barrel. The scrub bushes might conceal Cal's location, but the flimsy vegetation provided no cover.

Shots rang out.

Rifle shots zinged, cutting through the air, no doubt from the same rifle that reflected in the morning sun. His .38 didn't have the range of a rifle, most likely a rifle with a mounted scope. The same type scope Cal had in the trunk of his Packard.

He was definitely out-gunned. His stomach tightened. He should have brought Rodney with him. Hell, even Herb would be a welcome sight.

Cal ducked his head as close to the cliff wall as he could. Dirt and gravel dislodged and hurtled toward the bottom. Cal didn't know if his body caused the avalanche or if bullets had stuck the cliff.

Who was shooting? And who was the target?

Didn't matter. He hung in the middle of a turkey shoot. And he was the turkey.

*Do something.* Too bad planning and a firm grip were mutually exclusive. Why hadn't he taken his .38 out of his holster? If he reached for his rifle on the ledge, he might slip. Thirty feet was a long plummet. A fall would be as deadly as being shot.

The bullets were the immediate threat. Instinct and adrenaline combined forces, propelling Cal across the terrain toward a large rock at the cliff's edge. The big rock would provide cover from both sides, hide him from both intruders.

Cal took a deep breath. Then he dived for the rock.

Silence. Damn, he'd left his rifle on the ledge. How stupid was that?

He assessed the immediate situation: an unknown number of assailants in unknown locations shooting at his known location. Behind the big rock, which seemed to grow smaller with each passing second.

Something moved. Cal froze.

*No.* The earth shifted beneath his stomach. He'd miscalculated, jumped too far when he dived behind the rock.

He lay still as a corpse, hoping like hell the shifting ground could support his weight.

It didn't. Dirt began to trickle down the cliff wall. Cal grabbed at the ledge. More dirt crashed to the bottom of the ravine, making an explosive sound.

His throat constricted. He hadn't just miscalculated, he'd made a fatal error.

Another shot rang out. Cal lost his grip.

# CHAPTER 31

*Saturday, December 3*

Yesterday, his plan had been foolproof. Today, it was just foolish.

Cal hung onto a scrub pine jutting out of the steep hillside, cursing his stupidity. More shots echoed around him. Was the horse rider shooting, too?

*Zing.* A clump of rock blew away from the cliff wall. Seemed like inches, but the shot had probably missed him by a couple yards. A small consolation.

He clenched his eyes shut. No time for praying. He had to act.

Maybe if he swung his feet, generated enough momentum, he could propel his legs up and over the ledge. Another bullet whizzed over his head.

Maybe not.

Everything went silent. Cal froze. A shadow covered the cliff wall—probably someone standing on the top of the rocky terrain. Cal couldn't see the person, only the shadow. Damn man didn't seem concerned about being shot. Had he killed the shooter on the opposite bank?

Cal hoped to hell the man didn't see him. He held his breath until his body screamed for air. His lungs exhaled without him.

The shadow moved.

Cal tightened his grip but his arms ached. How much longer could he hang on? He estimated he'd fallen about half-way down the cliff. He tried to make out the ground below but flecks of dirt made his vision blur. From what he remembered, there were bushes at the base. If he managed to land on vegetation instead of rock or concrete, he might survive.

Or not. Even if he avoided breaking his neck, he'd be easy target practice for the person with the gun.

He looked sideways, spotted another protruding root four feet away. The thing looked more solid than the little pine he held in a death grip. There was a slight indentation for his foot there, too. If he reached the root, he might be able to brace his feet and draw his Colt. He'd have a shot. Maybe two. If nothing else, maybe he'd discover who'd killed Lily before he died. He stared upward, but the glaring sun obliterated everything else.

He held his breath, aware he needed to be as silent as death. The glare faded directly above him. Someone stood on the ledge. Watching.

Watching him?

Even with the shadow, Cal still couldn't see the person. He pressed himself flat against the rock, trying to disappear. A bit of dirt tumbled toward the ravine, the rock formations amplifying the sound.

*Damn.* His fingers ached, the muscles strained to the limit. He must hang on.

A shrill whistle surrounded him. Maybe he'd imagined the sound. Whatever he'd heard, the noise echoed from the wooded side, not from the person watching.

The shadow from overhead loomed larger. Cal twisted for a better look, hoping the person blocked the sun. Nothing but trees, dirt and rock.

The shadow moved, casting a silhouette over the rocks. Cal saw a man's outline, but the figure was distorted. Then the jerking shadow vanished.

The cap. Cal recognized the baseball cap.

The little pine's roots gave way. In a second, the little tree would dislodge. "Hell."

# Robin Weaver

# CHAPTER 32

*Boom.* Rocks and dirt raced down the cliff.

"No!" Grace yelled. She jumped off her horse and sprinted toward the edge of the cliff. "Oh, God!" She was too late. Dear God in heaven, she was too late.

At the edge of the bank, she dropped to her stomach, not caring one iota about the red clay dirt. "Cal?" Her voice echoed, but that's all she heard.

Her chest felt leaden, he couldn't be dead.

She struggled to regain her composure. She listened. Nothing. She'd never forgive herself. Never.

Instead of arguing with her father, she should have just stolen his damn car. No, she should have told Cal the truth when she had the opportunity. If she'd done the right thing, he wouldn't be at the bottom of the ravine.

She shaded her eyes for a better look. Probably a waste of time, she should start hiking down.

Wait. Was that him?

Grace leaned further over the edge for a better look. Cal. He looked dead.

*No. No, no, no.* She had to get to him. Only there was no direct way to the bottom. She'd have to hike at least a mile south, and then reverse directions to reach the bottom without killing herself. At the moment, the last part didn't seem like a bad idea. Only she had no time.

She had a rope in her saddlebag—the rope she'd used to pull a calf out of the stream last month. Thank God she hadn't put it away. She hurried back to the mare. Polly stood stock still.

"Good girl!" she patted the mare's flank before grabbing the rope. She hurriedly tied the rope around a sturdy oak and then tossed it over the edge of the cliff.

She lay flat on her stomach again for a better look. "Criminy." The rope stopped about fifteen feet from the bottom. She could probably jump that distance without getting hurt, but how would she get back up?

She winced. If Cal were dead, getting out of the canyon wouldn't matter.

Time to act. She wrapped the rope around her wrist and prepared to rappel down the cliff bank. Good thing she'd grown up playing with boys. The lady her father wanted her to be could never traverse a fifty-foot incline. Not with a thirty-five foot rope anyway.

She put her left foot over the edge. Then paused. Was that…?

*Movement.* She'd seen something move. *Please, let it be Cal.*

"Cal!"

A small branch moved. "Son of a bitch."

"Cal!" She thought she might just be able to breathe again. Until she leaned over for a better look. Cal lay flat on his back, one foot on a jutting rock.

"Grace?"

She nodded, feeling like a fool when she realized he probably couldn't see her. "Are you all right?" she yelled.

"Hell, no. Get out of here! People are shooting!"

# CHAPTER 33

"I don't see anyone," Grace replied. She didn't know how she'd explain her presence at the cliff, but she had to think of something. Fast.

"You sure?" Cal asked, his voice sounding ragged.

"Pretty sure." Better change the subject. "Anything broken? Any bleeding?"

"Don't think so." She watched Cal try to stand before he promptly sat back down. "Damn." He rubbed his arm.

She should feel bad, a fall like that had to hurt. That kind of tumble would kill most people. Only she was so relieved to see him alive and kicking, she couldn't focus on his pain.

"Cal, I have a rope, but…"

He looked up, still massaging his bicep. He gave the rope a cursory glance. Even from the distance, he looked none too happy. "Grace, what are you doing here?"

He would ask that. Didn't seem like the appropriate time for that conversation, not while she looked down from the cliff edge. The best time to have that little talk would be…never. She'd deceived him too long to fess up now. "The rope isn't long enough. If you don't need a tourniquet, I'll go to Vertie's house and get another one. Will you be able to climb?"

"I don't know. Tell me why you're here."

"I'll be back as quick as I can." She scurried away from the cliff edge before he could demand an answer.

The horseback ride to the main road seemed to take forever. When she reached the gravel, she spotted the car. "Criminy."

She checked her surroundings to make sure no one watched, then pulled Polly alongside the automobile. Polly skittered when she pounded on the window, but Grace held the reins firm.

The window rolled down.

Grace frowned at the driver. "Didn't you get my note?"

"What note?"

Grace groaned. "I told you not to come to the cliff."

The man chuckled. "Obviously not."

She wanted to hit him. How dare he laugh? "Did Cal see you?"

"Don't think so. Man was too busy trying to save his neck."

"Don't you dare say…" Grace glared at him. "Cal's expecting the bootlegger, so you have to come back to the cliff. At the correct time."

"Uh-uh. We barely dodged the last bullet. I'm not going to let the sheriff see me next time. He has no proof. Why would we give him some?"

"If you don't come back, Cal is going to know I'm involved."

The man laughed—a nasty, in-your-face sort of laugh. "Aren't you?"

She wouldn't dignify that question with a response. "Give me fifteen minutes to get the rope, then bring the car back. Park up top, behind the ridge of trees. Slam the door. Wait five minutes, then go."

"What if he sees me?"

Grace took a deep breath, determined to keep her cool. Did he have to be so blasted dense? "He won't. He's at the bottom of the ravine. If you don't go near the cliff edge, he won't be able to see your face."

The man started laughing. "What a bozo."

Grace glared at him. She wanted to insist Cal was no bozo, but that would only add fuel to an inferno. "Just do what I say. Otherwise…"

All humor left the man's face. "*Fine.* Anything else, *boss* lady?"

"Yes. What the hell are you doing in that smokehouse?"

He laughed, not a pleasant sound. "Not everyone has a rich grand-mommy."

"But bootlegging? Why would you do something like that?"

"So the good sheriff told you about that, huh?" He shook his head. "That darn dog."

"Dog?" she asked, confusion clouding some of her temper. "What dog?"

"Tanner. Remember how he growled at me that night?"

"Yes." The dog had always been protective of Lily and kept baring his teeth. Grace had taken him home with her and put him in the shed. She'd thought Tanner got out—there was a hole under the door—and ran away. "You took Tanner?" She shook her head, wondering if the nightmare would ever end.

"I had to take the dog. If the good sheriff saw him growling at me, he'd have put two and two together. Hell, Cal was probably looking for Tanner when he found the smokehouse."

"What else have you done?"

The driver shrugged. "Other than breaking in that safe? Nothing. Which reminds me, you still owe me for that actor."

Grace took a deep breath, knowing she couldn't raise her voice. Sound carried in the hollows. "Owe you? It was *your* baseball cap."

The driver laughed. "True, but hiring that man to act as a Fed and lure the sheriff away was your idea."

"Fine," Grace replied, not wanting to think about her desperate acts.

"I have to make sure we stay out of jail. You might want to act more appreciative."

"Jail doesn't sound so bad these days," she said, meaning every word. Things kept getting worse and worse. "Where's the dog now?"

"Think Cal has him. Was in the smokehouse. Now he's gone."

She'd worry about Tanner later. Right now, she needed to get back. "Get that note I left for you and destroy it," she ordered.

"Grace…" The man's tone had changed.

"What?"

"I know Lily said she was pregnant." The man hesitated. "That wasn't true."

She nodded. That didn't matter now.

Grace nudged Polly into a gallop and headed for her brother's house to get a rope. She needed to think of something to explain her appearance and disappearance.

\* \* \* \*

"*Stay put, Cal.*" Cal mimicked Grace's voice. Stay put? Not like he could shimmy up the cliff. How had he fallen that far and lived?

He lifted his head for another look. The distance took his breath.

Grace had long-since vanished. Before she left, he thought he'd seen what appeared to be the barrel of a rifle, but that too disappeared. Had it been fired?

So what was he supposed to do now? His head ached, his arm hurt like hell. Son of a bitch, every muscle in his body screamed.

Didn't matter. Despite Grace's contention that no one lurked, he believed someone still hovered. With him a wounded duck—right in the line of sight and Grace cavorting around as if she hadn't a care in the universe. Shielding his eyes from the sun and his skull from any potential gunmen, he tried to assess his situation.

Double son of a bitch. Unless he climbed up, he faced a five-mile walk down the basin of the old riverbed. Climbing the cliff was out of the question; his body was in no shape to play monkey in the trees. Unless he could somehow reach the rope.

Since he couldn't get out quickly, Cal sucked in a breath, trying to think logically. Why had Grace come to the cliff? Was she the killer? Didn't make sense she would shoot him and then try to save him. With a scope, she could hit a single stitch on the seam of a baseball from two-hundred yards. If Grace wanted him dead, he'd have already gotten the big kiss off.

So how did she know he'd gone to the cliff? He'd told her about the smokehouse, but no details about his plan. She hadn't followed him—Cal was sure about that. And how had she gotten to the cliff? Last time he'd seen her car, the automobile was flaming. Maybe she'd ridden. He thought he'd heard a horse.

Nothing made sense. Unless…

Had Grace seen his note in the smokehouse? That would mean she was involved with the bootlegging. At the least.

Only that made no sense. Grace seemed genuinely surprised when he mentioned the alcohol. He tried to board the logic train and make sense of Grace's presence, but he kept getting derailed. Nothing made sense.

He made a couple of lame attempts to reach the rope, but it remained elusive. Only six feet, or so, beyond his reach, but he might as well have reached for the moon. He sat back down, trying to form a plan. After a few minutes, he surrendered. He found the best cover he could, pulled the collar of his bomber jacket up around his ears, and settled back to wait.

"Cal?"

He blinked. Hell, he'd fallen asleep. How lame was that?

"Yeah." He sat up.

A thud. Cal flinched.

Grace had thrown down a rope. The hemp swung to the left and caught on a bit of scrub on the side of the hill.

"Need me to help you?"

"No. Don't come down—" Cal tried to stand, but his foot buckled.

Grace had already started shimmying toward the bottom. In any other situation, seeing her backside as she gripped and released the rope with her feet would be downright erotic. When she reached the bottom, she leaned over and placed her hand on his forehead. Her fingers were cold, so cold.

"Grace, I fell. I don't have a temperature."

She flashed a half-smile. "You could have hypothermia."

"Hypo-what?" Cal shook his head. "Never mind. Just help me stand up so we can get out of here."

Grace didn't move. "You sure? What if something's broken."

"Nothing's broken. Well, maybe a toe, but I can still stand. And walk."

Instead of helping him, Grace sat down beside him and took a deep breath, her exhale creating a mist in the bright sunshine. "You could have been killed."

And he still needed to catch a killer. "I'm alive and kicking, Grace. Let's get out of here."

He tried to stand only Grace still didn't move. Instead of leaning against her, he held onto the jutting boulder and forced his body upright. Cal reached for the rope, but lowered his hand. He needed to know if Grace had…seen his note. He couldn't even think of her and "being a killer" in the same thought.

"Grace, how did you just happen to be here?"

She smiled, a sad sort of smile that looked beautiful, but broke his heart at the same time. "When I ride, I usually come this way. Good thing I did, right?"

He nodded, wishing he hadn't. The least bit of movement turned him into a punching bag. Being punched. "You saw me?"

She shook her head. "No. Heard some shots. Then I heard a thud. Being nosy, I had to see."

That made sense. And he truly wanted to believe. Her excuse was utter nonsense though.

"Did you see anyone else?" he asked.

She squinted. "Yes. Or at least I think so. Walking away, I believe."

"So you didn't get a good look?"

"Why?" she asked.

Cal shrugged. He really needed to stop all unnecessary movement.

"You weren't the target of the shooting, were you?" she asked, her eyes wide.

"No," he replied. "Just deer hunters, I think." He studied her face, needing to test her reaction. She seemed totally oblivious to his killer trap, but perhaps he only saw what he wanted to see.

She reacted, narrowing her eyes. "Cal, why are you out here? Is this part of that bootlegging trap you told me about?"

Her questions eased his mind, made him more confident she hadn't seen his note. "I'll explain later. Right now, I'm really sick of this ravine."

"Fine. Let's go."

He reached for the rope. Grace reached at the same time. The rope swung sideways. Being taller, Cal grabbed it when it returned.

Grace tugged on his arm. "You sure you don't want me to get another horse? We can take the canyon trail. Riding out of here will be a lot easier than climbing. Especially in your condition."

The idea had absolutely no appeal. Cal shook his head and immediately wished he hadn't. "That'll take hours. I'm cold. And grumpy."

"Fine. I'll go first."

Cal blinked. He would have insisted on that, but he expected her to want to follow him. "Okay. Go."

Grace took hold of the rope with both hands, tugging. She shifted her feet several times, but made no move to climb.

What the hell was she doing? She'd climbed better than any of the boys when they were kids. Judging by the way she'd shimmied down, Cal didn't think going up should be an issue.

"Everything okay?" he asked.

"Yes. Just want to make sure the rope will hold the weight."

Cal stifled a grin, first time he'd felt like smiling in a while. Grace might weigh a hundred pounds after Thanksgiving dinner. "I think it will hold you."

She shook her head. "I meant *your* weight."

Cal grinned again. "I'll be fine."

She went. At a snail's pace. If Cal didn't know better, he'd swear she was afraid of heights. He knew better.

"Grace, can you move a tad faster. It's not getting any warmer down here." And he needed to find out if his plan had been completely shot to Mars.

She looked down at him from the halfway point. "Sorry. My hands are cold."

He'd been properly chastised. Her hands had been cold indeed. Only if she rode this way often, why wasn't she wearing gloves.

And why did she keep looking around? Almost as if she expected to see someone.

Cal would have smacked his own head if his body didn't already hurt in every conceivable spot. Of course Grace would look around. She'd heard the shots before and even if she bought his *hunter* story, she'd still be leery of stray bullets.

Grace moved faster. Once she reached the top she crouched, waiting.

He grabbed the rope, wrapped it beneath his hips, and started his ascent. The climb was slow because he had to stop every few seconds to rest his aching body. Still, he moved faster than he probably should in his condition. He'd pay for the exertion tomorrow, but he had to get back to the smokehouse.

He glanced up once. Grace waited. Patient as always. No lame words of encouragement. No unnecessary questions that required an answer—

315

nothing that would take oxygen away from lungs that already burned.

Finally. Only one more yard. Cal rested, one foot dug into a tiny indentation in the cliff wall, the rope encircling his bicep.

He heard a car. Could it be the killer had arrived? Or had he returned?

Cal could only guess at the time, but didn't dare reach for his pocket watch—assuming the thing still ticked. Still, the sun seemed right for noontime.

*Damn.*

"Grace, get down!" Hyped up on adrenaline, he yanked his body to the top. He rolled left to take cover under a spindly cedar, the snap of every twig echoing like artillery. He searched for Grace, spotting her behind a holly about ten yards to his left.

"Why are we hiding?" she whispered.

Words had never sounded sweeter. If she didn't know why they hid, it was possible she didn't know anything about his note. He held his finger to his lip.

She shook her head. "I can't leave Polly."

"Stay down." he whispered back.

"Why?"

Before he could respond, a car door slammed. Cal yanked his head toward the sound. Damn, his cover was too good. He had to see the man, or at least the car. Cal low crawled around the cedar. Only he still couldn't see, so he maneuvered his body around another bush. He still couldn't see anyone, couldn't see Grace either.

He heard footsteps. They came closer.

Cal's confidence rose. The jerk probably thought someone had already polished him off. That made sense. The killer would probably send someone else to do his dirty work.

Or maybe the shots he'd heard before were just hunters. Deer season had opened the week before Thanksgiving. If the man wasn't somehow related to the earlier shooter, that would mean he was just careless.

Cal waited, trying to form a plan. He wanted to rush the thug, but Grace might get hurt in the crossfire.

He guessed five minutes had passed. It seemed like an hour. He inched forward, determined to put a face with the footsteps. He smelled cigar smoke. With any luck, the man would leave a butt. Every bit of evidence would help.

Cal wanted to stand up, face the scum like an old-west marshal. If only he had his gun.

Instead, he inched toward a clearing, using slow, deliberate movements. The horse snorted again. Cal heard the zip of the bullet.

Damn. He had to find out who was shooting. He raced toward the clearing. Not smart, but hell.

He stopped in midstride. Grace marched toward the cliff bank, firing her rifle.

"Get down!" he yelled.

Grace lowered her weapon, staring into the distance. An engine started. Tires screeched.

Cal jumped up and raced toward the sound. He saw dust. Lots and lots of dust as the vehicle departed at a high speed.

"Damn."

Cal ran a hand over his head, wondering if a grown man could cry. Grace meant well. Hell, she probably thought she'd saved him. Instead, she'd spoiled everything.

He took a second to regain his composure. Then, he turned to face her. Grace was gone.

He kicked at the ground. Where the heck had she gone.

Then he saw it. A clue. A fat cigar, with the end pinched flat.

# CHAPTER 34

"Where have you been?"

"Good to see you too, Rodney. I'm fine, thanks for asking," Cal said, packing more sarcasm than necessary into his words. "Unless you count a sprained wrist, an aching arm, and at least one broken toe. Not to mention, I've just blown my only lead." He might have found a clue at the cliff, but he had a snowball's chance in a fiery pit of proving anything.

His deputy followed him back to his office. "Sorry, Cal. What happened? What can I do?"

Cal sat down in his chair, trying to ignore that jolt of pain that raced up his spine. He twisted his head toward his deputy, being careful not to move too fast. He'd made that mistake getting out of his car.

It had taken almost an hour to get to his car from the cliff. Even longer to get cleaned up and into a fresh uniform. More than anything, he wanted to crawl into a hole and sleep for a month.

"What happened?" Rodney asked again, concern etched into his expression.

Cal puffed out a breath. Answering questions ranked at the top of his *last thing I want to do* list. Only his deputy had a right to know and Cal needed another perspective. He explained, being as concise as he could.

"Shit." Rodney plopped down in the visitor chair near Cal's office door, looking rather pale. "Why didn't you tell me you were going out there? Ask for help maybe?"

Cal shrugged—a gesture he wouldn't be repeating until some of his parts healed. "I thought Herb might be involved. Was afraid he'd catch on if he caught us talking."

Rodney leaned back in the chair, lifting the front legs off the floor. "He might be. Haven't seen him today."

"Damn." Cal started to shrug, but caught himself. "If only I'd seen his face."

They sat for a few seconds, neither speaking.

Rodney lowered his chair back to the floor. "There's more, isn't there?"

Cal nodded. "I'm still not sure Grace isn't involved."

"Grace?" His deputy shook his head. "No way. She's as straight-laced as they come. You know that."

"I hope you're right."

"I know I am, Cal, but I'm afraid I have more bad news."

*Hell's bells.* "No more bodies. Please?"

Rodney grinned, although his eyes didn't light up in their usual manner. "Worse. The mayor wants to see you."

Robin Weaver

# CHAPTER 35

*Sunday, December 4*

Grace rolled over, wrapping her leg around Cal's body. He was so strong, so perfect.

And she'd almost lost him. Correction, she had lost him, but at least he was alive.

She encircled him with her arms, savoring his scent and the feel of his skin. She wanted to remember every bit of him, file the memory away to bring her comfort when things got tougher.

Cal turned to face her. She lifted her head, staring directly into his gray eyes. Why would God give her something so perfect, only to have him forever beyond her grasp? It was enough to make a woman question her religion.

"Morning, angel." His words were sweet, but his tone foreshadowed things to come. When he'd shown up at her door, she'd expected questions, had been prepared for questions. Instead, he pulled her into his arms and kissed her, a kiss so potent the recollection made her lose her breath. No, she hadn't expected the sweet, unexpected respite.

"Let me guess," she replied, running her fingers over his chest. "We have to talk."

"We do." He propped on one elbow to look at her, his gaze filled with something wonderful—a wonder negated by the tenseness in his muscles. "Doesn't seem appropriate to question you while we're naked."

Several wisecracks popped into her head, but the occasion seemed too somber. "Wow, first time you've ever told me to *put on* some clothes. I'll get my robe."

After she donned the garment and turned, Cal stood in front of her. He took her hands, kissing each knuckle before he pulled her into his arms for another kiss. Earlier, he'd kissed her with enough passion to fuel a power plant. This one was tender, almost timid, but no less potent. Both kisses would be eternally planted in her mind.

He released her, but still held onto one hand. "Let's go to the kitchen."

She understood. Her bedroom had been a little bit of heaven for a little bit of time. He wouldn't interrogate her there.

"Do you want coffee? Water?" she asked, stalling so she could think.

"Sit down, Grace."

She complied, her heart heavy. How much did he suspect? How much did he know? For a brief moment, she'd actually believed he bought her story about a midday ride. She should have known better.

"Let's start with where you went," he said, his tone kind but no one would ever question the authority behind his words.

"Where I went?" Why had she repeated the question. No matter what she said, Cal would think she was trying to come up with a story now. Which was exactly what she was doing.

He nodded. "Don't pretend you don't understand, Grace. When I got to the top of the cliff, you'd vanished."

Grace blinked. "I had to get Polly. I didn't tie her up. And why are you questioning me about that?"

He shook his head. "You wouldn't lie to me, would you, Grace? If you told Polly to stay, the horse would stay." He smiled. The situation would have been less heartbreaking if he'd snarled, or barked. "I know what you're doing, angel. You're not exactly lying, but you're not answering my questions either."

"I was in a bit of a hurry, so I didn't tell Polly to stay. I did go after her." True, but she couldn't admit the horse had trotted after the car. No she wouldn't lie, but she'd withhold as much as necessary.

Cal did that funny thing with his lip. "Why'd you have a rope? And don't give me that baloney about a calf in the stream."

Grace studied his face. Not a question she'd expected and not one that required evasion. Still, her throat felt prickly. "I went to Vertie's place for the rope. You know that."

Cal shook his head. doing that thing with his mouth again. "The first rope. The one that was too short. You had it with you. Almost like you expected you'd need it."

"Cal. I have cows. I keep a rope in the saddlebag. Are you going to arrest me for having a rope?" She tried to smile but wasn't sure she pulled it off.

He did that pursing thing with his mouth for a third time. How could he be unhappy about that answer?

"You were gone a long time, Grace. The ride to Vertie's place shouldn't have taken more than five minutes. Each way."

That was just ridiculous. She'd rushed to her brother's place for the rope. Sure, she'd stopped for a quick conversation, but that couldn't have taken more than a minute. "Maybe it just seemed longer at the bottom of that cliff. What would you have done if I hadn't shown up?"

Cal lifted her chin with his fist. "Grace, I saw the man—at least one of them. If you're involved, please tell me."

"Involved in what?" she asked. Dear Lord. "Why were *you* in the ravine, Cal?"

"I'm asking the questions, Grace. Don't make me ask them in an official capacity. Was one of your calves lost in the ravine? Is that why you brought your horse and a rope? I set the trap. And Lily's killer took the bait. He showed. I recognized the killer's hat."

She blinked. Pretending nothing was wrong might be the most difficult thing she'd ever done. At least the second most difficult. "The hat? I don't understand, Cal. If the killer showed up and you know who he is, why not arrest him?"

He sighed. "I only recognized the hat, Grace. A Mudcats baseball cap. Maybe even the same one stolen from my office."

Oh dear God. That blasted cap again. She ran her hands over her hair. "That's a start, but a lot of people in this town still have those hats."

"Including your ex, right, Gracie? You told me you never loved Ernest. Why are you covering for him?"

The question came from out of the gray. And fairly knocked the wind out of her. She didn't know whether to be relieved or mortified. "You think Ernest is the killer?"

"Don't act dumb, Grace. Why are you covering for Ernest?"

Why couldn't she just die and be done with it? Keeping her secret would plague her forever. She wouldn't make things worse by lying to him. Best to stop talking and let Cal think the worst.

"Or are you covering for your father?"

"My..." Dear God. Why did he think her father was involved?

"Are they in it together, Grace? Or are they covering for you?"

She swallowed hard. This was the part she'd dreaded. Might as well minimize the damage.

Grace stared up at Cal, memorizing his face, his slight cowlick, and even his stern expression. "Just stop," she whispered.

He blinked. "Stop?"

"Yes, stop. I love you." She touched his face, then quickly removed her hand. "I will always love you, but I can't answer your questions. If you insist on asking them, I'm going to insist on a lawyer."

# CHAPTER 36

Cal staggered toward the door. He wheezed like a lunger. Grace loved him? But she needed a lawyer? In what world did she need a lawyer? *Why* would she need a lawyer? He'd just made that "covering for you" comment to goad her into talking. He'd never considered her a suspect. Not really.

Not until now.

He should turn around, march back into her kitchen, and arrest her. March her sexy ass right down to the jail. Only he couldn't. Wouldn't. Not without concrete proof.

As a law enforcer, he was all wet. The man convicted of the crime was on the run and he refused to arrest the woman who'd probably given Lily the lead jewelry.

Didn't matter. He was done. He simply could not arrest Grace. Would not arrest Grace.

He'd turn in his resignation. With any luck, he could get his D.C. job back, put away real scum, not people he loved. Thank God he could resign at the end of the year. Bless the county seat and their contractual loopholes. Leeton didn't need a sheriff who couldn't make an arrest without gumming up the works.

Somehow he made it to his house, but had no memory of the drive. And he had no idea whose Chrysler was parked in his driveway. In his state of mind, he sure as hell didn't need a visitor.

When he got out of his Packard, a man walked toward him. Cal shielded his eyes against the wind for a better look.

"Mule?" Any other day he'd be thrilled to see the former manager of the Chattanooga Lookouts. Only today, Cal didn't know if he could form full sentences.

Mule held out his hand. "Cal Henderson, as I live and breath. Good to see you, son. You're looking fit, if a little green around the gills."

Somehow, Cal managed to invite the man inside. He even poured him a drink.

Mule didn't seem to notice his addled state. They talked, but Cal had a hard time keeping up with the conversation.

"So, Cal. Whadda you say?"

Cal squinted, as if seeing the man more clearly would make him remember the conversation. "Beg your pardon?"

Mule laughed as if Cal had made some Buster Keaton joke. "If that's a ploy for more money, there ain't any. Still, managing has to pay better than wearing country tin."

Managing? Was he for real? "They want me to manage? The Lookouts?"

Mule laughed again. "They really do. I'll be back down this way in two weeks. I'll stop by and see what you've decided then. You decide before then, call the main office. Better yet, why don't you meet me in Memphis, at the Peabody? We can get a legal drink there."

The former manager got to his feet and put on his hat. Cal remembered his manners and followed him to the door.

"Mule, wait. You don't need to come back."

The man leaned against the door frame and turned to face him. "Ah, hell, Cal. Think about it before you say no."

Cal shook his head. He didn't know if he really understood his own reasoning, but getting out of Leeton suddenly seemed like the best idea ever. He might change his mind if he thought about it, might let his guilt over Noverta and his heartache over Grace get in the way.

"No," he said, his insides feeling like lead. "I mean you don't need to come back because I'll take the job."

# CHAPTER 37

*Sunday, December 11*

Cal stood outside his office, staring at the street.
A full week had passed since he'd accepted Mule's
offer and he still hadn't told anyone. He scarcely
felt the bitter wind on his face. Damn cold for
Leeton. And he didn't just mean the weather.

"You wanted to see me?"

He turned to face Rodney. "I did."

Rodney shifted, hands in his pocket. "Can we
go inside? Freezing my ass off out here."

Cal blinked. "Sure."

Inside his office, Cal took off his jacket, shaking
the snowflakes away before he hung it on the coat
tree. Rodney made no move to take off his big
overcoat, didn't even take his hands out of the

pocket. The deputy kicked the door closed with his foot.

"What's so important I have to come in on a Sunday?" Rodney asked.

"Have a seat, Rod."

The deputy sat, tugging his collar tighter around his neck. "Everything okay?"

Hell's bells. Rodney had probably just gotten home from church. The single, good-looking deputy always got an invitation to Sunday lunch from someone. Cal had probably messed up his meal.

"Sorry to call you in today, but I'm going to see the county mayor in the morning, but wanted to talk to you first."

"The mayor? Hell, Cal. Must be really bad if you're talking to him."

"Not bad," Cal replied. "Not really. I'm leaving Leeton."

Rodney gave his head a little shake, as if to clear his mind. "Leaving Leeton?"

Cal nodded. "I've been offered another job."

The deputy frowned. "But you were elected. Can you do that?"

"Yes. The mayor will appoint an interim sheriff. I'm going to recommend he appoint you."

A big grin spread across the deputy's face. "Keen. Sure hate to see you leave, though."

Cal was glad someone would benefit from his misery. Since Rodney had never run for office, he'd assumed his friend didn't want the responsibility.

Guess he'd underestimated him. Or maybe Noverta's conviction had made everyone reevaluate priorities.

# Robin Weaver

# CHAPTER 38

*Tuesday, December 13*

Cal pulled into his driveway, but didn't get out of his car. A full week with nothing more serious than disturbing the peace and one drunk and disorderly. Wasn't that what he wanted? So why didn't he feel better?

No one, except Herb, had commented on his imminent departure either, which was also what he wanted. Only why did he feel so hollow?

He'd done the right thing by resigning. Cal knew in his soul that was the right thing, but his failure to clear Noverta still nagged at him. Probably always would.

He walked up the pathway to his house, wondering if he'd be able to sleep. He hadn't had a full eight hours in so long, he'd begun to believe he'd never get a good night's rest again. Every joint in his body ached.

He pulled out his key. Then pulled out his gun. His front door was ajar.

"Surprise!"

A *GOODBYE CAL* banner hung from his ceiling. A surprise party? For him?

Hell, he had his gun out. He hurriedly set the safety and put the .38 in his bomber pocket. Maybe he should have locked his door, but nobody in Leeton did that, not even after Lily's murder.

No, he should be happy folks cared. He had enough to feel guilty about without being unappreciative too. He smiled, he shook hands. He did all the right things. Cal even addressed Grace in a friendly manner, as if he wasn't still in love with her. As if he didn't think she was involved in Lily's murder.

He appreciated the gesture, was touched by the townsfolk's well wishes. Still, he was glad when everyone went home. He got into bed, but did more tossing than snoozing, finally giving up and heading into the office at six a.m. No matter that it was a Saturday.

He'd lost Grace and failed Noverta, but the support of the town made him want to step up to the plate again, to make one last attempt to find Lily's killer before he returned to the career he loved—even if he wouldn't be playing. He pulled out his notepad and started making a list.

1 – Grace lied. She killed Lily.
2 – Grace didn't lie. She'd didn't kill Lily but she knows who did.
3 – Grace really doesn't know who killed Lily.

"All right," he said aloud. So what if he talked to himself? Crazy couldn't be any worse than failure.

Ernest was his most viable suspect, but if Grace was correct, Ernest and Lily were...partners. Cal couldn't find a motive that fit. Still, Ernest had gone into hiding right after the murder. And his mother had also died mysteriously. Ernest hadn't reported the murder either.

*Only Ernest had told Grace he loved Lily.*

Hell, maybe Granny killed Lily. The woman sure wouldn't want some girl messing up the comfortable life Grace's money provided. Maybe Ernest got ticked and killed his mother for killing Lily? That was too far-fetched, right?

Damn, he probably should report Granny Gardner's death. Only most people still believed Noverta had been in that car. Unless Cal could prove who killed Granny, nothing would be gained by reporting her demise.

"You gummed up the works," he said to himself. He was the sheriff. Why hadn't he managed to get the full story out of Grace without her deciding she needed a lawyer?

Maybe he should focus on John Randolph, even though the man had a restaurant full of congressional folks as his alibi for the murder. The senator was drinking and smoking with colleagues until after one a.m. according to several sources. The man had *supposedly* been driving to Nashville when Cal found the cigar. Still, could he have paid someone?

"Morning, Boss."

Herb. Tired turned into bone crunching fatigue when he caught sight of the deputy.

"Morning," Cal replied, refusing to be a hypocrite and say *good* morning.

Herb took off his hat, but remained standing. "What kind of errands you got for me today?"

Cal blinked. "Excuse me?"

Herb grinned. "You've been sending me on one odd job or the other since the murder. Just wondered what you had in mind for today."

Hell. Cal leaned back in his chair, studying Herb's face. He'd underestimated the man. And he, not Herb, had been the crumb. From what he gathered, Herb had been one of the primary instigators of his farewell party. He suspected Grace had been the main instigator, but Herb's gesture was still nice.

He glanced at the clock. Already 7:30. The diner would be open. "I was thinking coffee."

Herb's stance went stiff. "I'm not making coffee, Boss."

Cal grinned. "Of course not. I mean let's get some decent coffee. I'm buying."

The tension visibly left Herb's body. "Well why didn't you say so?"

Cal really wanted to be decent to the man, but if Herb hid something, maybe in a more relaxed environment he'd let something slip. Nothing wrong with getting double duty out of a cup of joe, right?

Herb chatted on the short walk to the bakery. Cal listened, still preoccupied with *who could have* theories. The bell jingled as he opened the door to Della's place. The combination of cinnamon, coffee and bacon grease actually improved his mood. The waitress filled his mug then took his order—two eggs over easy with bacon. Herb rambled on about a eight-point buck he'd killed over the weekend.

"Good hunting, I suppose," Cal said, hoping he sounded casual. "You weren't over by the Broken Bridge Cliff by any chance, were you?" He seriously doubted Herb had anything to do with Lily's murder. Herb had been far too gleeful, but he'd also been surprised about the homicide. Still, wouldn't hurt to ask.

Herb's forehead furrowed. "Nah. Didn't think there were any deer over there since the creek dried up. Hard to keep up with the dogs there, too. Why you asking?"

Cal took a sip of his coffee. "No reason. Just heard there were some gunshots over that way. Hunters, I'm guessing."

Herb nodded. He started talking about the best places to hunt, leaving Cal's mind free to wander.

Cal decided he'd spent too much time on the who. Maybe he should focus on how the murder could be related to Kenny's abduction?

The deputy stopped talking. Herb probably expected him to talk. Or respond. Hell.

He searched his mind for something to get the deputy rambling again. "Whose dogs did you run on your hunting trip?"

The deputy mentioned three of his buddies. Not really interested and only half listening, Cal looked around the bakery and spotted Dodd, the undertaker, having breakfast. The man nodded.

"Sure wish I had Noverta's bluetick though. You know what happened to that dog? Is he for sale?"

*Noverta's bluetick?* Cal looked directly at Herb, his interest meter rising as if it were the final out of a no-hitter. "Say that again?"

"Said I wished I had Noverta's hound. That's some dog."

A suspicion triggered in Cal's brain. "Eh, Herb... Have you seen Ernest's dog lately? Isn't he from the same litter as Tanner?"

"Tanner is the name of Noverta's dog, right?" Herb asked.

Cal nodded.

The deputy shook his head. "Didn't know Ernest had a dog. I thought Noverta bought his dog full grown. Over in Jackson. Guess I was wrong."

"Damn." Cal instantly regretted his outburst. Still, how could he have missed that?

"What's wrong?" the deputy asked.

"Nothing." Cal pulled out his wallet. "But I just remembered I have some paperwork for the mayor. You know how he is if a report is late." For being a stickler about lying, he'd just told a whopper.

"Ah, shit." Herb reached for his hat.

Cal shook his head, trying to act nonchalant. "You don't need to go back because of my mistake. Stay here and enjoy your food." He pulled a bill and laid it on the table. "Breakfast is on me. And I think you're overdue for a day off." Cal tried to smile.

Herb frowned. Given the way Cal had barked at the deputy during the past few weeks, Herb probably thought he was in trouble.

"I'm trying to make up for all those errands, Herb. I really appreciate all your hard work, so I just mean you don't have to come back to the office today. If something comes up, I'll find you." Cal really did want to repay Herb—he probably hadn't treated the man fairly—but mainly, he wanted to talk to his other deputy. Alone.

Herb beamed. "Thanks, Boss."

Cal hurried away before Herb could ask questions.

Rodney was standing by the coffee pot when he entered the office. "Morning, Cal."

"We need to talk."

The deputy whirled to face him. "'Bout what?"

Cal gambled. "About the bluetick Ernest doesn't have."

"So you figured it out?"

Not the answer Cal wanted. "Was the senator in on it too?"

Rodney shook his head. "No. I thought I'd planted a good red herring when I dropped that cigar at Broken Bridge. But that's all it was, Cal. The senator still thinks his son murdered his wife. Fool man is actually proud of Vertie."

Cal swallowed hard, deciding to gamble again. "That night at Noverta's, I heard a car drive away. That was you, wasn't it?"

Rodney didn't look up, just kept stirring his coffee. "Question is, Cal, what do we do now?"

Cal didn't reply. He couldn't do anything until he had more evidence. Maybe Rodney wanted to confess. From his time in D.C., Cal learned silence often loosened people's tongues more effectively than questions.

Rodney sipped his coffee, acting like he hadn't a care in the world. "I really wished you'd just gone on to Chattanooga and left well enough alone, Cal. Why'd you have to go digging again? Vertie took the rap. And now he's out of jail. Problem solved."

"*You* were behind Noverta's escape."

Rodney shrugged. "The senator took care of that. Just like Vertie said he would. The senator takes care of everything."

The deputy pulled out his gun. "I'll be taking your weapon, if you don't mind. Lay it on the table. Real slow like."

Cal complied.

"Why couldn't you just leave well enough alone?" Rodney asked.

Cal stared at the man he had considered a good friend. For years. "Character flaw I suppose." Might as well go for the confession. Surely Rodney wouldn't shoot him. "Why'd you do it, Rod? Why did you shoot Lily?"

Rodney snorted. "Maybe you ain't the genius everyone thinks you are. Thought it would be obvious, especially to you. Lily and Ernest *were together*. I lost my head."

Cal scratched his eyebrow, never letting his gaze waver from Rodney's Smith and Wesson. "Not so obvious to me," Cal said, handing his Colt over. "You didn't have to kill Lily to protect Grace."

"Grace?" Rodney cackled, his laugh downright spooky. "You *are* dense. Sure, she's like a sister to me, but I wouldn't kill for her. Not everything is about Grace, Cal, though you probably don't agree."

That didn't make sense. "Don't tell me you were dizzy over Lily. Hell, Rod, you have a different babe every weekend," Cal said, stalling for time as much as anything. He didn't think Rodney would actually shoot him, but before, he wouldn't have believed Rodney could shoot Lily either.

The deputy's eerie grin faded. "I'm dense, too. I loved Lily, Cal. My real dumbness came when I told her about my alcohol distribution system."

"You're the…" Cal closed his mouth. "You told her about the smokehouse?"

Rodney grinned, looking a bit like one of those cartoon devils. "I knew you left that note, Cal. If you didn't want anyone to know where it came from, you probably shouldn't have left the newspapers on your desk with a lot of the letters cut out."

Hell's bells. He had been stupid. "Why would Lily care about your bootlegging?"

"Alcohol distribution." Rodney grinned again. Cal really wished he'd show some remorse. "She didn't. Even said she'd go away with me. Then I caught her and Ernest…together." Rodney dropped his gun hand to his side. Was he losing it?

Cal considered lunging for the weapon, but in the half-second of considering, Rodney raised his hand again, pointing the Smith and Wesson directly at his chest. He'd have to find another way to disarm Rodney. But how?

"Ernest was my partner. Has been ever since I covered for him after that incident at the Caged Canary. That's where we got the idea to start our own alcohol distribution. The Canary was having trouble keeping the liquor stocked. Lily knew we were partners and she screwed him anyway." Rodney shook his head. "Can you believe that?"

"So why didn't you shoot him instead of Lily?"

"Ernest didn't know about me and her. He wouldn't have been sniffing around if I'd told him. He told me that himself."

Cal's mind raced. "Did Grace know about this partnership? She know about the bootlegging?"

"Alcohol distribution, Cal. Get it right."

"Did Grace know?" Cal repeated.

"Saint Grace? Hell no. Not until your little cliff stunt anyway." Rodney's expression turned somber. "Thanks to you my dear cousin no longer considers me one of the good guys."

Cal had to buy time. Rodney was well trained, he wouldn't fall for any tricks. He was a good shot, too. He'd be a deadly shot in the small confines of the office. "Did you kill the old woman, too?" He prayed to every holy deity the deputy hadn't sunk that low. "I can almost understand that, she was a mean old coot."

"Granny might have been crazy, but she wasn't mean. Not if she liked you, and she liked me plenty."

Cal thought Rodney calling Granny crazy was a pot-kettle thing. "But you put her body in Grace's car. That was you, right?"

"Damn." Rodney waved his gun as he talked. "Everyone was supposed to think Vertie was dead. Why didn't you tell?"

Cal had kept his mouth shut because he'd feared Grace was involved, but he wasn't going to admit that to Rodney. "You wanted everyone to think Noverta's dead? Why?" Cal hoped Rodney would keep waving the gun as he talked. If Cal timed it just right, he might be able to lunge at the deputy.

Rodney nodded. "If everyone thought Vertie was dead, they'd quit looking for him. Figured I owed him that much. He knew I killed Lily, but agreed to take the rap. Said his dad wouldn't let him go to the big house, but knew the good ole senator wouldn't do a damn thing for me. Vertie always wanted an excuse to get out of Leeton anyway. He knew his dad would have to let him leave if he was convicted of murder."

Cal forgot about lunging. That crazy theory actually made sense. Noverta had always wanted to head west, but had never had the guts to just leave, knew the senator would find a way to bring him home. Maybe that's why Noverta insisted he find Tanner—so Cal would know Noverta wasn't guilty. Understand why he'd never see his best friend again.

Cal twisted his neck. Noverta's intentions might have been well intended, but his deputy was a murderer. Worse, Rodney was insane. "So you killed Granny so people would stop looking for Vertie?"

"I didn't kill her." Rodney waved the gun. "She up and died. Natural causes and all. I think she was about ninety. Very convenient, though. Grace told me the senator had put the fear of God into Ernest so I knew he'd be too chicken shit to come back for the body. So I took care of it."

Rodney laughed again, sounding even less sane than he had a few seconds earlier. "Old Ernie will have a steer when he finds out I burned his dear old mammie to a crisp. Still, that was a stroke of genius, don't you think? Letting folks think Noverta had died."

Cal experienced his first bout of real fear. Rodney might be a psychopath. "You made the call to the Mississippi State Police?"

The deputy shook his head. "Nah. I intended to, but somebody must of seen me. I intended to burn the car before the locals arrived."

"How *did* you set the car on fire?"

Rodney smirked, no doubt confident he had all the answers. "Granny actually took Grace's car. I'm sure that doesn't surprise you. The old bat stole a couple of cans of Grace's petroleum, too. Stupid cow had them stored in the back, but hey, worked out fine for me."

Cal shook his head. "But the fire started after we arrived."

Rodney grinned, the most unpleasant smile Cal had ever seen. "You almost messed up my plan when you told me to go talk to the Mississippi boys. But then you went sneaking up to the car and all I had to do was say, 'What's he doing?' Everybody watched you after that, so all I had to do was put a bullet into the car—at the right spot, of course."

Cal shook his head. "You had a silencer."

Rodney made a snorting, laughing sound. The man definitely had succumbed to his demon side.

"You kidnapped Kenny," Cal said, really needing to understand and really needing to keep the deputy talking. "How could you do that, Rod?"

Rodney shrugged, causing his gun to waver again. "I don't have to answer your questions, Cal, and I know what you're doing. I also know how you like to check things off your list. Least I can do is let you get this case solved in that brain of yours. Considering what I have to do."

*Hell.* Why in the name of everything holy had he given Herb the day off?

"I thought that boy saw me at Lily's house that night," Rodney continued. "Grace said he was wandering around, so I had to be sure."

Cal knew he was in the middle of a nightmare. Nothing made sense. His pal Rodney couldn't be so calculating. "But you were in the office that morning. How the hell could you take him?"

"Grabbed him before work. Disguised, of course. Kenny pitched a fit at first, but after I cut down a branch and told him it was a pirate sword, he was happy to go with me. Left him at my house and told him not to move or the boogieman would get him. Then, I went to the office. Boy didn't move. Can you believe it?"

Cal couldn't believe he'd ever considered Rodney a friend. "He didn't recognize you?"

Rodney shook his head. "Nah. Always wore a mask. And disguised my voice." Rodney's accent sounded almost exactly as Kenny described it.

"You were going to kill him?" Cal asked, not remotely able to understand. "Hell, Rodney."

"Don't get so high and mighty, Cal. I hoped all I'd have to do was convince him he hadn't seen me. You know how he is. If you say something three times, boy believes it's a fact. Hell, cause of you, he still thinks he's a pirate. Kenny told me, or my disguise, he wouldn't tell no one Miz Grace done killed Lily if I'd let him go. Can you believe it? Kenny thought Grace murdered Lily. I took the boy for nothing."

At this point, Cal could believe the moon was made of ice cream. "But Kenny was gone a week."

"Four days, Cal. And I would have let him go sooner, but you kept me pretty busy. Enough talking though. You really should have enjoyed your party, Cal. And then you should have gotten the hell out of Dodge like you were supposed to."

"You got away with killing Lily," Cal said, trying to make his voice soothing, whatever the hell that was. "But you won't get away with shooting me."

The deputy laughed again, but the sound completely lacked humor. "That's where you're wrong. After that big party we threw for you, everybody knows you're leaving Leeton. Way I see it, you don't have to be in Chattanooga for at least another month, maybe two. I'll send a note to the folks at Joe Engel Stadium saying you changed your mind. Nobody will expect you there and no one here will be the wiser. Since you and Gracie are on the outs, doubt anyone will even look for you."

"Grace? How do you know we're on the outs?"

Rodney shook his head. "Grace still tells me everything, Cal. Still helps me. She wanted to tell you everything, too. Begged me, but I made her promise she'd keep quiet."

Hell. Grace knew Rodney had killed Lily?

"Was Grace there when you shot that poor woman?" He could never forgive her if she'd been there and didn't try to stop the murder.

The gun barrel dropped a fraction of an inch while Rodney massaged his temple with his pistol-free hand. "She came to my house after she shot Ernest, needed me to drive him to the hospital in Memphis. Figured I could say we'd been hunting. Course we didn't know then it was just a little scratch. Ernest made such a racket you'd think he severed an artery. I made Ernest show me his wound. He didn't need no doctor. And I needed to see Lily."

*Keep him talking.* If he could distract Rodney, maybe he could dive behind the desk. He had a knife in his bottom drawer. "That explains how you knew about her shooting Ernest. How did she know you drilled Lily?"

A little smile played at the corner of Rodney's lip. For a second, the man looked like his boyhood pal. "You know how Grace is always creepin' around, not making a sound?"

Cal nodded, his eyes on the gun barrel.

Rodney shook his head, waving the Smith and Wesson as he moved. "She might have pale skin, but I swear that woman is one hundred percent Choctaw."

Cal waited.

"Anyway, she'd walked over and I didn't hear nothing. She just asked me what I was doing."

And naturally Grace would cover for him. Especially if she wasn't wise to Rodney's real actions. Grace wanted to believe the best. She was as close to her cousin as she was to Noverta. Maybe closer. "Did she know why you shot Lily?"

Rodney shook his head again. "Nah. She thought I was mad cause Lily cheated on Vertie."

Cal inched closer to the desk, but needed another small step before he dared jump. He needed to say something, needed Rodney to talk a little longer. "Guess blood really is thicker than—"

"Thicker than love? She does love you, Cal. Problem is, love don't mean shit to those Randolphs. Family comes first, and sorry as I am, I'm still her cousin."

Cal swallowed. Rodney was watching him. Diving for the desk was no longer an option.

Rodney gripped his pistol in both hands. "I really hate to do this, Cal."

"Drop the gun."

*Grace?*

Cal dropped to his knees. Rodney spun ninety degrees.

A shot rang out.

# CHAPTER 39

Grace had never been so scared in her life. She saw no way out. Well, one, but that depended on love being thicker than integrity and Cal Henderson had a lot of integrity. And how could he possibly still love her?

Holding the gun, she tried to think as she watched Cal wrap Rodney's little finger with a torn shred of an old uniform. She swallowed, and swallowed again. Something caught in her throat.

"I can't believe you shot me, Grace." Rodney stared at her. His expression implied she might be the Antichrist.

"Don't be a baby," she said, grateful for a distraction. "The bullet didn't even hit bone. You're worse than Ernest. And I can't believe you were going to shoot Cal. What's wrong with you?"

Rodney glared. "What's wrong with me? What's wrong with you? Cal will send me to the big house. Or have me hanged."

"I will arrest you." Cal's voice was so soft, she barely heard him. "A jury will decide about the big house."

Maybe if Rodney stopped yapping, she could reason with Cal. His face looked pretty determined though, so maybe not.

"Get out of here, Rodney," she said. "Leave town and don't come back."

"I can't let him go," Cal said, his voice a little louder.

She aimed the gun at him. "You can if you have no choice."

He made a little snorting noise. "You going to shoot me? Go ahead. Otherwise, give me the gun so I can cuff him."

"Don't listen to him," Rodney whined.

"Quiet!" So much for reasoning with Cal. Lord help her. "Let me think."

To her surprise, both men shut up. Only she couldn't think. She had one idea, the same stupid idea she'd had when she first saw Rodney aiming his gun at Cal. The man she loved would hate her forever, and she couldn't blame him. He probably already hated her. Even so, after everything she'd done to protect her cousin, she couldn't let Rodney go to jail now.

She dropped the gun to her side. "We're going to let him go, Cal. Rodney's your friend, too."

Cal crossed his arms. "It's murder. You *will* have to shoot me." He held up a finger. "You going to graze me or shoot it off?"

She had an insane urge to giggle, totally inappropriate, but every last one of her nerves had been shot with Rodney's finger. "Maybe I'll take the tip. You have ten fingers—don't imagine you'll miss one." She'd never shoot Cal, but wouldn't do to let him know that.

Cal's expression didn't change. "Grace, Rod killed Lily. He let Vertie take the rap. I didn't like the woman a lot either, but you can't let a man get away with murder. Even Rodney."

Maybe she'd just throw the gun in a river and tell everyone she shot Lily. Prison looked pretty good compared to her life. "Rodney didn't mean to shoot her, Cal. He made a mistake."

"A mistake? Don't be naïve, Grace. Even if you believe that mistake malarkey, he was going to kill *me*. Doesn't that matter?"

"He was not." She glanced at her cousin, praying to everything holy that Rodney wouldn't really have shot Cal. "He was desperate. He wouldn't have pulled the trigger."

"He murdered Lily!"

She waved the gun in Cal's face. "Stop talking. Here's what we're going to do." She nodded toward Rodney. "You're going to go home. If anyone asks, you didn't shoot anyone, got that?"

"But Cal will—"

"Cal won't say anything. If he does, it's our word against his. People know how obsessed he is with clearing Vertie, everyone will think he's grasping at hay." Cal would definitely hate her now. "I'll swear you didn't even have a gun."

"You'd do that?" Cal's voice had gone soft again. So soft, she blinked to make sure she'd heard him. Soft or not, his voice carried a lifetime of judgment.

She put the safety on her rifle gun and handed it to Cal. "I would. What's more, I'll say Vertie confessed, admitted he killed his wife."

"Damn, Grace." Rodney laughed. "Thank you."

Criminy, she could almost regret protecting the fool. "Get out of here, Rod. Do it now, before I change my mind."

Her cousin's face turned somber. "I'm going."

"You're not going anywhere." Herbert Smith said, his voice more menacing than she thought possible. He aimed a rifle at Rodney's head. Where had he come from?

Rodney laughed. The son of a bitch laughed. Didn't he know what a loose cannon Herb was?

"Herbie," she said, working hard to keep her voice steady ."I mean Herb. Please put the gun down."

The deputy didn't acknowledge her. He glared at Rodney, his stance wide.

"Herb," Cal said. "How much did you hear?"

The deputy nodded slightly in Cal's direction, but kept his gun steady as an andiron. "Enough. Let's just say it's our words against theirs, Boss. I heard a boom. Thought it sounded like a shot so I came to see what was happening."

"Lower you weapon, Herb," Cal ordered. "We have enough to arrest him, we don't need a shoot-out."

Grace rubbed her temples, trying to think. Everything had gone to hell. "Go, Rodney. Get out of here. It's still our word against theirs. Everyone knows Herb doesn't like you so no one will believe him."

"That right, Herbie?" Rodney moved closer to the gun-toting deputy. What the devil was that stupid cousin of hers doing? "What you going to do, *Herbie*? Shoot an unarmed man?" They faced off like old West gunslingers.

Grace grabbed the opportunity. She nudged Cal from behind. When he glanced at her, she nodded toward her rifle in his hand. If he raised the weapon, maybe the deputies would back down.

"Don't move!" Herb yelled.

Was he talking to her? Or Rodney?

Rodney took another step toward the armed deputy. "Shoot if you're going to, *Herbie*."

"I said don't move!" Herb yelled.

Rodney kept walking. Cal aimed her rifle. Only Rodney was between him and Herb.

A shot echoed.

# Robin Weaver

# CHAPTER 40

Grace rushed to Rodney's side. She wadded her skirt and pressed it against Rodney's chest. Cal couldn't look. He knew the damage a bolt-action Winchester would do at close range.

He had to do something. Cal yanked the weapon away from Herb, placing it on the floor. "Don't move," he ordered.

Herb's face had turned a scary shade of white. His hands shook. Cal wished he didn't give a plugged nickel, but he felt sorry for the jackoff. Not as bad as he felt for Rodney. Or Grace.

Hell's bells. No one would ever be the same. Two good men gone because Lily Carleton Randolph couldn't keep her legs together.

"I didn't want to kill him. I swear. You know that, right?" Herb whispered. "You saw him coming at me? Cal, you saw him, right."

"Yes, Herb. I saw him."

"Cal…" Grace's voice sounded like a bleating goat.

Cal didn't want to look. He knew what he'd see, knew Rodney was dead. No one could have survived that shot.

He had to offer comfort. No matter what she knew, no matter what she'd done. Cal understood now that she'd protected her cousin, but she should have been straight with him.

But no one should have to face death alone.

"Don't move," he repeated to Herb. He pulled Grace off the floor and into his arms. He hung on for dear life.

# CHAPTER 41

*Friday, December 16*

He hated funerals. Not so unusual, Cal supposed. Nobody liked funerals. Except maybe the undertakers.

Jackson kept shooting him the evil eye. The county mayor glared too. Why? The man they didn't want arrested lay in the coffin. Were they still angry because he didn't want to hush things up? Did they still believe he wanted to tarnish the reputation of Leeton High's all-time leading scorer.

Maybe the real crime was that he'd gone along with the county officials' whitewash. Cal had argued Noverta could never be free if they didn't announce Rodney had killed Lily. The mayor countered Noverta was dead. Cal couldn't correct that statement without opening another can of worms. He hadn't reported Granny's death.

He refused to say Rodney's death was an accident, but had agreed he wouldn't challenge the ruling. If anyone asked, he'd tell them the truth. Only no one asked.

Herb had surprisingly agreed to the subterfuge. "Doesn't matter much now, does it?" he'd said. Probably didn't hurt that the mayor appointed him interim sheriff.

As the minister talked about better places, he kept his arm around Grace's back, suspecting she'd collapse if he let go. Sooner or later, he would have to let go. Leave Leeton, leave Grace. As much as he wanted her, their relationship had been tainted.

After the surprise party, he'd decided to ask Grace to go to Chattanooga with him. She wouldn't, but he figured she'd know how he felt and maybe she'd wait for him. He couldn't even do that now. The wounds were too fresh, too deep. She hadn't trusted him and he didn't know if he could accept that. Ever.

Why hadn't she just encouraged Rodney to confess? Did she really think no one would find out? Maybe with good reason. One more day and the crime might have remained unsolved.

Finally, the service ended. Grace raised her beautiful face, staring at him with an expression that broke his heart all over again. In spite of her deception, Cal had done everything he could to shield her the horror of the past three days.

"Don't look at me like that," Grace said, reminding Cal they were still in the funeral home.

"Like what?" he asked, not much in the mood for conversation.

"Like you're thinking something bad. Even if you are."

He sighed. "Anyone would be thinking bad thoughts in a situation like this. For now, just cry, Grace. Just this once, it will be okay. Grieve."

She shook her head.

Just as he thought. There would be no crying in public. As a kid, Grace had refused to shed a single tear, even when John Randolph took a belt and whacked her backside.

"Crying won't fix this, Cal."

"Then let's get out of this place." He ushered her into the cold afternoon and walked toward his car. When they were beyond earshot of the attendees, he leaned closer and whispered. "Can you get word to Vertie? Let him know he can come home now."

She jerked her arm away and turned to face him. "I don't know where Vertie is."

He frowned at her. "Really? No lies this time?"

She grimaced. "I'm not lying, Cal." Good, some of her spark had returned. "I even asked my father, demanded the truth. He doesn't know where Vertie is either."

He didn't believe that. "You bought that?"

She shrugged. "I actually do. I think he arranged the escape, but to cover his own tracks, he probably made sure he wouldn't know where Vertie went. Sounds like my father, doesn't it?"

He nodded. "I guess so. Do you think Vertie will contact you?"

She shook her head. "Probably not. You know how he is—easy going until he sets his mind on something. Then, he's pigheaded. If my father told him to disappear, and I'm pretty sure that's what happened, Vertie will literally vanish. He'll avoid all contact rather than cause us even a little bit of trouble. Any of us."

Neither spoke as they walked. Their breaths made puffs of smoke in the cold afternoon.

Grace stopped moving and touched his arm. "Wherever Vertie is," she said, "he'll be all right. I know that." More likely, she *had* to believe that.

"At least he won't have to deal with Rodney's death."

Grace frowned. "Don't hate Rodney, Cal. He lost his head when he caught Lily cheating—on Vertie and me. Even though he got caught up in the bootlegging mess, he was a good man—his family just messed him up."

Cal rubbed his forehead. Might as well let her believe that.

"I suppose Vertie agreed with you," he said. "After all, he *willingly* went to prison for Rodney."

Grace frowned again. "He did. I imagine Vertie figured he'd have a better chance of getting a 'not guilty' verdict from a Leeton jury than Rodney did. I think by the time his trial started, Vertie and Dad had already come up with a plan. A *just-in-case* plan. Vertie refused to talk to me once he went to jail, so I knew then my father was involved."

He didn't have the heart to tell her what Rodney said, that Noverta was happy to get out of Leeton. Cal could understand Noverta's desire for freedom. He didn't think Grace could reconcile how easily her brother left her behind.

"What I don't understand," he said, "is why you'd protect Rodney instead of Vertie. I know you and Rodney have always been close, but Vertie is your twin."

She swallowed, then swallowed again. "You can't understand, because your family is normal. Rodney was damaged, he wouldn't have lasted a week in jail. My father was…bad, but Rodney's old man was plain evil."

She was right. He didn't understand. "And Vertie would?"

Grace shrugged. "I really didn't believe this town would convict Vertie. Stupid, I suppose, but everybody loves him. Or did. After the trial, I was going to talk to you, tell you the truth so we could stop the sentencing, but then…"

"Then Vertie escaped," Cal said, finishing her sentence.

She nodded.

"You ready?" he asked, tired of talking about the murder, tired of thinking about the things they'd done so no one would know. He didn't want to go to the cemetery, such a sadistic practice, but he'd go for Grace.

"I should probably ride with the family."

"You mean with your dad? I know that's the custom, but you don't have to do that, Grace."

She shrugged again. "I think I do. My father's hurting. Rodney might not be his blood, but dad did care about him. And with Vertie gone, the senator is all the family I have left. I have to give him a chance." Grace looked like she might cry after all. She stared at the line of parked cars, but Cal suspected she didn't really see anything.

"Shall I come by afterward?"

She blinked. "To be with me, or to talk?"

He looked down at his feet. They had to talk at some point. She knew it, he knew it. Only today wasn't that day.

"You don't have to answer," she said. "I can see it in your face. I need some rest, Cal." She turned and started walking.

He couldn't let her go. Not yet. "Grace?"

She stopped moving and faced him again. "Yes?"

"I haven't said anything about your involvement. To anyone. Nothing to be gained by arresting you for aiding and abetting." He tugged on his overcoat, suddenly all too aware of the chill.

"You can't arrest me anyway. You resigned, remember?" She tried to smile, but didn't quite succeed. At least she hadn't completely lost her sense of humor.

"That I did," he replied.

He watched her walk away. He didn't want to let her go, but he couldn't stay in Leeton. The wound was too raw, the ache too sharp. He'd return someday—after all, he loved her. Would always love her.

Would she wait this time? He hoped so, only he couldn't ask that of her. Not when he had no idea when one day would be. If ever.

# CHAPTER 42

*Tuesday, December 20*

Grace stared out her kitchen window, wondering if Christmas would ever be heralded without gut-wrenching melancholy. She gazed at the brown backyard and beyond to the barn. She watched Mr. Hess shoo a renegade Holstein into the protection of the stalls, but the only thing that really registered was cold. The weather seemed to mirror her mood—gray and frozen.

Three people she cared about, all of them gone or going. Her cousin and friend, dead. Her beloved brother, on the run, God only knew where.

And Cal. Her entire body ached with a physical pain at his desertion. His loss ranked as the worst of the three. He remained alive, vibrant. The love of her life and she was dead to him, dead to the man she loved more than blood.

The knock on her door startled her. No one had knocked on her door since the day before the funeral. She suspected people didn't know what to say. At any rate, the townsfolk seemed to avoid her. Understandable, but painful all the same.

"Grace?" a voice called out, seeming to crack like the icicles hanging from her roof.

*Cal*? She hurried to the door and flung it open, not caring about the Artic air that chased away the little warmth her iron stove provided. "I thought you'd gone."

He took off his hat, but didn't look at her directly. "I left yesterday, but I had to come back. May I come in?"

"Please." She stepped aside to let him enter, wondering why she tortured herself. He'd be leaving again, she could tell by his expression. Once, she believed she knew every nuance that flitted across his chiseled face, but now, everything about him seemed out of character, even the shadow of a beard on his normally clean-shaved chin.

She shut the door and waited, afraid to speak.

Cal tugged on his coat collar. "Why did you lie to me, Grace? Surely you knew I'd protect you."

The irony was enough to choke a milk cow. She thought she couldn't have Cal and live with the secret. That secret had been revealed, yet she still couldn't have him. Their love was more star-crossed than any Shakespearean characters.

"I never lied to you, Cal." Everything she'd said to him had been true. Only that didn't matter. The truths she'd left unspoken would forever form a barrier between them.

He glared at her, contorting his jaw in an unnatural way. "Stop with the word games. Not being honest is no better than lying."

The venom in his tone made Grace wonder if the earth had shifted. Maybe the world no longer rotated around the same sun. It had been the coldest winter on record

Only the weather had nothing to do with the chill she couldn't shake. "I should have told you everything," she confessed. "I see that now."

"You think that makes it okay?"

"I'm sorry," she said. And she was.

He crossed his arms over his chest. "That's all you have to say?"

What else was there? She'd done a horrible thing, but she'd do it again. Rodney was blood. Before Cal, he'd been her best friend. She protected the people she loved, even if it meant protecting them from people she loved more. Didn't make sense, but that was her.

She shook her head. "I did what I had to do. Noverta and Rodney are all the family I have. Rather, had left."

"You think that's what this is about? Hell, Grace. I don't care how many laws you broke to protect him."

"I'd do it all again. Arrest me if you have to."

"Saints protect me. You don't get it, do you? I'm asking why didn't you trust me, Grace."

She blinked. "I trusted you."

He shook his head. "No you didn't. Why didn't you trust me to help you?"

She blinked again. "You're the sheriff, Cal. Or you were. You're the most honorable man I know. I'd never ask you to compromise your principles."

She reached for his hand. He tried to pull it away but she held firm.

"Cal, Rodney killed Lily. Had you known, you would have been honor-bound to arrest him. You would have had to choose between a friend and the law. You could never compromise your integrity and I would never ask that of you. Thus I had no option but to keep the information from you."

"My honor? I was willing to look the other way when I thought you killed Lily."

She blinked several times. "You thought I killed Lily. That's absurd." She could more easily believe in those Martians from that War of the Worlds radio broadcast. She didn't know which was more earth shattering—his thinking that she'd committed murder, or his contention that he actually would have compromised his principles. For her.

Life was so unfair.

"Will I ever see you again?" she asked.

He smiled but looked forlorn, Grace thought her heart might break all over again.

"Who knows what the future brings," he said. "The Lookouts play the Chickasaws. Maybe I'll see you in Joe Engle Stadium."

Grace nodded, fighting back tears and a whoop. At least he hadn't said no. She experienced a sliver of hope. Not much, but so much more than she ever expected.

"You'll be a great manager, Cal. I know you will."

His smile looked a little less forlorn. He leaned forward, placing a kiss on her lips. She didn't move, didn't dare.

He stepped back, clearly as surprised by the gesture as she was. "I wish you'd told me about the baby, Grace. Given me a chance to do the right thing. Everything might be different now."

"You'd have done the honorable thing, Cal, and that would have been the wrong thing. You'd have given up your dream. I won't apologize for that."

He flashed a sad little smile but said nothing.

"Will you ever forgive me?" she asked, hating herself for being so needy.

He shrugged. "Yes. I already have. It's the forgetting part I need to figure out." His Adam's apple rose and retracted. "Bye, Grace."

He turned and hurried down the steps, leaving the door open. She didn't want to watch him go, but she couldn't seem to move, even to stop the blast of Artic wind whooshing through her living room.

Cal didn't turn back. Grace was glad. She could deal with her loss, she'd had more than enough practice, but she couldn't stand the sight of Cal's hunched shoulders. Seeing sadness in his eyes would be so much worse.

She kept watching as Cal headed toward his car, looking like a man who'd broken more than his wrist. Like a man who'd lost more than a starting position with the Washington Senators.

When his car disappeared around the curve, Grace finally closed the door and sat. She'd done the right thing, all those years ago, when she hadn't told him she was pregnant. Now she might be facing the same situation again. This time would be different, though. She didn't know what Cal would do, but if she was indeed pregnant again—and by all indications, she was—she'd tell him. But only if she carried the baby past the first trimester.

She'd have three months to deal with that problem. Right now, she needed to focus her energy to stop the tears.

She would *not* cry.

# ABOUT THE AUTHOR

Robin Weaver is the author of eight novels, including *Blue Ridge Fear, a* Golden Heart finalist and winner of the Daphne du Maurier contest. She teaches workshops on point of view and pacing, and is a regular blogger with Romancing the Genres (www.RomancingtheGenres.blogspot.com). She loves Latin dancing, most things British, and the five o'clock shadow, not necessarily in that order. When she's not writing or doing undercover work as a university computer geek, she's re-investigating the 1932 kidnapping of the Lindbergh baby or trying to figure out what Billy Joe MacAllister threw off the Tallahatchie Bridge.

Please visit her on Facebook, LinkedIn or via her website: http://www.AuthorRobinWeaver.com.

# Other Books by Robin Weaver

## Mystery
*Blue Ridge Fear*
*Artifact of Death*
*Styrofoam Corpse – Available January 2016*

## Young Adult
*The Secret Language of Leah Sinclair*

## Contemporary Romance
*The Christmas Tree Wars*
*Full Contact Decorating – Available December 2015*

## Fantasy (Writing as Genia Avers)
*Forbidden Magic*
*Forbidden Flame*
*Forbidden Twice*
*Forbidden No More – Available December 2016*

## *Blue Ridge Fear*

Can things get any worse?

After an intimate relationship with her former boss sours, Sienna Sanders is slapped with a lawsuit for breach of contract. Broke and jobless, she moves in with her airhead cousin in a too-small mountain cabin--their joint inheritance.

But things get worse when a hiking misstep leaves Sienna stranded. That is, until a hunky stranger comes to her rescue. A zing of attraction has her thinking he might be the one. But there's a psycho stalking the area who's already killed four women-- women who look a lot like Sienna. Her stranger insists his name is Carson Addison, but Sienna discovers that isn't true. Plus, her dreamboat protector, a.k.a. possible stalker, only materializes when she's alone. Can she trust her heart and believe he's not a killer? Or is she making herself an easy target for the monster lurking in the mountains?

Available at www.Amazon.com or
www.TheWildRosePress.com

# <u>Coming Soon</u>

## *Styrofoam Corpse*

Shannon Summers is secure inside her property
with no sign anyone else entered.
So how did a dead man get into her pool?

Read the excerpt below:

### Chapter One

"Not again."

The acid in Larry's tone caused Casey
Randolph to halt the tedious task of stirring his
coffee. Both the deputy's nostrils and his biceps
flared as he stared at the caller ID.

His second-in-command jerked the handset
from its cradle. "Sheriff's office... Look, Welch."

*Welch?* Every muscle in Casey's body seemed to
cramp in unison. The involuntary clenching of his
right fist shifted his mug, sending droplets of coffee
sloshing across his pristine, starched shirt.

"Damn." He wiped at the specks on his shirt,
hoping the caller wasn't *that* Welch—the
voyeuristic freak who lived behind Shannon, the
new woman in his life who might be the one. Even
if he hadn't been able to share his good news.

He forced his fingers to loosen the grip on his

cup and leaned over to look at the address on the display. *Shit.* It was that Welch.

The deputy grimaced and crossed his eyes. Translation: another crazy. "I've already told you once today, there's no noise ordinance outside the city limits. We...whoa." Deputy Lawrence Johnson stopped rolling his eyes and sat straighter. "Slow down. Say that again?"

The deputy glanced at Casey, his expression a mask of tension. "If this is your idea of a joke... Okay, okay, we're on our way."

The deputy put the phone back into its cradle and scrawled the address on a yellow sticky note. "Guy claims someone got stabbed in a swimming pool."

"Stabbed?" Casey's stomach lurched upward, pushing all the air out of his lungs. The address scribbled in Larry's almost illegible handwriting, 615 South Run, belonged to Shannon.

Holy hell. What if it wasn't a crank call? "Was the vic male or female?"

Larry pushed himself upright. "Welch didn't say." The deputy donned his aviator glasses and tugged on the collar encircling his eighteen-inch neck. "So much for enjoying my cheeseburger. Wonder what time that loser started drinking."

"I'm driving." Casey grabbed his hat and checked his weapon.

Larry stared at the coffee stains on Casey's chest as he pulled the address off the pad. "I got this one, boss. You go change your shirt."

"What the hell's wrong with you? We get a call about a stabbing and you stand there jawboning about my uniform?"

"Well, Mr. G.Q., I know how finicky you are about your uniform and—"

"I said I'm driving."

"Suit yourself, but what if there really is a body? You forget about your necrophilia?"

"Did you forget to keep your mouth shut?" Casey glanced over his shoulder to make sure no one else had entered the office. Larry wouldn't intentionally betray him, but he talked too loud. "And the word is necrophobia, you moron, not necrophilia. I *hate* dead bodies. I certainly don't plan to hump one."

"You're running for sheriff when you're scared shitless of corpses and I'm the moron?" The deputy made a sputtering noise as he buckled his equipment belt.

"Get your ass moving," Casey ordered, refusing to debate the wisdom—or stupidity—of his bid for the sheriff's star.

Larry groaned. "What's the rush? Welch calls about some shit every goddamn week. Last week, he complained about the neighbor's stereo. When we wouldn't send a cruiser, he reported a prowler. Carmichael said Welch called twice yesterday about that same stereo."

"Just get in the friggin' car." Casey rushed toward his cruiser, not looking back to see if Larry followed. He started the engine and accelerated before the deputy got both feet inside the vehicle.

"Geezus." Larry braced one hand against the fake leather dashboard and struggled to close his door with the other. "Take it easy. I'll bet you a six-pack of Sam Adams there wasn't a stabbing. And if there is a stiff, we'd better call your shrink."

"Not funny." The deputy had been a friend since junior high, but Casey's forebodings zapped his patience with Larry's good-natured ribbing. Normally, he gave as good as he got, but Casey hadn't heard from Shannon all morning. He clamped his lips together to refrain from telling Larry to shut-the-F-up.

His bad feelings about Shannon's neighbor fueled the heartburn churning in his chest. He didn't believe in any psychic, voodoo crap, but every time he got a bad feeling in his gut, something bad happened.

"Yo', boss!"

"What?"

"You're going almost eighty. Maybe you ought to turn on the damn siren if you're going to play NASCAR. You think you're Jimmie Freakin' Johnson?"

Casey snorted. He trusted his driving skills, but to appease his deputy, he turned on the turret lights. He left the siren silent. He didn't want Welch, or anyone else, forewarned of their arrival. Glancing right, then left, he tapped his horn and blew through a red light.

"That's okay," the deputy muttered. "Stayin' alive is probably overrated."

On any other day, watching Larry execute a death-grip on the door handle and stomp on imaginary brakes would amuse him, but the very air seemed charged with anything but ordinary. The creeps crawled out of the woodwork on Halloween, especially when the temperature hovered near seventy degrees. Casey just hadn't expected them to slither over to Shannon's house.

He maintained his break-neck speed until he zoomed into her driveway. Slamming on the brakes, he stopped his SUV an inch from her hybrid. Music blared, but not at the glass-shattering volume he expected.

Crawling out of the vehicle, he ordered, "Check the back."

Larry headed toward the rear of the house. Casey knew the deputy couldn't scale the eight-foot stone fence surrounding Shannon's backyard. Her property was a virtual fortress, but diverting Larry would allow him to get inside and assess the situation without the deputy's scrutiny.

When Larry disappeared from his line-of-sight, Casey raced up the front steps and jabbed at the doorbell, generating a series of ding-dongs. No response.

He pummeled the door with his fist. Still no response. "Dammit, Shannon."

Fishing in his wallet, he produced the single key she'd given him, the key he'd never used.

Holding his breath, he slid it into the lock. When the deadbolt turned, he exhaled. Shaking fingers punched in the code to silence the security alarm. He hoped he remembered the right numbers.

*Beep, beep, beep.* The system flashed a green light.

"Shannon!"

He waited for a reply. None came.

Apprehension sent a wave of indigestion pounding at his gut. He did a quick check of the living room and kitchen.

Nothing.